The Crossing

Andrew Miller
The Crossing

SCEPTRE

First published in Great Britain in 2015 by Sceptre
An imprint of Hodder & Stoughton
An Hachette UK company

1

A CIP catalogue record for this title is available from the British Library

Hardback ISBN 978 1 444 75349 3
Trade Paperback ISBN 978 1 444 75350 9
Ebook ISBN 978 1 444 75351 6

Typeset in Janson Text by Hewer Text UK Ltd, Edinburgh

Printed and bound by Clays Ltd, St Ives plc

Hodder & Stoughton policy is to use papers that are natural, renewable
and recyclable products and made from wood grown in sustainable forests.
The logging and manufacturing processes are expected to conform to
the environmental regulations of the country of origin.

Hodder & Stoughton Ltd
Carmelite House
50 Victoria Embankment
London EC4Y 0DZ

www.sceptrebooks.co.uk

To the memory of my mother and my step-father.
Those we love travel with us always.

ONE

To be serious only about sex
Is perhaps one way, but the sands are hissing
As they approach the beginning of the big slide
Into what happened.

John Ashbery

1

Early spring, the new millennium, a young woman walks backwards along the deck of a boat. She goes slowly, is bent almost double, holds in her left hand a ladle and in her right a pot of hot pitch. From the spout of the ladle she pours a thin ribbon of pitch into the seams where all yesterday she tapped in lengths of oakum with a mallet and bosun's chisel.

So it begins, simply, with work.

The boat is raised on wooden stilts, the deck twenty feet above the ground, that hard standing of rubbled concrete and brick where the warmth of the new season has brought out unlikely patches of pale flowers, their roots in shallow veins of earth. Around the boat is the yard, a place where ships were once built – ferries, coal-lighters, trawlers, a wooden minesweeper during the war – but now given over to the servicing and maintenance of pleasure craft, some on their stilts, others tied up at the pontoons. There is a sound of power tools, radios, the now-and-then rapping of a hammer.

She is alone on the deck. For the work, for ease of movement and access, the mast has been unstepped, and all the rigging, together with stanchions and guard rails, has been removed and stowed away. When she finishes one seam she immediately begins the next. In the pot, the pitch is cooling. As it cools it thickens. She will have to stop at some point soon to light the gas-burner in the galley and heat it again, but not yet.

Below her, standing in the shadow of the boat's steel hull, a young man is dipping bolts into white lead and softly singing to himself. He is tall, blue-eyed, patrician. His fair hair, luxurious at a distance, is already starting to thin. His name is Henley but he is known and prefers to be known as Tim. There is some question, still unresolved, as to whether he and the girl on deck will sleep together.

He pauses, a bolt in his gloved fingers, calls up, 'Maud! Maud! Where art thou?' and getting no answer, grins and goes back to his work. He does not know her well but knows she does not do banter, does not in fact seem to understand what it is. This he finds funny and endearing, a trick of character, a benign absence, to be numbered among those things he most likes about her, such as the bluntness of her blunt brown stare, the curls of her hair that are flicks and half-curls because she cuts her hair short as a boy's; the inked lettering on her arm (the underside of her left forearm), a surprise the first time you see it that makes you wonder what other surprises there might be. The hint of Wiltshire in her voice, the way she sucks on a cut but does not mention it, the way her breasts are not much larger than peaches and hard, he thinks, as peaches. Yesterday, when she pulled off her jumper, he saw for the first time two inches of bare belly above the waistband of her jeans and felt an entirely unexpected seriousness.

They are both members of the university sailing club. The two others who came down with them have driven back to Bristol, perhaps, thinks Tim, to give them a bit of space, a bit of privacy. Is that what Maud thinks too? That the scene is set?

He can smell the pitch she's using. Also the faint sweet rotten smell of the river, the old piles, the mud, the amphibious vegetation. This is a drowned valley, a place broken to the sea, salt water heaving in and out twice a day under banks of dense woodland, at high tide lapping the roots of the trees, at low tide leaving little creeks of thigh-deep mud bare and glittering. In places, further up river, old boats have been scuttled and left to find their way back to nothing – blackened staves, blackened freeboard, some so old and rotten they might have carried Vikings, Argonauts, the first men and women of the world. There are herring gulls, egrets, cormorants, a resident seal that rises without warning at the side of boats, eyes like a Labrador. The sea itself is not in view but it's not distant. Two curves of the river bank, then the harbour, the town, the castles on the headlands. Open water.

Outside the boat shed a figure in red overalls and welder's goggles is standing like a boxer under a fountain of blue sparks. By the offices, a man in a suit is leaning against an iron pillar, smoking. Tim stretches – a luxurious feeling – but as he turns back to his work, to the boat, there is a movement through the air, a blink of feathered shadow, that is also a movement across the surface of his eye like a thorn scratch. There must have been a noise too – no such thing as silent impact – but whatever it was, it was lost in the hissing of his own blood and left no trace of itself.

He is staring at the ladle, which has come to rest by one of the patches of white flowers, pitch drizzling from the scoop. Maud herself is further off, face up, her arms flung above her head, her head tilted to the side, her eyes shut. It takes an immense effort to keep looking at her, this girl newly dead on the rubbled brick, one shoe on, one shoe off. He is very afraid of her. He holds his head between his gloved hands. He is going to be sick. He whispers her name. He whispers other things like fuck, fuck, fuck, fuck . . .

Then she opens her eyes and sits up. She's looking, if she's looking anywhere, straight ahead to the old boat shed. She gets to her feet. It does not appear difficult or painful though somehow she gives the impression she is reassembling herself out of the bricks and flowers around her, rising out of her own dust. She starts walking – bare foot, dressed foot, bare foot, dressed foot – twelve or fifteen steps until, without warning, she crumples to the ground, face down this time.

The welder has been watching it all through the tint of his goggles. He shuts the valves on the tank, pushes up his goggles and starts to run. The other man, the one smoking outside the office, is also running, though more awkwardly, as if running was not really his thing or as if he did not want to be the first to arrive. The welder kneels beside Maud's head. He puts his lips close to the ground. He whispers to her, rests two fingers on her neck. The man in the suit crouches, Arab style, on the other side of her, the cloth of his trousers tight over his thighs. From somewhere a bell has started to sound, high-pitched and continuous. Others are coming now, more yardsmen in red overalls, the woman from the marina office, somebody in salopettes who must have just come off one of the boats on the pontoon. 'Don't crowd her!' says the welder. Someone, breathless, passes forward a green box. Three or four times the woman from the office says she has called the emergency services. She says emergency services rather than ambulance.

At some point they all notice Tim, the way he is standing there fifteen feet away as if nailed to the air. They notice him, frown, then look back at Maud.

2

No stanchions, no guard rail. And she was, perhaps, affected by the fumes from the pitch. The ambulance could be heard coming from a long way off. It had, among other things, to cross the river. When they arrived, the paramedics put a neck brace on Maud then turned her like some precious archaeological find, a bog girl old as Christ, fragile as ashes. Once she was stabilized, one of the paramedics sat Tim on the back step of the ambulance and explained to him that he was suffering from shock but that he wasn't to worry because his girlfriend was doing pretty well, all things considered. They were going to drive up to the top of the valley to meet the helicopter. The helicopter would fly her to the hospital in Plymouth. She would be there in about half an hour.

When Tim wakes to himself, when the shivering stops and his head begins to work again in a way he can recognize, he is sitting in the marina office with a tartan blanket round his shoulders. Pot plants, filing cabinets, maps of the river. A poster, sun-faded, of a sailing boat, one of the old kind of racing yacht, low, over-canvassed, a dozen crew sitting along the windward side, legs dangling. The woman who called the ambulance is talking in a low voice to the man in the suit. She brings Tim a mug of tea. It's scalding hot and undrinkably sweet. He sips at it then stands and folds the blanket. It takes him a moment to shrug off the idea that he too has been injured, that there is an injury he should find and look at. He thanks the man and the woman (he is nothing if not polite – those schools!) then goes out to where his old Lancia is parked and drives to Plymouth.

It's nearly dark when he arrives. The hospital seems among the most terrible places he has ever been. He cannot find A&E. He stands for a time in the lit doorway of the genito-urinary unit until a porter asks him if he is all right and points out his way – a path between bushes that leads to a forecourt where ambulances are clustered around wide, rubber-fringed doors.

At reception the woman behind the glass wants to know what he is to Maud and after a pause he says he's a friend. She won't tell him Maud's condition, her status. He thinks she probably doesn't know. He sits in the waiting room on a worn red bench. An elderly couple is sitting near him. They have the look of people who have recently escaped from a bombed city – or what he imagines such people would look like. A half-hour passes. He goes back to the desk. The woman has been replaced by another woman. This one is friendlier.

'Hold on,' she says. She calls the nurses' station, somewhere on the far side of the swing doors. 'Stamp,' she says. 'Came in on the helicopter this afternoon?' She listens, she nods. 'Yes,' she says, 'OK . . . Yes . . . Yes . . . A friend . . . yes . . . right . . . Thanks.' She puts the phone down. She looks at Tim and smiles.

Maud is in the hospital for three nights. Her first night is on ICU, then they move her to an assessment ward in an older part of the hospital. From the windows of the ward you cannot see the sea but you can see the light from the sea. Ten women either side of the room, one behind screens with a voice like a child's, so obese she cannot bear to be looked at.

Maud's parents, alerted by the hospital, visit from Swindon. They're both schoolteachers, busy people. They have brought a bag of Maltesers with them and some magazines from which certain pictures have been carefully cut out and already, perhaps, laminated on the machine in the kitchen, images of the physical world or pictures illustrative of the human condition, those aspects most readily taught to schoolchildren. Her mother calls her Maudy, her father polishes his glasses. In the middle of speaking to them Maud falls asleep. Her parents look at her, the wax-white face on the pillow, the bandages on her head like a skull cap. They look round to see if there is anyone calm and medical who might take charge of things.

When she leaves she has a cast on her leg and a pair of crutches. Tim drives her back to Bristol. He has spent the last three nights in a hotel near the docks where Chinese seamen wandered the overheated corridors in their underwear, a wide-hipped strolling from room to room, every room with its door open, parties of men strewn on the beds, smoking and watching television.

He stows her crutches in the back of the car. She is very quiet. He asks if she wants the radio on and she says she doesn't mind. He wants to know if she is in pain. He asks if she remembers anything. He says he is sorry, and when she asks why he says he doesn't know. He's sorry anyway. Sorry she's hurt.

Her flat is on Woodland Road, not far from the university biology department where she is doing her master's degree. She has lived there for at least six months but to Tim, when he has followed her up the stairs, the place has an oddly uninhabited air. He has sisters – the twins – and certain ideas about the spaces girls live in, the scented candles on the mantlepiece, dresses on hangers hanging from the backs of doors, throws, wraps, photographs in heart-shaped frames. He can see nothing of this at Maud's. There are two pairs of trainers and a pair of walking boots lined up in the little hallway. In the living room the furniture is three types of brown. There are no pictures on the walls. Light from the street drains inwards through a big window and falls onto a carpet of the kind intended to endure all insult. Everything is tidy. If there's a smell it's just the smell of the building itself.

She sits in one of the armchairs, her crutches on the floor beside her. He makes tea for her though there is no milk in the fridge. She is pale. She looks exhausted. He says he thinks he should stay the night on the sofa, unless of course there was someone else she could call. 'You're not supposed to be alone,' he says. 'Not for the first twenty-four hours. It's in the notes from the hospital.'

'I'm OK,' she says, and he says, 'Yes, well, you're probably not. Not yet.' Her cupboards are bare. He hurries out to do some shopping. In the supermarket he wonders if he is taking advantage of her, that far from being just a helpful friend he is in fact a manipulative scheming shit. This thought does not go deep. He fills the basket, pays and strides back to the flat, city wind in his face.

He cooks a cheese soufflé. He's a good cook and the soufflé is light and appetizing. She thanks him, eats three forkfuls. She sleeps upright in the chair. It's slightly boring, slightly worrying. When she comes to, they watch television for an hour then she goes through the door to her bedroom. He cleans up, lies awake on the sofa under his coat. He would like to find a secret diary and read her secret thoughts. Her sex fantasies, her fear of loneliness, her plans. Does she have a diary? His sisters have diaries, volumes of them, mostly with little locks on them, but he's pretty certain Maud does not and that if she did she would not be recording her sex fantasies, her fear of loneliness. Through the netting over the window he sees a smudge of moon and when he shuts his eyes he sees Chinamen drifting like cigarette smoke.

He is woken by the noise of Maud throwing up. She has made it to the bathroom; the door is open, the light on, a hard light. He has a back view of her in her nightshirt, bent over the pink sink. She doesn't have much to bring up. He hovers by the door waiting to catch her but she has wrapped her fingers round the taps, has braced herself.

The Infirmary is a five-minute drive, certainly at this time of night. They admit her straight away, wheel her off in a wheel-chair. He doesn't get to say goodbye or good luck.

When he returns the next morning he is told she is on Elizabeth Fry, a ward on the fifth floor at the front. He goes up flights of stairs, broad green steps, a window at every turn, the city opening out as he ascends, revealing itself as several cities, dozens perhaps, each wrapped around the bones of what it grew from. He cannot find Maud at first. The patients in their beds, in their gowns, are all strangely similar. He walks slowly past the ends of beds until he finds her in an annex with five others, her name and date of admission written on the whiteboard above her head.

She already has a visitor, a woman with long grey hair worn free, a pair of leopard-print kitten heels on her big feet. She is gently holding one of Maud's hands and keeps her hold as she turns to look up at Tim.

'She's asleep,' says the woman. 'She's been asleep since I got here.'

'But she's OK?'

'As far as I know.'

'It's probably what she needs.'

'Sleep?'

'Yes.'

'It's certainly,' says the woman, 'the sort of thing people say.' She has a northern accent – Midlands, north Midlands, somewhere like that. He doesn't really know the Midlands.

'I'm Tim,' he says, 'Tim Rathbone.'

'Susan Kimber,' says the woman. 'Maud's professor at the university. She called me this morning. She had a tutorial scheduled for this afternoon.'

'She called you?'

'She's conscientious. And they have a sort of phone on wheels, somewhere.'

'I brought her in last night,' says Tim. 'She was being sick.'

'It was lucky you were there.'

'Yes. I suppose it was.'

'You're a friend.'

'Yes.'

'Are you at the university?'

'I finished the year before last. I did English.'

'So you read novels for three years.'

'Actually, a lot of it was reading *about* novels,' says Tim. 'But it must seem a bit thin compared to what you do, you and Maud.'

'Not really,' says the professor. 'Or if it is that might be the point.'

'I would rather have done music. I should have.'

'You play something?'

'The guitar. Some piano. Mostly guitar.'

'Ah,' says the professor, her expression softening a little. 'You're the guitar player.'

'Yes. She's mentioned me?'

'I quiz all my students relentlessly, particularly about their private lives. Maud of course I had first to teach that she had a private life. I mean something between work and sleep. Something discussable.'

For a moment they both glance over at the bed, the sleeping girl.

'How well do you know her?' asks the professor.

'We've sailed a couple of times on the university boat. And once she came to a concert I put on. A lunchtime thing at the church at the bottom of Park Street.'

'You like her.'

'Yes.'

'You want to help her.'

'Help her?'

'Rescue her. You're not alone, I'm afraid. They flit around her like moths, though as far as I can tell she does nothing obvious to encourage it. Boys and girls. It's her pheromones perhaps.'

He nods. He is not sure what to say to this. She has started to remind him of his mother, though the professor is clearly sober.

'On the phone,' says the professor, 'she told me she had fallen from the deck of a boat. Presumably not into the sea.'

'The boat was in the yard. She fell onto brick. About twenty feet.'

'And then?'

'Then?'

'You were there, weren't you? What happened next?'

Tim frowns. For some reason – for several reasons – he has

failed to play it back to himself, the half-minute that followed. After a while, in which he seems to see pictures, like portraits hanging in a gallery – the welder under his shower of sparks, the man in the suit smoking, and some white bird, a gull or even an egret, wings spread in emblematic flight over the curled green heads of the trees – he says, 'She got up. She started walking.'

The professor smiles. 'Yes,' she says. 'Yes. That sounds like our Maud.'

For a second time he leads her from the doors of a hospital. He has a fresh set of guidance notes. She swings on her crutches at his side. The sky is tufted with small, perfectly white clouds.

He goes shopping again then cooks her a herb omelette with a side salad of imported leaves. She finishes her food, wipes her plate clean with a slice of bread.

He says he will play for her if she wants and when she agrees or does not tell him she does not want it, he drives the Lancia to his flat in one of the tall white houses overlooking the river, views of the suspension bridge on one side, the old bonded warehouses on the other. He rents the place with a Spaniard who works all hours at a restaurant, at two restaurants, at least two. Tim's share is paid from the family money stream, those trusts, the echo of old work, set up by his grandparents, and which provide him with an income never much more than modest but enough for this, the flat in the white building, the airy views.

The Spaniard's Spanish girlfriend is asleep on the window seat. She has a nose like a shark's fin and blue-black hair so thick you would have to cut it with gardening shears. He goes softly past her to his room, chooses a guitar, settles it into its case, clips the case shut and drives back to Maud.

She has showered, changed. Her hair is still damp. He asks if she is feeling better and she says she is. They drink tea (he has bought some milk). She reads for half an hour a volume entitled *Medical Physiology (2nd Edition)*, though her eyes are sometimes shut and the book teeters in her grip. As evening comes on he takes out the guitar and shows it to her. He tells her it's a reproduction of a René Lacôte and that Lacôte was a celebrated nineteenth-century guitar-maker. This is maple, and on the top, this is spruce. He draws her attention to the abalone rosette, the diamonds and moons on the headstock. He says, in fact, he has an original Lacôte, one that he bought at auction a couple of years ago. He keeps it at his parents' place. His parents have an elaborate security system. He laughs, then turns on the only lamp in the room and sits under its light.

He plays, she listens. He might imagine this a model of their future together. One piece, a short study by Fernando Sor, she asks to hear again. The guitar has a light sound compared to a modern guitar. It is clear and sweet and seems an instrument designed to play children to sleep.

At ten she rocks herself onto her good foot, readies herself for bed. When she comes out of the bathroom she has a nightshirt on and hangs between the crutches. He is thinking what to say to her – another quote from the hospital guidance notes perhaps – but it's Maud who speaks first. 'You can stay in my room,' she says.

'OK,' he says. 'With you?'

'Not to have sex,' she says.

'Of course,' he says. Then, more gravely, 'Of course not.'

In her bedroom the bed is not particularly large, not a full-size double. She gets under the covers, he quickly strips down to T-shirt and boxers. He gets in beside her. She smells – despite the shower – of the hospital, and when she reaches to put off the lamp he sees she still has the hospital ID bracelet on her wrist. She lies with her back to him. She has a small patch of shaved scalp around the wound on her head. They don't talk. He has an erection he knows will not subside for hours and he keeps his hips back a little so she will not feel it press against her. He listens to her breathing, thinks he hears the moment it settles into the rhythm of her sleep. He wants to stay awake all night and imagines that he will, that he will have no choice, but her warmth enters him like a drug and when he opens his eyes again there's a fine silt of dawn in the room. She is still there, the broken girl, the miraculous girl. All night they have lain like two stones in the road. He rests a hand on her shoulder. She stirs but sleeps on. In sleep, her nightshirt has ridden up a little and his right knee is touching the back of her left thigh, skin on skin. Under the window the occasional car drones past.

This was their courtship.

3

Maud alone for a moment, sitting on the bed nude as an egg, her foot sunk in the cast, no watch or bracelet or jewel of any kind on her, her skin lit by the light of an ancient and implicated city.

Her bedroom – as undecorated as the rest of the flat – is heated by a plug-in and possibly unsafe oil radiator that heats only a rose of air in the immediate vicinity of its grey fins. She has a good tolerance for the cold. All those hours of dinghy sailing in gravel ponds, on the Thames, the seaside. Wet shorts, wet feet. Then all the rest: the stubbed toes, rope-burn, your face slapped by a sail, a bruise on your thigh like a peony in full bloom from losing your footing among the weeds on the slipway.

As a schoolgirl she belonged to the school judo club. The club was in a kind of Nissen hut in the grounds of the boys' school across the road. It had no obvious ventilation and the small windows ran with condensation, summer and winter. The instructor was a middle-aged man called Rawlins, a one-time European champion but by Maud's time a semi-cripple who chain-smoked throughout the classes and whose hands were huge and red and murderous. The smell of the place. The thump thump thump of bodies hitting the mat. How to grip up, how to point your feet. Your balance as a secret you carried and your opponent guessed at, reached for. Rawlins saw how she stood her ground, how she was not intimidated by bigger girls, never gave up even when giving up made sense. For a while he thought she might have the necessary oddness to do well in a fighting art. She reminded him of a dog he had once owned that had been killed by a car and that he still sometimes thought about. When she dislocated a finger throwing a girl with tai otoshi he asked if she wanted him to reset it, right there on the mat. This was one of his tests. With Rawlins everything was a test, a way of seeing who you were. She nodded. He took her white hand between his red ones, his gaze made crazy by the smoke drifting up from the cigarette between his teeth. You just keep looking at me, he said, you keep your eyes on old Rawlins, and she did, obediently, while his thumbs felt out the joint.

Tim calls to her through the door. 'You OK in there, Maud?'

'Yes,' she calls back.

'Decent?'

'Yes.'

He opens the door. 'Oh, Jesus,' he says. 'So sorry.' He blushes but she doesn't. Several seconds pass. 'I'll be in here,' he says.

4

In July they drive down to his parents' place. It turns out they grew up within a hundred miles of each other, in neighbouring counties, but while she was in a terraced house in a town, semi-industrial, a transport hub, he was among open fields, stables, copses, lawns. (The local hunt takes twenty minutes to cross his parents' land, a line of black and scarlet riders, mud like shrapnel from the horses' hooves.)

They bump up the driveway. It is the Rathbone summer gathering and there are already four other cars parked casually in the yard of the house, big cars dappled with mud. All the way from Bristol he has talked about his family. As they came closer to the house he became more convinced she would not get on with them, would not like them, would find them strange, difficult. Unpleasant.

'You won't want to speak to me afterwards,' he says. And then, 'Please be as rude as you like.' And then, definitively, 'They wouldn't even notice.'

In the hallway – if that's what it is, the room (with its own fireplace) that lies beyond the front door (if this is the front door) – a dog puts its snout in Maud's crotch while other, smaller dogs, chew at her heels. There are old newspapers, dog leads, twenty hats from straw boaters to waxed caps. Waxed jackets, rows of boots upturned on the boot racks, a riding crop propped against a windowpane. In a crystal bowl a dozen brass-ended cartridges are like loose change from somebody's pocket.

Between the hall and the kitchen are other rooms that seem to have the freedom to simply be rooms. There are dog baskets, armchairs, a table that looks even older than the house. From one of the armchairs a dog, very old, tracks them with milky eyes. Tim's mother is in the kitchen. She is doing something with flour and fat, her hands sunk in a glass bowl. She is tall with hennaed hair in a tight French plait. She has a floral dress on, laced patent leather boots, a butcher's apron. She offers Tim her cheek, smiles at Maud. 'I have cool hands,' she says, 'which is perfect for making pastry.'

Children come in – two boys and a girl, the eldest perhaps eight. They are chasing each other but, seeing Maud, become suddenly self-possessed. The girl holds out her hand.

'I'm Molly,' says the girl. 'This is Ish and this is Billy. Are you Tim's girlfriend?'

The children's parents arrive, Tim's brother, Magnus, and his wife, the former model. 'Is it gin o'clock?' asks the brother. He and Tim slap shoulders. Magnus looks at Maud, welcomes her to the asylum. Through the kitchen window, on the shining lawn, two teenage girls, their hair in heavy plaits, are playing croquet. There is nothing dainty in the way they handle the mallets. The balls fizz over the mown grass.

It turns out that it is gin o'clock. Magnus spends twenty

minutes preparing the drinks, slicing limes, breaking ice in a clean tea-towel, measuring, stirring.

The dog with the occluded eyes has got on to a bench and is eating a biscuit it has dragged from a plate. It has an expression on its face like a martyr in a religious painting.

At the sound of an aeroplane, a thin buzzing in the air, the children all run outside. Tim leads Maud out behind them. They walk towards the stable block. The plane has disappeared but suddenly reappears thirty feet above the road, skims the treetops, then the hedges. Magnus's wife calls to the children but her voice doesn't carry. They are running towards the field behind the stables, waving. The plane falls delicately to the grass, bounces, settles, slows, turns and taxis towards the stables. It is a very small plane, silvery and trembling in its movements. It stops a short distance from where the adults and children are now gathered. A door swings up, a large man struggles from his seat. 'Points for the landing?' he calls.

To Maud, Tim says, 'Meet Daddy.'

Lunch is long, noisy. The family has manners that are beyond manners. The food is delicious, clever. There is wine from a decanter; there are crystal glasses, none of which match. Maud has been sat next to Tim's father. She calls him Mr Rathbone and he says Peter will do or shall I call you Miss Stamp? He has red corduroys on, a thick wreath of grey hair, a weathered and immaculately shaved face, a voice that seems to have no back to it, that effortlessly subdues all others. He flew that morning over Salisbury Cathedral and felt proud to be of the race that built it. He says there was a queen called Maud, wasn't there? Married one of the Plantagenets. He wants to know about her work at the university, her research. She explains, carefully though not at length.

Pathological wound healing, tissue repair response, particularly in the elderly.

'People like me, you mean?'

'Older,' she says.

'Well, that's something.'

When she speaks about defects in oestrogen signalling, he seems able to follow her. He tells her he was in the army and since then a dabbler – reads a lot, does stuff in the workshops, a seat-of-the-pants pilot. He asks about her accident. The story of her fall has already been recited three or four times. The children particularly like it. The cast came off last week.

'Do you have any scars?' asks the ex-model.

'A couple,' says Maud.

'And tell me about this,' says Tim's father, taking hold of her left arm with hands utterly unlike Tim's. He has glasses on a cord round his neck. He puts them on, reads the ink along her forearm (ink that took four hours over two sessions to put in place, her arm bloody on a padded rest).

'*Sauve . . . Qui . . . Peut. Sauve Qui Peut?*'

'Every man for himself,' says Magnus, refilling his glass.

'I'm not sure it's quite that,' says Tim. 'Is it, Maud?'

'Of course it bloody is,' says his brother.

'Better,' says Mr Rathbone, 'than runes or some Maori nonsense. At least it means something.'

'By that token,' says Magnus, 'she could have had *Arbeit Macht Frei*. That means something.'

'Don't be an ass, Mags,' says his father.

One of the twins says, 'There's a girl at school who's going to have the Song of Songs tattooed in a spiral around her belly button.'

'No she's not,' says the other twin.

'But did you know what it meant, Maud,' asks Tim's mother, 'when you had it done?'

'Mum, please,' says Tim.

She smiles. 'It was just a question, dear.'

They are given the upstairs guest room at the western end of the house. This is sometimes called the blue room on account of the wallpaper, or the Chinese room on account of a framed scroll that hangs between the windows. They take their bags up there. The room is packed with afternoon sun. Tim frees a fly batting the glass of a window. 'The children already love you,' he says.

'They don't know me,' she says.

He puts his arms around her from behind. 'How long do you have to know someone before you love them?'

'More than a morning,' she says.

'Did you like any of them?'

'Of course.'

'Any in particular?'

'Your father?'

'When I was a boy,' says Tim, 'I was completely in awe of him. Everyone talking about him like he was God. But you need to be careful. I can remember all of us hiding behind a sofa, Mum too, while Dad went from room to room looking for us. It wasn't a game.' He holds Maud more tightly, draws her against himself. 'Anyway, they'll all be drunk in an hour,' he says.

The long twilight, blue and violet, blue and purple. They stroll in and out of the French windows. They drink gin poured from a blue bottle. The children chase the dogs around the croquet hoops. Tim's mother, speaking about the light, the loveliness of it, the way it seems to simply *fold* over everything, becomes incoherent and tearful and plucks at the material of her dress. To Maud, Tim's father explains that there are three twilights. 'This one,' he says, sniffing it, 'is civil. Later we will have nautical.'

Blue and violet, blue and purple. The twins, their big backsides in pale jodhpurs, kneel on the lawn and dreamily tear at the trimmed grass. Magnus wears an expression of tragic boredom. His wife, in a dress she has sewn herself, drifts after the children.

By the time they sit down to eat it's nearly eleven and no one has much interest in the food. Tim's mother has wept and recovered and is now elaborately precise in everything she says. When they have finished, the picked-at food is simply pushed aside. Someone is coming in in the morning. Everything will be taken care of.

The family disperses. Tim takes Maud's hand, leads her through a door into a passageway and along the passage to a short flight of steps. Here there is a door with a metal face, a keypad at the side of it. This, Tim tells her, is the treasure room. He laughs as he taps in the code and says it's like the burial chamber in a pyramid. Inside, the room is noticeably cooler than the rest of the house. The walls are whitewashed, lined with shelves and cabinets. There is no window.

He shows her things. 'I don't really know what any of this is worth,' he says.

There's some heavy Victorian jewellery. A portrait, palm-sized, attributed to Ozias Humphry, of a young woman with red hair. There's a first edition of J. M. Barrie's *The Little White Bird* (with a dedication to 'pretty little Lilly Rathbone'). There's a portfolio of watercolour sketches by Alfred Downing Fripp, mostly of children on the sea-shore. There's a wind-up gramophone, a Webley revolver someone in the family carried at the second battle of

Ypres. There's a ritual mask from somewhere in central Africa carved from a dark and oily wood, an artefact that seems to speak a dead or irrecoverable language but not itself to be dead, not at all. Tim poses with the mask over his face, the revolver in his hand. 'My place or yours,' he says, his voice muffled by the wood.

On a low shelf, in a creased brown case, is the guitar. He lifts it out, and after a second of hesitation, puts it into Maud's hands. Lacôte, Luthier, Paris 1842. Breveté Du Roi. It appears to be in almost immaculate condition. It is surprisingly light, buoyant. Around the sound hole is a pattern of tortoiseshell with gold and mother-of-pearl inlays. She hands it back. He sits on a stool and begins to tune by ear.

'Old guitars,' he says, 'don't necessarily improve with age. Most of them lose tone. But this one's exceptional.' He runs his fingers over the strings, sounds a chord, adjusts the tuning. He plays the beginning of something, fifteen, twenty bars of a dance. 'The acoustic here is shit,' he says. 'But you get the idea.'

In her own house – her parents' house – there was a laminating machine, the television, her mother's wedding ring. Some painted plates on the wall in the living room. Paperbacks.

'Why do you keep it in here?' she says. 'It's like having a boat you never sail.'

'It costs about the same as a boat,' he says. 'And it's a lot easier to steal.' He puts it back in its case, lifts the case back onto the shelf, turns to find Maud looking at the African mask as if the mask were looking back at her. He has not seen anything quite like that before. He decides not to think about it.

When the treasure room is locked again, sealed, the alarm reset to active, they move together, quietly, through the part-lit house. It's late. There's no one around. He opens doors for her, invites her to peer into the empty rooms. Each room has its particular smell. The drawing room is leather and flowers; the little drawing room is last winter's last fire. The study stinks of sleeping dogs. The music room smells of the beeswax worked into the black wood of the piano. Everywhere, on every surface, there are pictures of children and dogs. Upstairs, it seems they must be the last ones to bed, the last awake, but when Maud with her wash bag finds her way to the nearest bathroom the light is on and the shower running. She sits on the step opposite the door and waits. The shower stops and a minute later Magnus comes out with a towel round his waist. At supper, while topping up her glass with good wine he told her, in a voice he might, in other circumstances, have used to pass on sensitive financial information, 'This is an all-or-nothing family. We tend not to take prisoners.' Now, seeing Maud on the step, he grins at her, whips off his towel, slowly wraps himself again and plods away along the corridor. 'Goodnight,' he calls over his shoulder. 'Funny girl.'

In the blue room, the Chinese room, one o'clock in the morning, Tim hunches over Maud like a man who has stumbled, a man preparing to be flogged. Every few seconds he makes a quivering, doggish thrust, sinks into her, slides out a little. They have been lovers for five weeks. Each time they do it he wants to drive her mad but each time it's himself he drives mad. The gasps, the hushed exclamations, are all his. With Maud there's just a subtle thickening of the breath. Has she been louder with other men? He frets over whether he is doing it right; if he should, for example, be crashing into her frenziedly rather than this slow stop-start fucking that, at twenty-six, appears to be his sexual character, his sexual fate.

He has not told her what Professor Kimber said in the hospital about the flitting moths. He is not sure how much he wants to know. If she didn't encourage them, does that mean she didn't go with them? Or does it mean they didn't need encouragement, that Maud as Maud was encouragement enough? That quality in her he has not yet found the word for but that seems located in her gaze, something undesigned, vulnerable, subtly immodest, that might suggest to all manner of people who approached directly enough, boldly enough, she would simply lie down and let them do it.

What has he found? Who has he found? Is this a wise love?

The room is not entirely dark. Electric light seeps under the door from the corridor, and there's a scattered light in the air itself, the light of summer nights, like phosphorescence at sea. Her eyes are shut, her arms loosely by her head, *Sauve Qui Peut* a block of shadow on one palely gleaming forearm.

He changes the rhythm. The old bed jangles. It is, in some curious way, like a children's game. He kisses her throat and she lifts her hips to him. It's too much. He has a condom on but feels he is flooding her, has access to her blood and is flooding her. He buries his face in her shoulder, is briefly blind, erased. For a few joyful seconds the whole world rests on the peeping of a nightbird in the trees by the stream. Then the room reassembles itself. She reaches between them, touches the end of the condom. It means – for they have learnt this last month to read each other's sexual dumb-show – that he should come out of her and carefully. He kneels up. She shifts off her back and swings herself to the side of the bed. For a while she sits there looking towards the uncurtained window, then wipes the sweat from under her breasts with the blades of her hands.

5

A night sail to the Île-de-Bréhat in the university boat. Twenty-four hours if the wind is fair, the course as south as they can sail it, cut the shipping lanes at right angles, raise the La Peon lighthouse or Les Heux, pick their way in through the currents.

There are six of them – three young men, three young women. In experience there is little to choose between them though some, like Maud, know more about dinghies than yachts, are more at ease working purely with sail and wind than passage planning and tidal curves. As a matter of club policy they have (in the pub in Bristol) appointed a captain. The choice was made by ballot, the names written on Rizla papers, the papers folded and dropped into a clean ashtray. Tim won by a single vote and promised to flog them all for the merest indiscipline. Maud received two votes, one of them from Tim. As for whether Maud voted for him, he knew there were two who did not and prefers to assume she was not one of them.

They leave on the morning tide. The wind is from the west,

force three to four, the boat moving in stately rhythm and heeling just enough to make a pencil on the chart table roll slowly to the leeward side. As they come clear of the shelter of the bay there are cross-currents, fields of green water stubbled with short choppy waves that make the hull jitter and send wisps of spray to darken the wood of the deck. But this is sailing at its easiest, its most pleasant. Summer air, the boat's shadow like black silk hauled just beneath the water's surface, the crew fresh, fresh-faced, the forecast excellent. In the afternoon the wind backs towards the south. There's a rain squall they watch arriving from miles off that leaves the boat's hundred surfaces shining and dripping. England disappears in the murk astern then appears again in uncanny green detail as the weather blows through.

In the last good hour of daylight they prepare a supper of chilli con carne (chilli sin carne for the one vegetarian), have a single glass of wine each, mugs of coffee. They switch on the navigation lights and begin the watches. In another hour they will be up in the shipping lanes with vessels of fifty thousand tonnes, a hundred thousand tonnes, some moving so fast that a light on the far horizon could be on top of them inside of fifteen minutes. Ships that by rumour and repute travel blind or nearly so, some man or other dozing on a part-lit bridge sixty metres above the water.

At ten to three in the morning, Tim and Maud are woken for their watch and move from thin sleep into the life of the boat, the tilted world. The off-going watch has made hot drinks for them. A voice, amused, calls Tim 'skipper'. On the chart table under a red lamp the English Channel is pinned by weights of lead wrapped in leather. Soft lines show their progress. The last fix places them thirty miles west of Jersey. In the cockpit Maud takes the tiller. Tim goes forward to look for shipping. Off the starboard bow are the heaped lights of a RoRo ferry; something much smaller off the other bow – a trawler, perhaps, from the odd way she's lit up. He watches for a while, sees how her bearing changes, then makes his way back to the cockpit.

'OK?' he says.

'OK,' she says.

She has a blue Helly Hansen jacket on, jeans, sea boots.

'You should have a hat,' he says and points to his own.

The light of the binnacle on her face, the eeriness of that light. She's peering up at the mainsail, the dove-grey ghost of it under the masthead light. She lets the boat fall away from the wind then brings it up a point and settles it. Tim puts half a turn on the headsail winch. The ferry is already passing them. He thinks he hears its engines. Perhaps he does.

'Turn right,' he says, 'and we could sail for America.'

She nods. She's concentrating.

'Would you like that?'

'Yes,' she says.

'Good,' he says. 'I'll pop below and cut their throats.'

'OK,' she says.

'You may have to help me heave them over the side.'

'OK.'

'Or would *you* like to cut their throats?'

'Are you keeping watch?'

He reaches across, touches the cold cloth of her jeans. 'OK,' he says. 'I'll behave.'

At twenty-minute intervals they swap roles, one to the tiller, one to the slatted bench on the leeward side to keep watch under the foot of the sails. The urge to keep talking to her, to keep her attention, is disturbingly strong. Love is making him slightly foolish. Here they are, crossing the English Channel at night, and he, the nominal captain, is thinking of the chocolate in his pocket and whether she would let him feed it to her so that he could feel for a moment the slight damp heat of her mouth on his fingertips. He should shake this off. He should assume his responsibilities. Come on, Rathbone! But beyond all admonition is his belief that the world is secretly powered by people in exactly the condition he is now, melodic, lit up, the nerve-trees of their brains like cities seen from the air at night . . .

Over the eastern horizon, the morning star. At twenty to six the sun is rising. Briefly, sea and air appear as things new made and they are Adam and Eve drifting on a vine leaf, a morning in Eden. Then fog comes down as fog can, long fingers of it winding shyly around the things of the boat and thickening until visibility is down to thirty yards, then ten. Tim fetches the horn, shouts up the rest of the crew. They stand by to start the engine, to drop the sails. The sea rustles at the side of them. The fog is theatrical, impenetrable. Tim sounds the horn – one long blast and two short. There's someone below watching the radar, everyone else is on deck, leaning into the fog. They begin to hear the horns of shipping. They speak in whispers, see shapes, imaginary headlands, vessels of smoke. On the VHF, the open channel, comes a sudden voice in a language none of them recognize. The cadence is unusual. It may be a warning of some sort but it sounds more like a recitation or a call to prayer.

6

In her pigeon-hole in the biology department she finds an advertisement for a job. It's been cut out of the *New Scientist*, and in the margin, in Professor Kimber's handwriting – *Interested?*

The job is for a project study-manager leading, in a year or two, to a position as clinical research associate. The company is called Fenniman Laboratories, American-owned but with a UK base in Reading. She applies and is called for an interview. She takes the train from Bristol. The journey takes her through Swindon, and as the train slows she looks up from the papers in her lap (the glossy folder of information about the company) and takes in the utter familiarity of the view – the car parks, the billboards, the old engine sheds and workshops, converted or derelict. The station is a bare half-mile from where she grew up and where her parents still live. Further off is the school she went to (not one her parents ever taught at) and beyond that, at the not-quite-visible edge of the town, the house on the estate where, at fifteen, she lost her virginity to the father of the children she babysat for. Twenty minutes on his marriage bed, the satiny counterpane, late-afternoon light on the wall and strict instructions about which towel she could use when it was over.

There is no one she knows on the platform, no girl from school with a pushchair, no one she remembers from the terraces of the football ground, the narrow turnstiles she used to push through to watch the team slide down through the divisions, the players steaming like cattle on the muddy pitch, the manager in his big coat tearing pieces of air to shreds. Then they are off again, past posters advertising days out by the sea, past warehouses, a trading estate ('Swindon Vehicle Solutions'), the rind of meanly windowed new-builds, the first fields . . .

She goes back to the folder. There are headings such as 'You and Fenniman Laboratories', 'Our Philosophy', 'Into the Future'. There are charts of company performance, market share. There is an open letter from Josh Fenniman, CEO (*I have a passion for excellence in all fields . . .*). At the back of the folder is a list, with short descriptions, of the company's current research areas – diabetic neuropathy, post-herpetic neuralgia, nerve blocks, kappa-opioids. One study in particular catches her eye, a project involving a chemical called epibatidine discovered on the skin of an Ecuadorian frog, a type of toxic sweat that has also turned out to be powerfully analgesic. Fenniman's has produced a derivative called Fennidine and is starting a phase two trial at a hospital in Croydon. If she gets the job, the study might, conceivably, become one of those she monitors.

The next time she looks up – alerted by some alteration in the quality of the light – they are passing beside water. It's the gravel ponds where she first went sailing in the Mirror Ten dinghy she and Grandfather Ray built from a kit in his garage. On the water they had nothing to guide them other than the how-to book that came with the kit. Grandfather Ray was a railwayman. He sat in the boat wearing his yellow fluorescent jacket with British Rail Western Region on the back. They had a tartan thermos, sandwiches, no life jackets. They spent an hour crashing softly into the reeds that grew by the banks before they worked out how the boat was turned. She was two weeks short of her eleventh birthday.

At the interview she recounts something of this story. Professor Kimber, who has learnt, through patient questioning, much of Maud's past, has encouraged her to ('They'll like it,' she said. 'They'll like that side of you.') The interview is conducted by a woman from Human Resources and a man called Henderson, a South African, who is himself a keen sailor and grew up sailing out of Port Elizabeth with his father. He thinks it's delightful that Maud learnt to sail with a railwayman, that they sat on the bank of a pond with a how-to book.

The woman, however, has no interest in sailing. She is tall, impeccably turned out, has a small silver cross showing at the opening of her blouse. From the beginning, she seems suspicious of Maud, ill at ease with her, this candidate who shows no interview nerves, who makes eye-contact, who *maintains* eye-contact, in a way that is, frankly, not quite right.

For twenty minutes Maud and Henderson talk about the pathology of healing. Henderson uses the phrase 'the wound's journey'. They talk about methodology, health outcomes, trial protocols; about the pharmaceutical market place, the industrial angle. Maud is strong on the science, less so on commerce.

When the talk has lulled and Henderson has leant back in his chair, the woman from Human Resources says, 'If you were a drink, what would you be?'

After a moment Maud answers, 'Water.'

'With ice and lemon?' asks Henderson.

'No,' says Maud.

'Just plain old water? Straight up?'

'Yes.'

Henderson grins. The woman jots something onto her pad.

'Any questions for us, Maud?' asks Henderson.

She asks him about the trial in Croydon.

'Ah, yeah,' says Henderson. 'The little frog. Epipedobates. That's beautiful, isn't it? The chemical has a profile similar to nicotine. So maybe smoking will turn out to be good for us after all.' He smiles at her. 'I don't think I'm giving any secrets away if I tell you this is one of Josh Fenniman's pet projects. If there's a breakthrough, the consequences, human and financial, would obviously be pretty significant.'

From somewhere, someone's bag or pocket, there comes a faint electronic chime. Henderson looks over to the woman. The woman is looking at Maud.

'We don't,' she says, 'have an official policy, but do you mind if I ask what's written on your arm?'

She gestures to the half-word visible below the cuff of Maud's jacket. Maud undoes a button and pulls up her sleeve. She offers her arm, lays it on the table as if Henderson or the woman were going to take blood. The woman leans forward but keeps her hands in her lap. She has attended half-day seminars on appropriate and inappropriate contact. Henderson moves a finger in the air about an inch above the black ink, the white skin. He sounds out the words. 'Oh,' he says. 'Yeah. Yeah, I get it.'

After a second interview a fortnight later and a reference from Professor Kimber (*Maud is dependable, deeply resourceful and notable for the determined way in which she sees all projects through to conclusion*), and despite the reservations expressed by the woman from Human Resources ('I thought she was arrogant. Is she going to get on with people?'), Maud is offered the job. She accepts.

7

Six weeks before Christmas, seven months into the relationship, Maud and Tim begin to live together. Tim finds a first-floor flat in a small, half-hidden crescent on the hill above his old place. It's hidden from the main road by three plane trees that have grown as tall as the buildings. The houses (that must once have belonged to wealthy and perhaps fashionable families) have been converted into flats by someone more interested in rent than architecture, but the big sash windows are unspoilt and admit a tree-filtered light that shimmers when the sun is low and throws shadows of branches onto the back walls of the rooms. Tim puts down the deposit, rents a van. The van is almost entirely taken up with his own stuff; Maud's few boxes are squeezed in by the rear doors. All of it – the relationship, the move – feels inevitable to Tim and several times, as they carry their things up the common stairs he says, 'Doesn't this feel inevitable?' After the first time, she's quick enough to agree with him.

They have a flat-warming party. Tim plays flamenco (not on

the Lacôte or the Lacôte copy but on a guitar of highly polished cypress from the workshop of Andrés Dominguez in Seville). Among the guests are Tim's former flatmate, Ernesto, and his girlfriend with the blue-black hair. While Tim plays, she dances some private version of flamenco then sits on a table and looks at Maud, studies her, before leaning over to Ernesto and whispering, '*Ella, la novia. Una bruja.*'

'*Una bruja? Qué va! Es como una chica que trabaja en una pastelería.*'

Professor Kimber is at the party, dress split to her thigh, a silk camellia in her hair. She has brought two bottles of prosecco and a bunch of small yellow hothouse roses. She has also brought three or four of the moths, who look innocent, sane and gentle, entirely unpredatory. At some point during the evening, the party in its last fling, the moths flown home, Tim finds himself alone with the professor. 'Congratulations,' she says, touching her glass to his, and when he thanks her she says, 'Now which do you think she is, Tom – very fragile or very strong?'

'Tim,' he says, 'rather than Tom.'

She smiles. 'I suppose you'll find out in the end,' she says. 'I suppose we all will.'

At Christmas they are invited to his parents' house. He puts them off with the promise of being there the following year, and he and Maud spend Christmas Day alone eating tinned sardines, peaches in brandy, chocolate money. He has bought for her several small lovely things. A little brooch of antique jade in the form of a salamander. A dozen bangles of thin, beaten silver. A trinket box of polished rosewood (though she possesses no trinkets). A book of Chinese poems full of lovesick minor officials setting off for remote provinces. Also, a pot of winter jasmine, flowering.

To Tim, Maud gives a sailor's knife with a cork handle and a marlinspike. 'This is perfect,' he says, not mentioning the two he already has in a drawer somewhere. 'A perfect present.'

On New Year's Eve, frigid air tangled in the branches of the plane trees, Tim prepares them a private feast. First, a dozen oysters that have been sitting in their woven basket on the narrow balcony; then steak tartare made by hand-mincing best fillet, a raw egg stirred in, a chopped shallot. She has never eaten steak tartare but is happy to try it. He cannot imagine what he might suggest that she would baulk at. Sago pudding? Calf's brain? In restaurants, when she chooses from the menu, he does not get the impression she particularly *favours* one dish over another. And he loves the way she steadily clears her plate, the way at the end she puts her knife and fork together, tightly, a dead knight and his lady.

With the meal over they sit on the sofa and drink gin. Glass after glass of it. The room is snug, a faint odour of seafood, the sea.

'Have you ever done anything you're ashamed of?' he asks.

'No.'

'Have you ever done something, you know, deliberately to hurt someone?'

'No.'

'Have you ever stolen anything?'

'No.'

'Did you ever lie to your parents?'

She shrugs. 'I didn't tell them everything.'

'Aha! What didn't you tell them?'

'Just not everything.'

'Like?'

'Where I'd been. Who I went with.'

'Who did you go with?'

'When?'

'I don't know. When you went.'

'We're drunk,' she says.

'Of course we're drunk,' he says. 'Have you ever kissed a girl?'

'What?'

'Have you ever kissed a girl?'

'Why do you want to know?'

'I bet you kissed Professor Kimber. I know she wants to.'

She laughs at this, that short laugh of hers that always seems to catch her unawares. 'Why don't you play the guitar?' she says.

'I want to know everything,' he says. 'Swindon 1975. Daylight. Your first breath.'

'That tune you played when I came out of hospital.'

'When did you start being you?' he asks.

'I don't know,' she says.

'Try.'

'I don't know.'

'You never ask about my girlfriends,' he says.

'Why would I ask about them?'

'Curiosity?'

'I'll ask if you want.'

'No,' he says. 'No. The past is the past. Isn't it?'

'Yes,' she says.

'It's just us now.'

'Yes.'

'Tim and Maud.'

He tops up their glasses. They've been drinking it neat. Their colour is high, their mouths burned with gin. They decide to go for a walk but get no further than the bedroom. They kiss, they topple on to the bed. The curtains are open but the room is unlit.

They seem to have been sewn into their clothes. Buttons do not operate in the usual way. He licks her wrists, she strokes his ears. Half an hour later he floats into the bathroom, kneels in front of the toilet and throws up. Oysters, raw meat, acid, gin. He's there a long time. When he comes back to the bedroom, cold, shaky, he stands in the doorway looking at her as she sleeps in a pool of thin light that falls past the netting over the window. His heart fails him for a moment, for there is nothing there, nothing in her shape on the bed, compact as a seed, to suggest she has any need of him, that she is not already complete. He has been fooling himself! He has not reached her, has not understood her at all. He should get out before it's too late. He should pack a bag and get out. He will change his name. He will work on a trawler. Maud, in time, will marry a passing god, a moth god. Or become a temple prostitute or an assassin or the first woman on Mars. She will think of him sometimes. She will look at the bangles, the jade salamander. She will not cry.

He whispers her name. She is snoring lightly; a girl, a woman, dreaming of snakes. Or whatever. You don't know. He unhooks his big towelling bath-robe from the back of the bedroom door, lays it over her with elaborate care, then settles himself on the bed beside her, shudders, shuts his eyes, plays music in his head, thinks wow, 2001. Wow.

In the morning, he remembers neither insight nor fantasy. He feels ill and cleans the kitchen. He decides – kneeling in the middle of the brightening floor – that the only thing that matters is being brave and he shouts this news to Maud in the bathroom and after a second or two thinks he hears her call back her yes.

She starts work at Fenniman's. She has bought two new outfits from the department store near the bus station. One is dark blue, one is black. Dresses with jackets that make Tim think of the sort of outfits a woman detective might wear to give evidence in court.

She gets up early, perhaps two hours before it is light. By lamplight he watches her dress. If she notices him she doesn't object. The clever way women put their bras on. Deodorant, camisole. He likes to watch her pull her tights on, how the act of pulling up the tights to her waist is somehow childlike, so that it's easy to imagine her at eight or twelve, dressing for school on a winter's morning. Depending on the outfit, she sits on the edge of the bed for him to zip up her dress. Each morning for the first two weeks he offers to make her breakfast but she doesn't want it. She cleans her teeth then leans in to say goodbye, her coat in her arms.

The first month is induction. She goes up on the train, eats a sandwich, drinks tea, looks out at the grey fields, houses in their morning privacy, the light coming up over England. Certain faces become familiar – the man who never takes off his cycling helmet, the man who appears to be meditating, the woman with eczema. When the carriage is very warm she sometimes falls asleep and twice in one week she dreams of the desert – or some place, scuffed, waterless, inchoate, that she thinks of as desert for lack of any term more exact.

At the laboratory they introduce her to everyone, including the cleaners. Fenniman's has bright, egalitarian policies. First names, no titles. The atmosphere is relaxed but focused. The walls are painted a fine silvery grey. The furniture is moulded plastic in primary colours. Here and there, on walls and doors, there are squares of board printed with inspirational quotes – Martin Luther King, Einstein, Gandhi. On the door of Meeting Room 2 there's a poem by Marianne Moore:

If you will tell me why the fen
appears impassable, I then
will tell you why I think that I
can get across it if I try.

The air of the place is odour neutral. The staff wear no perfumes or colognes, no one smokes. Even in the animal room, where three hundred rats live in carefully indexed cages, there is no strong smell. Heat in the room is strictly maintained at between twenty-two and twenty-five degrees. The lights come on and off at twelve-hour intervals. The animals themselves, or those not subject to experimentation, are sleek with health, gentled from regular, careful handling. At break-times, rather than sit up in the staff room, Maud sometimes goes down to help the technician, a man called Keith who plays at the weekends in a bluegrass band and who sometimes winks at her as if he and she alone can see through it all, the Fenniman vision, the Fenniman mission.

At the end of induction she is given two hundred business cards and two lab coats (Fenniman Laboratories embroidered over the breast pocket). She is given a phone, the Nokia 8260. She is given a computer – one of the iBook 'clamshells' that come in a variety of colours (Maud's is blueberry). There is also a company car, a Vauxhall Corsa (purple), 78,000 miles on the clock, the driver's seat moulded to the shape of someone larger than Maud, someone who has left the company.

She will monitor three projects in three different cities. A study of nociceptors and allodynia at the Radcliffe in Oxford, liver enzymes at the Royal Infirmary in Bristol, and the epibatidine trial in Croydon. Each project has its allotted day. One day a week will be spent at the headquarters in Reading; the remaining day she will be at the flat, working on the clamshell. She is not highly paid but paid well enough and she will have more if she successfully completes her probation. Promotion to Clinical Research Associate could happen as soon as eighteen months. On the last day of induction, Henderson, despite the cold, the blustering wind, walks her the length of the car park to where the Corsa is waiting. 'For luck,' he says, and gives her a small origami crane he has made from red paper. It almost blows away as he passes it to her.

8

Spring comes, and with it the sly greening of the city. Doing yoga in the living room while Maud is at work, Tim is struck by a beam of sunlight and imagines himself a saint in a painting.

He decides to write a concerto, quite a short one perhaps, which he will call CYP2D6 after the liver enzyme that converts codeine into morphine and which, for the pleasures of her teacherly gaze, her fluency, he has made Maud explain to him at length and in detail. He will, of course, dedicate the concerto to her. For Maud, for M. For M with love. He will give it to her on her birthday or some other auspicious day. The little concerto! It will be proof of many things.

Elated by this – the prospect of the work, the already perfectly imagined moment of the presentation – he cycles to a music store at the bottom of Park Street and buys workbooks bound in blue card. Urtext. Merkheft für Noten und Notizen. He buys a dozen (they are so beautiful) then cycles to the delicatessen on Christmas Steps and has the plump girl lift ribbons of pasta from the wide floury drawer under the counter. He buys fennel sausages (that he will split from their skins), dried porcini, single cream, imported yellow courgettes. Also a bottle of red wine with a painterly label that seems to show Eve companionable with the serpent, the pair of them under an umbrella pine in some dangerous southern garden.

When she comes home – it's been a Croydon day, a three-hour meeting about the biosynthesis of alkaloids, then a talk, endless, entitled 'What can we learn from ABT 894?' – the wine is open, the mushrooms soaking in warm water, a large pan on the gas coming slowly to the boil. She takes a shower. When she comes back to the kitchen towelling her damp hair he says, 'Today was a true spring day, wasn't it?'

He watches her sit, watches her set up the little blueberry computer. He pours her a glass of wine. 'Check out the label,' he says. 'It may not be theologically sound.'

The sideboard by the cooker is spread with good things. His technique with garlic – crushing the clove with the flat of his knife, slipping it from its skin, dicing it – has an almost professional flair. He chatters to her over his shoulder. He hears the computer keys, now slow, now as though she is dropping fistfuls of dried peas. He has finished his first glass and pours himself a second. The wine, which had been interesting at first, with notes of rosemary and black tobacco, now seems bizarrely heavy, syrupy and heavy, with notes of tar, dead flowers, bath oil. How stupid it is to buy wine for the label! How stupid to go shopping because you have been touched by a beam of sunlight while practising yoga!

On the wall above her head the plaque of evening light is crisscrossed with the shadows of the plane trees. He takes a plate from the rack beside the sink, holds it at arm's length over the floor, waits some eight or ten seconds, then drops it. She looks at the shattered plate, glances up at him, turns back to the columns on the screen. 'Sorry,' he says, and fetches the dustpan and brush from the narrow cupboard at the far end of the kitchen where all the cleaning things are kept.

9

Something he would like to tell somebody. That when she sucks him it is no more lewd than if he were being sucked by, I don't know, a heifer, something of that kind. It is thorough and patient. And when he comes she drinks every last drop of him so that he wavers over the abyss and for several minutes afterwards is unable to meet her gaze or even say her name. In fact, there is no one he could possibly tell this to, not even his brother.

10

Though neither of them is now officially connected to the university, they are allowed to stay in the sailing club. They are the type of members the club cannot easily do without. They work on the boat, they pay their subscriptions, they know how to sail.

The boat is out of the water again but there is no caulking to be done, no bolts to replace. Some scrubbing of the hull and keel, on deck some sanding and varnishing. The most pressing job is replacing the stern gland around the propeller shaft. By the end of last season a steady drip had become a thin persistent trickle. It is not a job to attempt in the water, sea water flooding the engine compartment while someone flails with a spanner.

On the Saturday before Easter, they drive down to the coast in the Lancia. At the boatyard they meet two other members of the club, Angus and Camille. They pull on overalls. Camille, a fourth-year medical student, has brought two thermoses of coffee and a tupperware box of madeleines she has baked herself. Angus tucks copper dreadlocks under a woollen cap. Tim fetches the ladder and lashes the top rung to a cleat on the deck. He does not want Maud going up, feels his stomach turn at the sight of it, her blithe stepping from ladder to deck. He suggests she wears a safety line though he does not expect her to agree to it. She does not agree to it.

They work until two; coffee and madeleines sustain them. The men scrub the hull – neither is remotely mechanical – while Maud and Camille kneel either side of the access hatch on the cockpit sole, skinning their knuckles undoing clips and loosening bolts. To shift the locking nut they have to wrap four hands around the handle of the wrench. The capping nut is no easier. Camille hisses, '*Merde, merde*,' and when she catches her wrist, hard, on the edge of the hatch, is briefly tearful, then, laughing to find herself so ignored, comes back to the work. To free the old packing they need a tool they do not have – that may not, in fact, exist. Maud goes down the ladder and crosses to the boat shed. The shed is a hundred years old, an expanse of roofed air like a provincial railway station from the heroic days of steam, one of those places always grander than the town it served. There is no one in view – the yardsmen are still at lunch perhaps – and she is about to leave when a man leans from a shadowed tangle of ribs and struts, the beginnings or end of a boat, leans out and looks at her a moment and says, 'You're the girl whose flying lesson went wrong. I was here when that happened.'

His name is Robert Currey. He is forty, perhaps a little more, short and broad, his hair in dark curls. She tells him what she is trying to do, what she needs. He nods and crosses to a canvas tool bag, roots around (the bag is like an old canvas fish, a pantomime fish) and comes out with a tool, steel handle at one end, then a length of hawser, then, at the tip, something like a corkscrew. He smiles at her. 'Good luck,' he says.

The old packing is dragged out. Tim and Angus drive into town to buy crab sandwiches and a box of new packing. Maud and Camille wash in the marina toilet block. Camille brushes her fingers over the ink on Maud's arm. 'I love this,' she says. 'You want to see one of mine?'

She unbuttons the overall, peels herself, undoes her jeans and hooks down the waistband to show, just above the black cotton of her pants, a pair of elegantly drawn ideographs, Chinese, Japanese.

'What does it mean?' asks Maud.

'Fuck me until I cry,' says Camille. She rolls her eyes. 'Actually, it means harmony.'

'It's nice,' says Maud.

'Yes,' says Camille. 'It's nice but I like yours better. Yours is *speaking*.'

In watery sunlight they saunter in the yard. There are yachts on stilts, a few power boats, some upturned wooden boats like wherries or ships' pinnaces; a fishing boat hauled up on the slip, half-way through a fresh coat of blue paint. At the far end of the yard, the point where they will have to begin their loop back towards the water, Maud stops beside one of the chocked boats, looks up, walks slowly around it, first one way then the other. Everything suggests it has been there a long time. Even the wooden props are darker than those of the other boats, have more weather in them. The hull – fibreglass – is spotted with old red paint. The keel is long, deep, substantial. When she steps back she can see the end of the unstepped mast poking out like a bowsprit. All the rest is under a green tarpaulin streaked with bird shit and lashed so low over the transom they cannot see a name, a home port. From the mast tip, hanging like something someone has slung there and forgotten, is a small wooden board, the words 'For Sale' painted on it, and a telephone number, of which only the first few digits are legible.

They stand there looking up at it, two young women in overalls. Camille takes Maud's hand. 'It's like,' she says, 'one of those little houses you see in the country. You know, at the end of a long track. When you look through the window, there's a tree growing inside.'

When Maud returns the tool she asks Robert Currey about the boat. A nice boat, he says, an old Nicholson, but no one's been on it for at least two years. If she wants to know more she should talk to the broker, Chris Totten. Office by the car park. He gestures with his head. She thanks him, and is about to step out of the shed when he calls, 'Has it caught your eye, then?'

By four they have finished with the stern gland. The new packing – carefully cut loops of greased flax – is snug around the propeller shaft. Lock nut and capping nut are back in place, tight but not too tight. They won't know how successful they've been until the boat's back in the water but it looks right. They settle the hatch and go down to where Tim and Angus are sitting on drums of marine paint, eating chocolate. Camille tells Tim that Maud has found a beautiful boat for sale and that all he has to do now is pay for it.

'Maud?'

'Just a boat we saw,' she says. 'An old boat.'

He wants to see it and she takes him. 'It's probably too far gone,' she says. 'As for what it's like inside . . .'

'It might be fine inside,' he says.

They circle the boat, look mostly at the boat and sometimes at each other. She tells him what Robert Currey said.

52

'Two years?'

She nods.

He shrugs, makes a face. They both reach up to touch the boat, the red swell of it, then walk along the side of the boat shed and turn down towards the car park and the broker's office. The broker is at his desk, smiling as though he has been expecting them. He listens, nods, goes to the metal filing cabinet and pulls out a photocopied sheet with a picture of the boat that seems to have been taken during a blizzard.

'*Lodestar*,' he says. 'Not a vast amount I can tell you. The owner passed away. The family doesn't want it. It's got seventeen thousand on the ticket but if you made an offer that got their attention . . . Are you selling anything? That nice boat you've been working on, for example?'

'No,' says Tim. 'We were just curious about this . . . What was it again?'

'*Lodestar*,' says Maud.

'Well, she's a Nicholson 32. You probably don't need me to tell you about the pedigree. Serious blue-water cruisers. Wear their age very well. Potentially a lovely boat.'

'Is there a survey?' asks Maud.

'Not here,' says the broker. 'Perhaps not anywhere. As far as I know she's sound. Do you want to have a look at her?'

There is a hunt for keys. The keys are found. A ladder is found. The broker, who in his office looked like a character actor, someone employed to play the ex-husband, the ex-sportsman, his yellow hair slightly too long for his years, turns out to be both nimble and quietly efficient. He ascends (in leather-soled shoes), frees the tarpaulin, rolls it up to reveal the cockpit, the coach-house roof. There is no rigging of any sort; the deck is bare. He springs the padlock on the wash-boards, shoves back the hatch.

Maud and Tim stand behind him in the cockpit. The entrance to the cabin is set just right of centre. To the left are switches, a depth gauge. The tiller has been removed but the binnacle is there, the compass settled under clouded glass. Maud wipes the glass with her sleeve, sees the needle steady at 270. Due west.

The broker stands back and invites them to go ahead of him. Maud goes first, three steps down into the twilight of the cabin. A smell of damp fabric, a whiff of diesel, but mostly just contained marine air, a salty emptiness that comes cleanly to the nose. Galley, chart table. Brass-bound clock, stopped. Benches either side in some hopelessly faded green velour. Little green curtains. A folding table folded, a barometer; then the heads, the forecabin berths, sail locker, chain locker. Behind fiddle rails in the cabin a clutch of books that in the damp air have taken on the character of sea vegetables. Tim leans to read the titles. *The Shell Channel Pilot*, Joshua Slocum's *Sailing Alone Around the World*, a Penguin Classics edition of the *Dhammapada*. Near the books is a picture screwed to the bulkhead, a photograph of what appears to be the boat, moored somewhere, the hour of sunrise or sunset.

They go on deck though there is nothing much to see. There is not even a guard rail. Tim holds Maud's sleeve. 'She has a tendency to fall,' he says. 'I remember it,' says the broker, quietly. He smiles at Maud. 'They make them tough wherever you come from,' he says. 'Where do you come from?'

Outside his office they shake hands and the broker says those things that rise up in him effortlessly – have a think about it, a very nice example, hold their value, any questions don't hesitate. He knows he will not see them again, not to talk about that strange unloved old boat, but the next weekend they are back in his office and he walks them to the ladder, climbs up behind them.

The girlfriend, the girl who fell then *got up and walked*, has a torch with her, a little knife. In the cabin she removes the companionway steps and studies the engine. She lifts the cabin sole and peers into the bilges, tries the sea-cocks, wipes the beaded moisture from the steel surround of a window, comes up on deck and crouches over a cracked U bolt, rattles a grab rail, wears all the while a face that gives nothing away. The boyfriend sits in the cockpit. Now and then he calls to her but mostly he lets her get on with it. He's the friendly type, an amiable leaner against walls, an amiable loafer. The decision about the boat will, presumably, be hers. There is nothing that he, the broker, the salesman, can do to make it more likely, not really. The boat must sell itself or not at all. He lights a Café Crème cigarillo, talks to the boyfriend about the Camper & Nicholsons yard in Gosport, the history of the class, and when there is no more to say on it they talk about music. On his right hand the boyfriend has varnished nails, long nails for plucking strings. 'Be honest now,' asks the broker, 'who's the greater player, Jimmy Page or Jimi Hendrix?' The girlfriend is back below again, her shadow reaching into a sail bag. The boyfriend laughs. 'You've got to be kidding,' he says. 'Are you kidding?'

The following Thursday, at nine-thirty in the evening, they ring him at home. He is heating up his supper; he is halfway down a bottle of Argentinian red. They're sorry to call so late (it's the boyfriend, a bit breathless) but they've been talking for an hour and don't trust themselves to wait until morning. They call him Chris now. He calls them Tim and Maud. 'How does fourteen thousand sound?' says Tim.

'Fourteen? A good place to start,' says the broker. 'A smart offer.'

Next morning he calls the owners. He has never met them and never knew the man who sailed the boat. It's a London number. The woman who answers seems at first not to know what he's talking about, then: 'Oh gosh, Daddy's boat. Are they serious? Do they have the money? What are they *like*?' She accepts the offer immediately. She would, he realizes, have accepted a lot less. He puts the phone down and sits looking through the office window at the river, the wooded banks. Sometimes his life feels small, sometimes boundless. On the desk he lines up his tin of cigarillos, his ashtray, his lighter. He picks up the phone again and dials Bristol.

11

Among other things, Chris Totten passes on the name of a local surveyor. When Maud speaks to him the surveyor says, 'I'll be working for you. Not for the vendor, not for the broker. I'll say it as I see it.'

By the beginning of May they have the report. Items in green print are mostly cosmetic; those in blue describe work that should be undertaken in the next two years. Those in red are urgent and must be attended to immediately. On the list of urgent items – a list that runs to two pages – is a new cutlass bearing, replacement of engine mounts, of fuel hoses (compliance ISO 7840). There are two seized sea-cocks, no fire extinguisher. Stanchion feet one and two on the port side are unsafe. Likewise, the port-side coach-house roof grab rail.

'It's not going to sink,' says Tim. 'There's nothing here that says she's unsafe.'

Maud agrees. 'If we have to replace the engine mounts,' she

says, 'we might as well replace the engine. Put in something more powerful.'

'And we need new upholstery.'

'The spinnaker is torn.'

'How about red?'

'A red spinnaker?'

'Red upholstery. But a red spinnaker too, if you like. And new red curtains.'

'Red paint for the hull,' she says.

'Imagine her,' he says, 'freshly painted.'

'He hasn't even looked at the rigging,' she says.

'What does it say about osmosis?'

' "Consistent with the age of the boat".'

'Do you like her name?' he asks.

'What?'

'Her name. *Lodestar*.'

'The name doesn't matter,' she says.

'It sounds,' he says, 'like an intergalactic battle cruiser.'

They start to gather the money they need, to pool their resources. Much of what Maud earns she saves, not knowing what to spend it on, not desiring many things. Tim has savings too, of course, money that hangs slack in various accounts, fifteen or twenty thousand at the last look (he rarely opens the statements the bank sends) but that's money for an easy mind, a cash-mattress that ensures he can spend his days with his guitars, his yoga, his exper-imental cookery, his walks across the city, his not-yet-fully commenced life of serious composition, the music he will soon start to put down in the little blue Merkhefte, his concerto. For *Lodestar*, he decides to visit the money stream a little closer to its source. He goes home on his own during the week, says nothing the first day, then on the second, choosing the half-hour before evening drinks, he finds his mother in the kitchen, takes hold of one of her cool hands and explains, with an earnestness he knows she likes, what it is he wants. Money is called 'funds' or 'help'. She listens to him, a very slight smile on her face. They have horses, a plane, land. An old yacht is neither here nor there. She agrees the upholstery should be red. Not poppy red, not cerise. Brick, perhaps, or Morocco. She thinks young people should have a project. When she says 'strive' her cheeks tremble a little. He embraces her. The Aga sends out wave after wave of generous warmth. He fetches the gin, the blue bottle, the accoutrements.

'Maud's not who we would have chosen for you, Tim. Not, I suppose, what we expected. But love is love. If you're happy.'

'I am.'

'Are you?'

'Very.'

She nods and looks into her gin, touches the ice with the tip of a heavily ringed finger.

They never meet the boat's owners and learn almost nothing about the man who sailed her. Name of John Gosse. Retired from the law. Tim calls him ghostly Gosse and suggests they make an offering to him, placate his spirit to keep him from walking the decks above their heads at night.

'What sort of offering?' asks Maud.

'Our first born,' says Tim, then laughs at her, the strange, almost anxious expression on her face. 'I'm just kidding, OK? The Gosse has gone. He's not coming back.'

Maud puts in four thousand. The rest is gusted from Tim's mother's account to Tim's and then to the account (Coutts, the Strand) of Amelia Shovel (née Gosse). Ownership documents are sent together with a card from Chris Totten wishing them many years of successful sailing. It's suddenly theirs. A thirty-two-foot boat. A sloop, a blue-water cruiser. Deep-keeled. This thing they saw, she saw. The old boat. The new boat.

For a while the boat is everything. He pores over atlases; she researches engines – Bukh, Yanmar, Volvo, Ford. At the weekends, late Friday or early Saturday, they drive to the coast and spend hours clambering up and down the ladder. They have an account with the chandlers. In a single weekend they spend over six hundred pounds on paint, on nylon and polyester rope, on bolts and varnish. With the help of Robert Currey and the tools in his canvas bag, they replace the cutlass bearing. Other work is given over entirely to the yardsmen. Bills are pinned to the board in the kitchen, a fat sheaf of them fluttering in the breeze from the window. 'We'll die poor,' says Tim, 'but we'll die at sea.'

He writes a song about the boat in which *Lodestar* is rhymed with far and guitar; love with curve, rove, Noah's dove. He plays it for her while she sits on the sofa in a towel after showering. The song ends with ten bars of sea-shanty. He has tears in his eyes. He lays down the guitar and rests his hands on the roses of her knees.

'What about India?' he says. 'Or New Zealand? Cape Town?'

'I have a job,' she says.

'The Tuamotu Islands, the Red Sea, Tahiti, Cape Breton, Cuba.'

'I have three weeks leave a year.'

'It doesn't have to be tomorrow,' he says.

12

When she tells her parents about the boat – one of the every-third-Sunday phone calls – her mother says, 'Oh, Maudy. Whose idea was that?'

'Ours,' says Maud.

'No,' says her mother. 'It's always *somebody's* idea.'

13

She tells Henderson too. It's the Fenniman annual conference, a hotel in Surrey, a Victorian mock-Tudor mansion with notable gardens and a restaurant described in the information pack they have all received as 'imaginative'. There are sales people, research and development people, money people, legal people. The American leadership fly in from Orlando. Everyone has been asked to reflect on the question: 'Can I do my job better?'

Meetings with Josh Fenniman are scheduled throughout most of Saturday. Maud is booked in for eleven-ten sharp. The meetings are taking place in the Tennyson suite on the first-floor mezzanine. Maud takes a seat outside the door and a moment later a young male PA ushers someone out and with the briefest glance at his watch asks Maud to come through. Fenniman stands to greet her. He is wearing a white, open-necked shirt, a jacket of charcoal Italian cashmere, blue jeans, gleaming nut-brown brogues. They talk for exactly ten minutes. He asks her about the trials. He makes no notes – it's understood that he's remembering everything. As the morning is warm, a fine June morning out in the notable gardens, Maud is in short sleeves. '*Sauve Qui Peut*,' says Fenniman, reading her arm and pronouncing the words with a good accent. 'It's an interesting choice.' He regards her a while in the way his rank entitles him to. Then, 'We're all team players in this outfit, Maud. I guess you understood that?'

'Yes,' she says.

'You like your room?'

'Yes,' she says.

He holds out his hand to her. 'Hope we'll see you at the party tonight.'

The party is in the Gladstone room. An eight-piece mariachi band has been bused down from London. There's a bar, a free first glass of champagne. Maud wears a dress of dark chocolate silk, a short jacket of a lighter colour, the salamander brooch pinned on the left side, the Indian bangles around her right wrist. The dress has been her party dress for at least five years. On the back, under the jacket, is a small hole where somebody embraced her while holding a cigarette. She wears no tights. Her bra and pants are black and from the same department store where she bought her work outfits.

Henderson brings her a flute of champagne. 'Love this sort of thing or loathe it?' he asks.

'Neither,' she says.

'How did you get on with the great leader?'

'He wanted to know if I was a team player.'

Henderson laughs. 'I'm not sure you are a team player, Maud. I hope you don't mind my saying that. But you're twice the scientist he'll ever be. He's a Harvard MBA. I don't think he's opened a science textbook since high school. How's the sailing?'

'We've bought a boat,' she says.

'Bought a boat! Hey. I'm impressed. What kind of boat?'

She tells him, leans close to make herself heard over the noise of the band. Henderson, it turns out, has sailed Nicholsons – 32s, 44s – and thinks they're beautiful boats, beautifully put together. He says you could sail free of the known world in a boat like that, sail straight off the map. They have a second glass of champagne. He invites her on to the dance floor but she shakes her head. He leaves her alone for a while. Twenty minutes later he reappears carrying two shot glasses of tequila. 'For luck,' he says. She doesn't mind drinking, doesn't care that much what she drinks.

He tells her things about himself. The music is too loud to follow it closely. At some point he starts to speak of himself in the third person. Henderson was restless. Henderson got it into his head he should marry. What sort of man was this Henderson anyway? She nods, looks out at the dancers, sees Josh Fenniman making the rounds, is mildly surprised to find Henderson holding out another glass of champagne, which she drinks down for thirst's sake. Somewhere around eleven she goes up to her room. She has sat on the bed and taken off her shoes when there's a quick double tap at the door.

'A nightcap,' says Henderson, holding up a little bottle of brandy from a minibar. 'Two minutes?'

As soon as he is inside and the door is shut he puts down the bottle, speaks her name, touches her cheek, leans down – he's at least ten inches taller – and kisses her. She's tired but not very; drunk but not very. He's kissing her, kissing her, kissing her. One hand goes down to the hem of her chocolate dress, scrapes it up, strokes her thigh then moves round to press between her legs. He presses so hard it lifts her on to tiptoes. She slides off him and steps back. 'I know,' he says. 'You have someone, I have someone.

But this is not about relationships. It's two grown-ups alone in a room. It's what makes the world go round.'

He reaches for her again but she brushes his hand aside. He puts on an expression of offended puzzlement, exaggerated, theatrical. 'Come on,' he says. 'When you opened the door what did you think we were going to do?' He puts a hand on her shoulder. Again, with a movement of her own hand she breaks the contact. 'Jesus, Maud,' he says, 'you're behaving like a child. Relax, will you?' This time he reaches with both hands, takes hold of both her shoulders. There's a moment of dancing familiar to her from her years on the mat with Rawlins (lame Rawlins wreathed in smoke). She finds some space for herself, a half-yard between the desk and the trouser press. She has the television remote-control in her left hand. She swings it in a clean half-arc that catches him flush between temple and eye. He drops soundlessly, kneels on the carpet, both hands to his head. She steps clear of him and watches. Behind her the television has come on with its personalized message of welcome, its slideshow of the garden, the restaurant. Henderson gets to his feet and goes into the bathroom. There is the noise of running water. When he comes out he is holding a wad of damp toilet paper over the place where she hit him. He doesn't raise his voice, doesn't look at her. 'I'll tell you this,' he says. 'Someone like you comes to a bad end.'

He squints through the spy-hole in the door, opens the door, slips out and closes the door quietly behind him. Maud puts down the remote-control, then picks it up again to switch off the television. In the bathroom there are three small drops of blood on the lip of the sink. She washes them away, washes her face, cleans her teeth, sits on the toilet to urinate. In the bedroom she strips off, lays her dress carefully over a chair. The room is much warmer than the bedroom in Bristol. She climbs naked between the sheets and puts off the light. She is asleep very quickly but wakes an hour later, two hours, with dry mouth and dry lips, the shadow of Henderson's hand between her thighs. On the window, between the wooden slats of the blind, the glass is smeared with orange light. And there's a sound, a sound so soft, deep and continuous, it takes her several seconds to know it for what it is, the hushed tumult of the rain. She listens until it lies inside her like her own voice but when she sleeps again she does not dream of rain but of fog, and of herself, alone on deck, waiting for the noise of surf.

14

In July, *Lodestar* is lifted and laid in the water. The keel enters like a blade, the hull dipping then rising as if the touch of water has, in an instant, woken all the latent possibilities of its form. Tim whoops. Chris Totten opens a bottle of cava, pours it into plastic glasses. On board the boat, Robert Currey is freeing the sling. The crane operator polishes his sunglasses on the hem of his T-shirt. He looks at Maud and Tim then at Maud alone. Gulls circle. A day-trip boat on its way down river sounds its siren, idly.

All the work in red type on the report has been attended to. There is, as Maud wished, a new (a reconditioned) engine. The mast has been stepped, the hull is a glossy new red, a single line of cream at the boot top. Other work can be done while she is on the water. Anything that can't be done on the water will have to wait until she's lifted at the end of the season.

Maud has taken a week off work. For the first three days they are moored alongside one of the yard pontoons. They sleep in the forward berths, wake to seabirds and the singing of halyards.

They have bottled gas on board, a functioning galley. They make coffee, toast. They boil eggs and throw the empty shells into the water, watch them spin on the tide.

Tim takes up smoking. It is, he says, a considered decision. He rolls his cigarettes and smokes them up at the bow. He watches the life of the river, the ceaseless coming and going, the enchantment of it.

They have a list of jobs they will not come to the end of. Coming to the end of them is not the point. Tim sands and varnishes. Maud, below deck, is fitting the new diesel stove. People drop by. They want to see how the young couple are getting on, and because they are young the sense is that they are not simply fitting out their boat but fitting out their lives, their life together. Robert Currey helps Maud install the stove chimney (a five-inch hole drilled into the deck), fit the deck cap. He looks at Maud as other men do, puzzled and interested, looks sidelong at her face as she frowns at the work in her hands. He is not gallant or flirtatious, or he is both, though in ways she does not notice. ('That man,' says Tim, 'with the right tools, could build an entire city.')

On the fourth day – they have water on board and ninety litres of fuel – they move to a swinging mooring in the middle of the river. Tomorrow – at last! – they will sail. They will go out on the morning tide, raise their sails and see. They will learn what this boat of theirs can do. As night falls they sit opposite each other on the old green benches and eat bowls of mussels. They cannot light the stove because the pump is not yet fitted but it's not cold, not with a jumper on, a glass of wine in your hand. They stay up to hear the midnight shipping forecast then go to their bunks, their skin smelling of varnish, marine paint and mussels. Where the V of the bunks meet, their heads are close enough for kissing but their bodies slope away from each other. They sleep lightly.

The boat adjusts itself on the tide; water sounds the hull. In its locker the anchor chain shifts like money.

For the rest of that summer and on into the autumn, the coast of England is strung with helpful winds. The boat is at the centre of their lives; time away from the boat is time spent waiting to be back on board. Each weekend the Lancia heads south, then (sometimes by starlight, moonlight, ribbons of stray lights from the river bank) they row out in the tender with a holdall of clothes, bags of food. And there she is still, the river sliding beneath her, the deck gently dipping as they pull themselves on board.

The stove is functioning now and on cooler nights Maud twists a length of tissue, lights it and drops it into the burner pot. Then a bottle is hunted out of a shopping bag, there's food in tupperware boxes, things Tim has cooked while Maud was at work.

The boat becomes what perhaps it was before, in John Gosse's time. A true sailing yacht, sound, undecorated, dry where it matters, the cabin more workshop or garden shed than living room. They make few plans; they sail where wind and tide suggest, one weekend flying past Start Point on the tidal race, the next running across Lyme Bay on a westerly and spending the night anchored off Exmouth Dock. They are still sailing at the end of October. The pleasure boats, the few that keep going, are mostly empty. The banks of the river grow paler, barer. They tell each other that this is the season's long tail, that there's no real reason not to sail until Christmas, to have Christmas on board, sneak in to somewhere like Newtown and have the place to themselves. It's effortless. They're confident, increasingly careless. The second weekend in November they find themselves miles from home in a wind forecast to be four gusting five ('Isn't that what they said?')

but which feels nearer to six gusting seven, and rising. It comes suddenly, or seems to. No time to dog things down, to remember what's been left out below. Tim looks for the life jackets and safety lines, cannot find them. They furl the jib to a scrap then Maud crawls over the coach roof to reef the main. She knows how to reef but she's never reefed on *Lodestar*. While Tim keeps the boat on a close reach she eases the halyard, tugs at the sail, gets nowhere. Something is jammed or she's forgotten something. The boat's movement tips her against the mast, again and again. Tim is shouting advice or encouragement, she cannot hear which. She tears a nail dragging the cringle down to its hook, then moves along the boom to haul down the back of the sail, the rain and spray washing away the blood from her nail the moment it touches the deck. The sea heaps up. For a while it's exhilarating. They trust the boat, the boat can take it, but after an hour they are silent, their eyes fixed on the blurred and featureless coastline. They are motor sailing and doing the best part of seven knots but nothing seems to get any closer. The only other vessel in sight is some sort of coaster, steaming away from them. They are hungry, the light's going. They are children on an adventure that has gone wrong. From the cabin there have been two or three reports, gleeful smashings, and when Tim ducks below to snatch a handful of biscuits he sees the glimmering of broken glass, crockery. It's nine-something by the time they read the lights off the castle headland and know they are back. Forty minutes later they drop the main and motor into the wind's shadow. The wind falls from their faces. They see the lights of houses, the lit tower of a church, headlights of cars moving untroubled through the narrow streets of the town. Their hands are mottled from the cold; their fingers close stiffly. When the boat is moored they go below and stand among the broken things on the cabin floor, strip off wet clothes and pull on anything dry and warm. Tim makes tea while Maud sweeps up the mess. They slop whisky into their tea, tell each other it was quite a blow, that perhaps they were foolish but at least they know now how the boat performs in heavy weather. And where were the harnesses? Are they perhaps lying in the back of the car? They shake their heads, drink more whisky, climb into their sleeping bags, praising the boat in voices that grow quieter and quieter. The last voice is Tim's trying to explain something about the huts of Arctic explorers, and how everything was always hanging out to dry and the oil lamps were burning and someone in a white turtleneck was tamping tobacco into his pipe and it was so terribly, terribly snug . . .

In the early morning, tying on the mainsail cover, Maud steps briskly to the side of the boat, leans over the rail and vomits. Tim, in the middle of fixing breakfast, pokes his head out above the hatch. Maud wipes her mouth with the back of her hand, looks at him and shrugs.

15

It turns out she's pregnant. For the next six weeks she is sick every day, several times a day. She carries plastic bags in the pockets of her winter coat. When there is no bathroom to go to she can use one of the bags and drop it in the next bin she comes to. Tim asks: 'Is it supposed to be like this?' He tries to persuade her to take time off work but she says she's not ill, she's pregnant. In the car park of the hospital in Croydon she passes out, comes to a few moments later lying in grey snow. She cleans herself, picks up her briefcase and goes to the meeting where, after a few minutes, someone politely leans over to tell her she's bleeding, a little ooze of blood from above her left eye. Two days later she's in Reading, Fenniman HQ. The woman from Human Resources stops her in the corridor. She wants to know what happened in Croydon. 'Let's have a chat,' she says. In the course of the chat – red furniture in a silver room – the woman learns of Maud's condition and puts on, fleetingly, her disappointed face. Women who start work and then, a matter of months later, announce they are pregnant are no friends of the sorority of committed professional women. 'I see,' she says. 'Well, congratulations of course. Are you intending to leave us?'

'No,' says Maud.

'But you will need to take maternity leave.'

'Yes.'

'How long did you imagine you would need?'

'I don't know,' says Maud. 'Two months?'

'That would involve childcare for a very small baby.'

'Yes.'

'You might feel differently later.'

'About the baby?'

'You might want to stay with it. Him or her.'

'Perhaps.'

'Do you have a due date?'

'June the twenty-fourth.'

'Then let's schedule another chat for – what? – a fortnight from today? Obviously we need to agree on a timetable, get some firm dates in the diary. In the meantime you should have a look at your contract. Make sure you understand the relevant clauses. Our responsibilities, yours. Any questions for me at this point?'

To the woman, Maud looks like a child on a bench in a long corridor waiting for someone who is not going to come. A child with her knees politely pressed together, who does not even know she's lost. If she liked her more, she might pity her.

With Tim, she visits his parents, the Rathbone house. She is embraced by his mother who holds her for a full half-minute. She is thinner than Maud remembers her and has a number of small burns on her arms. Tim's father cups Maud's face then shakes his son by the hand. 'Bloody well done, the pair of you,' he says.

The twins, home on an exeat weekend, wrinkle their noses: 'Really preggers?'

Magnus, just back from a week of meetings in Stuttgart, all his movements weary and imperial, laughs at her but seems, like his father, genuinely touched by the news. His wife mouths, 'Caesarean.' Under the kitchen table the children sing, 'We hate babies! We hate babies!'

At supper – 'And all this is *very* baby friendly,' says Tim's mother, pointing to the dishes – Magnus asks where they will live when the baby is born.

'Where we live now,' says Maud.

'Well,' says Tim, 'we haven't given it much thought. Not yet.' Maud looks at him. 'What's wrong with where we live now?' she asks.

'A child needs a garden,' says Tim's father.

'Not to mention grandparents,' says his wife, peering at the buttered swede.

'Do you know,' says Magnus to Maud, 'why grandparents and grandchildren get on so well together?'

She shakes her head.

'They have a common enemy.'

Almost everybody laughs at this.

The next weekend they drive up the motorway to Swindon. The town has just twinned itself with somewhere in Poland and Maud's father points the place out in one of his atlases. 'Apparently it's quite pretty,' he says, 'as Poland goes.' While her mother is filling the kettle for tea Maud tells her the news. She looks round from the sink, the tap still running, something like fear in her eyes. Mr Stamp goes out to the garage to look for the bottle of wine he thinks might be out there. He comes back with home-made sloe gin he won in a school raffle. To his wife he says, 'I suppose Maudy can have some, can't she?'

'I wouldn't think so,' says his wife.

'I'll have tea,' says Maud.

'Do you want some, Tim?'

'I'm fine with tea too.'

'I'll pop it back then,' says Mr Stamp.

After tea they go to visit Grandfather Ray. He used to live two doors away but since his strokes (the year Maud went up to the university in Bristol) he lives at The Poplars.

'Maudy's got some news,' says Mrs Stamp. 'Haven't you, Maudy?' She wipes the old man's mouth. 'Look,' she says. 'They've put odd socks on him.' When Maud calls the old man Grandpa, Tim's heart staggers. This was the man who built the boat for her, who taught her to sail! British Rail Western Division. Very slowly, and with obvious effort, the old man turns his attention from Mrs Stamp to Maud. Impossible to say whether he understands what she's telling him. Mrs Stamp changes his socks. He has feet like a troll. On the wall is a picture of a steam train flying through a country station of the kind long since abolished. There is also a picture of a woman, his dead wife presumably, stout, friendly looking, sexless. They leave him. Find their way out through the large, frightening building.

At home the parents have work to do. They're sorry but there it is. Maud and Tim sit in the living room with the TV and a plate of sandwiches. When Mrs Stamp puts her head in Tim says, 'These are delicious.' They watch the last half of *A Room With a View*. When it's over and the news comes on he squeezes Maud's shoulder. 'Why don't you go to bed, love?' he says. She goes. He takes the plate through to the kitchen. Mrs Stamp has also gone to bed or gone somewhere (where is there to go in such a small house?) but Mr Stamp is still sitting in a circle of lamplight carefully tracing the delicate coastline of somewhere. If he wants to speak to Tim, to ask him perhaps for some account of his life with Maud, of his intentions, this would be a good moment, but he goes on with his work, utterly absorbed, a level of concentration, of lostness-in-the-task Tim has seen often enough in his daughter.

He has already been shown his bed in the spare bedroom – the only double bed in the house belongs to the parents – and he is about to step quietly out of the room when he sees a photograph on the cork board by the fridge. It's pinned between a milk bill and the dates for the Christmas bin collections, a girl in school uniform photographed standing against a wall, satchel over her shoulder, socks pulled up, skirt falling to somewhere about the knees. Her hair is shoulder length; her fringe needs cutting. You can see the curls, curls that would come again if she let her hair grow. He takes the picture from the board. On the back of it someone has written the date – 1987. That makes her twelve. Eleven or twelve. No grin, no frown. Nothing to say if this was a good girl, a bad girl, a humorous girl, an unhappy girl. A small badge on the lapel of her blazer. Could be anything. 1987. He puts the pin back in the board, puts the picture in the pocket of his shirt. 'Goodnight,' he says.

'Goodnight,' says Mr Stamp. He's looking at Tim now but if he saw the thing with the picture, the quiet theft of the little picture, he seems to have decided to accept it.

16

She stops being sick. She swells. The soft structures of her pelvis ache. She has certain cravings. One is for pomegranates and Tim buys them from a stall in St Nicholas Market. He cuts them open, scrapes out the seeds, feeds them to her, likes that dull look of pleasure that comes over her face at the taste of them. She also has what he calls 'an offal thing'. She keeps it in bags in the fridge. Kidneys, liver. Once a lamb's heart in a spattered bag on the shelf beside his yoghurts. He does not see her eat it. The heart is there and then one evening it's gone, the bag in the swing bin, empty, a fine haze of cooking smoke under the kitchen ceiling.

She has not become tearful or irrational. She is not subject to mood swings. The way she moves has changed, slowed, become a little clumsy. Now and then, watching her, he thinks of one of his mother's words – *slovenly*. He notes that she goes a week without washing her hair. He offers to do it for her; she says she'll do it herself but doesn't. And one morning, emptying the laundry basket on the floor by the machine, he sees a brazen shit-streak on the soft cotton of her knickers. He soaks them in hot water and too much detergent. He puts on yellow Marigolds and scrubs them. He would rather break a thumb than mention it to her.

There is not much sex, almost no penetrative sex. They touch each other, though on the last few occasions she has gently removed his hand from between her thighs then gone on with him until he was finished. It's a connection of sorts but it feels like something a paid woman does to a man in his car.

They watch television. They look at the house brochures his parents send them. *Lodestar* is out of the water, covered over until the spring. Spring or whenever, in this new world, they can get back to her.

'How do you feel?' he asks, taking her hand, a Sunday dusk in the living room, her four-month belly soft under a sea-blue jumper.

'I'm OK.'

'Really?'

'Yes.'

'Not just physically,' he says.

'Not just physically,' she says.

'And you're not sorry?'

'About what?'

'About this.'

'You know I'm not.'

'I'm checking.'

'I'm not sorry.'

'It would be OK to be a bit sorry.'

'I know.'

'You're going to be a lovely mum.'

'I hope so.'

'The Inkling will worship you.' Inkling is his name for the baby.

It's a name the Rathbones have used before for unborn children. The Inkling. 'Tell me if you're frightened,' he says.

'OK.'

'Are you frightened?'

'No.'

'A little?'

'No.'

'That's good.'

There's a white plate on the floor, white china with red gravy. She looks at him, he looks at her.

'Hello,' he says.

She nods and he thinks how close everyone is to a kind of madness. Maud, his parents, himself presumably. There is nowhere obvious to take this thought.

17

In April they settle on a house. As Maud has shown so little enthusiasm for the project the choice is mostly Tim's – well, Tim's and his mother's. It's a three-bedroom semi-detached cottage on the Dorset–Wiltshire border, a short drive from the Rathbone family house. There's a garden, beams, a big wood-burning stove, a Rayburn, a wooden gate with roses growing at the side, no onward chain. The money stream buys the place outright. Tim and Maud will pay the money back at so much a month.

At the beginning of May, Tim hires a van. Friends give up half a day to help them. Maud, heavy now, folds clothes into suitcases, wraps crockery and glasses in newspaper. She drops a glass and Tim's old flatmate, Ernesto, cries, '*No le toques, Maud!*' He sweeps up. He embraces her. He puts his hands on her belly, his expression like a priest officiating at the Mystery.

By mid-morning the following day the last oddments – a box of teabags, a pot plant, the cork board with *Lodestar*'s bills still pinned to it – are wedged into the back of the van and they set off, south then west. A-roads give way to lanes with lacy hedgerows and unmown verges. Tim's parents are waiting for them at the cottage. Also the twins and someone called Slad, a middle-aged man, four-square, who, if not entirely a servant, is something similar – a retainer, a housecarl.

All the windows of the cottage are open. There is honeysuckle growing around the door. The path is laid with a blue-grey stone that Tim's father, dropping stiffly to his knees, identifies as blue lias, ancient seabed of the Jurassic, rich in fossils, ammonites in particular.

Inside, in the cool of the low-ceilinged rooms, there is already some furniture, pieces the Rathbones had in storage. A dresser for the kitchen, dining chairs of dark varnished wood, a leather armchair, its leather mottled and dented as if the chair were made out of old heavy-bags from a boxing gym. There is even a bed – Slad has somehow wrestled it up the stairs – with a headboard of brilliantly polished walnut. Other things arrive in the afternoon: a fridge, a washing machine and dryer, things delivered by the vans of local firms the Rathbones have done business with for thirty years.

Slad lights the Rayburn. At first it stinks of oil but the fumes disperse. By dusk the house is a house to be lived in and they gather in the warmth of the kitchen to eat supper. Tim's mother has brought a casserole in a red Le Creuset pot. Tim's father brings in a half-box of Burgundy from the back of the car. Slad goes home. He makes a kind of shallow bow to them all. Everyone tells Maud she must be exhausted. She says she's not but falls asleep after supper on the leather armchair and only wakes when the others are leaving. She comes outside with Tim to wave them goodbye.

'They ran out of things to drink,' says Tim. 'But they'll be back in the morning.'

They stand, hand in hand in the doorway for several minutes after the car's engine note has dwindled to nothing. Over the silhouettes of the trees the sky is crowded with southern stars. An owl calls; an owl calls back. The moment rests against perfection.

'Let's leave the door unlocked,' says Tim, 'we're in the country for God's sake,' but later, when Maud is in bed, he finds the keys and locks it, puts the bolts over. If nothing else, he has the guitars in the house.

She begins her leave from Fenniman's. She is given a 'good luck' card signed by everyone, including Henderson who just puts his name, Karl Henderson. She will start back in October. After that Tim will stay at home with the child, an arrangement he seemed eager to accept but which his father mutters about, claims not to understand at all ('Is this modern? Is it modern to have a child and then simply leave it?')

A midwife is appointed. There are only two in the local town and Maud is given Julie – ruddy, stout, motherly, though only a year or two older than Maud. 'Are you planning on a big family?' she asks, and when Maud says no she laughs as if this is something she has heard before, women who seem not to really want babies but who end up with a houseful.

She examines Maud. 'You're very strong,' she says. 'It'll come out like a lemon pip.'

She plays the baby's heartbeat through a speaker while Maud looks up at the mobile of slowly drifting birds she thinks at first are swans but later, after watching them for half a minute, realizes are intended to be storks.

Julie shows Maud the unit. One mother who looks, at best, fourteen, sitting up in bed nursing her baby. One mother lying on her back as if shot. One walking slowly to and fro in the company of a man with a snake tattoo around his neck.

Back in the office Julie asks for the birth plan but Maud doesn't have one. Her plan is to do what is necessary when the time comes. That doesn't seem to need writing down. As for pain control, they agree she will simply ask for it if she needs it. She does not mention to Julie her work in this area, the project in Croydon, the trial packs of Fennidine she has in the glove compartment of the Corsa. So far, the trials have been extremely promising, though there have also been reports of side-effects, some of them worrying. One volunteer suffered extreme nausea and had, briefly, to be hospitalized. Another – who is suspected of having an undisclosed history of recreational drug use – claimed to have had hallucinations, both visual and auditory. This subject, known as Volunteer R, has been excluded from any future participation in the trial.

At the cottage, as advised, she packs a crash bag, something she can pick up in a hurry when the moment comes. Breast pads, nappies. Nightie, underwear, wash bag, torch.

'What's the torch for?' asks Tim.

'Just in case,' says Maud.

'Of a power cut?'

'Put it back,' says Maud.

He puts it back, suppresses a smart remark about adding a hand flare.

At about this time, in the morning post (the nice post lady who already seems to know them well), Maud receives an unsigned letter, or not a letter at all but a sheet of paper bearing a quote from someone called Marguerite Duras, and copied out in black ink, in careful handwriting. It reads:

Being a mother isn't the same as being a father. Motherhood means that a woman gives her body over to her child, her children; they're on her as they might be on a hill, in a garden. They devour her, hit her, sleep on her; and she lets herself be devoured, and sometimes she sleeps because they are on her body. Nothing like that happens with fathers.

She has no idea who has sent it to her, cannot tell if the writing belongs to a man or a woman. The postmark on the envelope is illegible. Nor can she tell if the words are intended to encourage her or warn her or simply inform her. She folds the paper and puts it between the leaves of a book (one that Tim's mother has given her, *What to Expect When You're Expecting*). A short while later she takes it out of the book and carefully slides it between two oak boards on the bedroom floor. Posts it into darkness.

She does small jobs in the garden, plants French beans and lettuces while Tim plays slow scales on the guitars (the Lacôte copy, the Andrés Dominguez, the Taylor with the ebony fretboard, the cocobolo backstrap). The people next door, a childless couple who seem to live a highly organized and orderly life, who dress each Sunday in black lycra and ride their expensive bikes for miles, have already said they have no objection to the sound of a guitar, though they hoped he did not have an electric guitar, did not belong to a rock band. Their names are Sarah and Michael. It is already perfectly clear there will be no intimacy between Sarah and Michael, Tim and Maud.

due date comes, passes. Another week goes by. Maud

sweats in the July sun. Her ankles swell; whole days pass when she hardly speaks. She is awake when Tim goes to sleep, awake when he wakes up. Julie comes out to the cottage. There is no sign of distress from the child. Maud's blood pressure is a little elevated but not a cause for concern. They will wait a few more days then consider their options.

Tim's mother visits. She offers to massage Maud's belly, looks relieved when Maud turns the offer down. The twins, broad-hipped virgins, can barely look at her without squirming – the horrid, comical outcome of the secret act! – but it is the twins who are with her, sitting in the little front garden braiding each other's hair, when Maud's waters break. They gape at her as she lifts her dress to watch the fluid run down the inside of her legs, can do or say nothing as she trudges towards the cottage.

Inside, Tim's mother is sitting on the leather armchair, head back, eyes half shut. It's her second month on Seroxat and she has, after some adjustment of the dose, achieved a passage of glassy calm. 'I'll take you,' she says. 'Tim will only drive into a wall. He can come along later.'

She spreads newspaper on the passenger seat. Maud sits on it with the crash bag on her lap. A dog in the well of the seat licks her legs, timidly. They speed away, the car's dust falling on campion, moon daisies, creeping buttercup.

'Try and stay awake,' says Tim's mother.

'I haven't taken an overdose,' says Maud, who may as may not have intended this to be a sharp remark. The dog is still licking her, its tongue flickering around her knees.

'When I had Magnus,' says Tim's mother, her bone-thin fingers wrapped tightly around the wheel, 'when I was in labour, I had a sort of huge spontaneous orgasm. Very unexpected. Rather embarrassing if anyone noticed. But at that age I could lean against the tumble dryer and be in heaven in about a minute. I've never understood those things you read in the magazines about women who can't. Makes you wonder if something's missing. You know, anatomically. I'm not going to ask about you and Tim. It's obviously very healthy. I remember Magnus having an enormous collection of pornography that he used to rent out to other boys in his house at school. He always had a good business head. Very good. But babies are what matter, Maud. You'll know that soon. Babies and children. Especially babies but children too . . . Well, this is odd . . .' She brakes, hard. They are at the edge of a village of low, thatched houses. A man in white is riding on a beautifully decorated horse. Around the horse women in gold and green and red are tapping sticks together and singing.

'Looks like a Hindu wedding. There are only about two Indians in Dorset.' She slides the window down, edges the big car forwards, and to every surprised or frowning face says, 'This girl is about to be delivered of a child. Thank you! No time to wait, I'm afraid!'

When they've reached the front of the procession she puts up the window, accelerates. 'You can call it Shiva,' she says. 'Or what's the other one? Kali?'

In the unit two other women are giving birth, each with her attendant team. The noises are what you would expect – life tugged around its spindle. Maud is doing well, people tell her so repeatedly. It's lunchtime, it's three o'clock. She has an hour in the birthing pool (it's new and they seem keen to use it). She has, in her seventh hour, lungfuls of gas and air (this, too, they seem keen to use).

The midwife wears a plastic apron like a dinner lady. 'Good girl,' she says, 'almost there.' The feel of the midwife's hand, the sight of her own knees, her stirruped feet. And visions – caused no doubt by the gas – a woman, for example, walking naked through some barren place, a desert, a shiny grey desert like the moon, just the view of her back, her hunched shoulders, the relentless rhythm of her walking and no end in view. Her back, her hips like an anvil, her shadow rippling in the grey dust of the place . . .

Then the promised burn, Tim weeping at something she cannot see, and in two drenching pushes it's out and lifted, still roped to her, and settled on her pounding heart. She touches its seamed back, rests her fingers there. The clock over the door says ten past ten at night. A bus passes on its way to the station; a moth dances under the ceiling. She has given birth. She has given birth and she is a mother. A mother, come what may.

18

The baby is a girl and they call her Zoe. Neither Tim nor Maud knows any Zoes. It is a name with no shadowy pairings of others, a name unhaunted.

She latches on. She feeds hungrily at Maud's breasts. Julie is pleased, the health visitor is pleased. When the health visitor, who is older than Julie, visits the cottage, she weighs the baby in a sling and writes the weight in a book that Maud keeps. The baby has a way of arching its back as though trying to shed its skin. Maud asks about it and the health visitor says it's fine, normal, completely fine. When in doubt, bosom out. 'It's the cure for most things,' she says. She laughs.

Maud loses weight. Her T-shirts have little yellowish crusts of dried milk on them. By early September she looks gaunt. Don't let baby eat you up, says the health visitor. She leaves some recipe cards that Tim drops in the wood-burner. He cooks a leg of pork with pistachio nuts and garlic. He cooks chicken with a sauce of cream and eggs (Madame Brazier's recipe). Maud picks at it. It's too rich, too something. She wants things like the electric-green lettuces still growing in the back garden. When Tim points out these are mostly water she says yes, she's very thirsty.

October is warm still. Hazy clouds collect in the distance. The last ragged stalks of evening primrose flourish in the dusk. Maud's parents visit. They say they are sorry they haven't been able to come before. First the walking holiday in Slovakia, which had been booked months ago, then the new term, an OFSTED inspection in Week Two, for heaven's sake. They bring a toy with them – coloured wooden blocks threaded onto curling wire, the whole thing screwed to a wooden base and designed to assist with hand-eye co-ordination, with motor control. Mrs Stamp has the baby on her lap. She looks quite comfortable. She does not look as if she will drop the baby. She handles the baby, thinks Tim, like a vase she has not yet decided to buy. Mr Stamp wrinkles his nose at her. He waves to her and says how nice she looks. He has a habit of glancing over at his wife for cues to the expected behaviour, the posture, the language. The only time he seems at ease is standing with Tim in the garden gesturing to the hills, evoking glaciers.

The Rathbones are at the cottage three times a week, sometimes more. They too bring gifts – a cashmere bonnet and blanket, a silver christening bracelet, a wooden goose, an onyx egg, a succession of soft toys, animals remarkably like the animals they imitate. They dandle the baby. Tim's father holds the child with real and obvious joy. In the warmth of the last warm afternoons he likes to lie in the unmown grass, the baby sprawled asleep on his chest, on the heavy cotton of his shirt. To anyone who visits him there he whispers, 'This is bliss.'

And there is a present for Maud and Tim. A belated

house-warming present, a new-baby present. Tim peels it from layers of bubble wrap and when he can see what it is he calls excitedly to Maud, holds it out to her. It's one of the Alfred Downing Fripp watercolours from the treasure room, a picture of a young girl with a basket of cherries. Big blue eyes, pink cheeks and pink lips, a straw sun hat askew on her thick blonde curls. The picture has been framed by some excellent people in Sherbourne. It has been put behind non-reflective glass. It has been insured. Tim walks around the living room with it, trying it out in different places. His mother, from the centre of the room, gives her opinions. His father is holding Zoe, talking to her, softly, privately. Maud is looking out at a stranger's cat on the lawn. The rooted lightness of its walking. The purity of its attention.

At the end of the month she weans the baby. The baby is frantic, pushes away the teat of the bottle, writhes in Maud's grip. Tim tries. He sits with her on the leather armchair, wets her lips with the milk, forces nothing. It takes the best part of an hour. The noise is remarkable, inhuman. Then, with a sudden uncoiling of her body, the child gives in. She lies back in Tim's arms and feeds, the new appetite as blind and powerful as the old. Tim looks at Maud, grinning. Maud goes upstairs and sleeps.

A week later she starts back at Fenniman's. Within days the drive to work through morning darkness, the drive back through evening darkness, feels entirely familiar. The Bristol project is with someone else now, the Oxford project is finished, but she still has Croydon, and is given a new project in Southampton investigating the use of kappa-opioids in short-term pain relief, including pain during labour. Because she herself has recently experienced the pain of labour this is, perhaps, thought to be a suitable project for her, though no one says this.

When she comes home in the evenings she often finds Tim and Zoe asleep in the warmth from the wood-burner. She does not wake them. She eats then sits with them a while. Sometimes the baby wakes first, sometimes Tim, sometimes they wake together as if, through the course of the day, the week, the several weeks, they have become perfectly synchronized.

There's nothing wrong with the baby, nothing at all. She loses her raw look. Overnight, it seems, a face appears. 'Christ,' says Tim, 'it's little Maud. Look!' Though to Maud it's obvious – the brow, the chin, the eyes above all – that the child is a Rathbone.

On winter Sundays they wrap up and go on walks. Zoe hangs on Tim's chest in a baby carrier, a kind of back-to-front rucksack called the Snuggler. He has a stick and on his thinning hair a Barbour waxed cap. They climb the stiles, cross shallow streams, walk up the blown green faces of Dorset fields. There's a pub they stop at for lunch, with swept stone floors, an open fire, a stuffed fox in a glass case. People there like to see the child. They learn her name, ask after her, admire her hands, her wispy hair, her mild, intelligent gaze. Soon, she is crawling over the stone flags. She pats the dozing dogs. The dogs, warming their bellies, ignore her. In the spring she experiments with standing and takes her first steps not at the cottage but in the pub, sliding from the bench to the floor then swaying into the lounge bar where she stops under the fox in the glass case, looks up at it warily, the sharp snout, the dead bird in its mouth, the brilliant eyes. She is laughed at; she is gently applauded. Tim follows her at a respectful distance. He is, he thinks, like a monk put in charge of a reincarnated lama. How did he fill his days before this? What were his days for?

'Whoops,' he says, returning her to her feet for the ninth, the tenth time. 'Whoops.'

*   *   *

Her first birthday: all manner of tender celebrations. In the morning, Tim mixes red paint – non-toxic, entirely safe – spreads it in a pyrex baking dish, and while Zoe and Maud watch him, lays his hand in the paint then presses it on the white wall by the back door. 'There,' he says, looking at the mark, the red ghost of his hand. 'Now you guys.'

Zoe goes next, excess paint dabbed from her wrist with a paper towel. Tim steadies her, helps her flatten her hand against the wall. The child looks with amazement at the mark she has made. She makes three more, each a little fainter. 'Now Mummy,' says Tim. 'Come on, Mummy.'

And Maud wets her hand with the paint, leans over Zoe to make her mark. 'Keep going,' says Tim, who is dipping his own hand again.

The fainter prints are more detailed, more truly a copy of the hand that made them, the pattern and texture of the skin. With a felt-tip pen, Tim writes the date on the wall, then they wash their hands together in the kitchen sink, red paint, red water, swirling round the plughole.

At noon the Rathbones arrive – Mr and Mrs Rathbone, the twins, Magnus's wife and children (Magnus himself is in Zurich).

A little later, Maud's parents arrive in a yellow car, the make and name of which nobody recognizes but which will do over sixty miles to the gallon. They park it carefully, though not too close to the Rathbones' Range Rover, and come in under the rose bush and along the path, the old seabed, in single file. In the crowded living room, Tim's mother kisses them both and this they endure with the flushed miming of a type of conviviality that is utterly foreign to them. For several minutes the women pair off and Mrs Rathbone speaks to Mrs Stamp like the prime minister's wife to the consort of an African president, a prime minister's wife who has started the day with some Qi Gong exercises and then a few drinks, or one particularly strong one. Mrs Stamp, who is clever, who has a face like a small flower or like an insect looking out of a small flower, says, 'Oh yes, yes,' a great many times and tries not to stare at Mrs Rathbone's hands when Mrs Rathbone touches her.

The men have their own kind of failure. Mr Rathbone does not know how many miles to the gallon his Range Rover will do, which is, anyway, his wife's car. He is not interested in roads or the different routes one might take to get somewhere, unless of course one were in a plane at, say, ten thousand feet, when he likes to follow the courses of rivers. He asks where Mr Stamp went to school, nods and says nothing when he answers. Mr Stamp does not ask where Mr Rathbone went to school, though not because he has anticipated the answer but because he is largely unaware of the basic rules of conversation. They stand at a distance that precludes any accidental touching, where they will not even have to smell each other.

'Let's go outside!' says Tim, watching it all from beside the front door. 'Come on, everyone!'

There are bees in the foxgloves, rose petals scattered by the gate from yesterday's rain. They sit on the warm, slightly damp grass. The adults, even Mr and Mrs Stamp, drink champagne, Perrier-Jouët, quite a lot of it. A dab of champagne is put on Zoe's lips and everyone agrees she seems to like it. Tim's father is a favourite of the child. She has a name for him, an apparent name. 'Ubu!' she calls whenever she catches sight of his scarlet corduroys. 'Ubu!' This, it seems, is the name Tim's father (Major Peter Ensleigh Rathbone JP, son of a general, great-nephew of a viscount) has secretly been waiting for. 'I'm Ubu!' he booms at Sarah and Michael as they wheel their thin bikes from the shed, the

93

expressions on their faces suggesting they have been driven from their house by the noise of the party. 'I'm Ubu!' he calls to the new young vicar walking with his wife in the lane.

There are party games – pass the parcel (with a present in every layer), hide and seek, pin the tail. There is a cake of mashed banana, cinnamon and yoghurt, a single candle on top. The older children pick Zoe up and put her down. They squeeze her and push their faces into hers. Now and then she looks for Tim, his assent to these strange happenings. By three o'clock she's dazed, pale, the rosebud mouth (the juicy perfection of that mouth), smeared with what looks like earth. 'Why don't you take her up, Maud?' says Tim's father.

'Yes,' says Maud. 'Do you think she's tired?'

'Of *course* she's tired,' says Tim's father. He chuckles but there's no humour in it. 'She's out on her feet. Don't you think?'

So Maud lifts the child and Tim's father looks at Tim, who looks away and starts collecting plates, carrying them through to the kitchen where the dry handprints on the wall have taken on an unintended character. He should not, he thinks, have chosen red.

In August they make the trip down to the coast. Maud drives her new company car, a cherry-coloured Honda, a great improvement on the Corsa. Tim sits in the back with Zoe, keeping her mild with dried apple rings, milk formula, songs. They stop at a service station to change her nappy. In the boot of the car they have a great bundle of things devoted to the baby. The pushchair alone (a rugged cross-country affair) fills half the space.

When they pick up the key from Chris Totten's office, the broker makes friendly noises to the child, lets her leave small fingerprints on the stainless steel body of his lighter, asks Tim and Maud about their sailing plans.

'Nothing too ambitious,' says Tim. 'We'll have to see what sort of sailor this one is first.'

Lodestar is on her mooring in the middle of the river. Maud frees the tender from where it has wintered on the pontoon boat rack. Curious small things have found their way into the boat. A mussel shell, a bottle top, a feather. Most curiously of all, the shed skin of a snake, papery, almost weightless.

Zoe has fallen asleep in the Snuggler but at the first pull of the oars she wakes and begins to twist her head in what is obviously a mounting panic. By the time they reach *Lodestar* and she is passed over the guard rail she's howling. They take her below, console her, but each time she's brought up (each time with soothing words), her terror is reignited and she is hurried below again. They had planned to stay down for the bank holiday but after a day and a half they drive back, service station by service station. The second attempt is equally hopeless; the third, if anything, slightly worse, the child staring at the water as if at some old enemy, suddenly, monstrously, present. They cannot speak to her, cannot reassure her. Robert Currey, witnessing some of this, the child writhing in her father's arms, a sound like heartbreak, says maybe it's just too soon. All that water, and a world that tips when you step on it. Why wouldn't that unsettle a body? He smiles at them. He has tiny corkscrews of metal shavings in his hair. 'None of my business, of course,' he says. But Tim agrees with him, vigorously. 'Too much too soon,' he says, and laughs with the relief of it.

Two weeks later, Maud goes down on her own. There are jobs that need doing, things that cannot wait, or can be seen that way. Tim will go next time, though when the next time arrives he says, 'It's OK. You go.'

'Don't you want to go?'

'I'm OK,' he says.

'You're sure?'

'Yeah.'

'I don't mind staying,' she says.

'I know.'

'I can look after her.'

'Of course you can. What are you talking about?'

They look at each other a while. She shrugs. 'If you're sure.'

'I am. Completely.'

'OK.'

'Mummy's going down to the boat,' says Tim to the child in his arms. 'But Zoe's going to stay here with Daddy.' The child gazes at him then turns to Maud, regards her with big, solemn eyes. From her fingers she unlaces a scrap of green ribbon and holds it out.

'The young queen's favour,' says Tim. 'All new discovered lands must be named in her honour.'

Maud takes the ribbon. 'Thank you,' she says, and after a moment, softly, 'Yes.'

Though she must have more than five hundred hours alone in small boats she has never sailed a yacht on her own. On Sunday morning, dressed in jeans, trainers, a thick blue shirt like a working man's shirt, she motors out of the harbour on the ebbing tide. It's the last of the high season and boats criss-cross the river ahead of her, a good many of them little bobbling motor-boats rented by the hour from the kiosks and commanded by people who have, perhaps, never been on the water before. Here, then, is a first difficulty – being in the cockpit at the tiller, being five foot six, and having no one up front to call a warning, to watch for the ferries, spot a length of drifting rope ready to wrap itself around the propeller. She's on edge for a while, dances from one side of the cockpit to the other, keeps glancing back as though the river were full of silent liners that would overhaul her in minutes, reduce *Lodestar* to splinters. Then she stops. She can see enough, and the movement of her boat is a proper part of the river's morning business. The engine thumps reassuringly beneath her feet. She likes the smell of diesel. She likes the unexcited way the boat is moving, like a confident swimmer pulling out, stroke by steady stroke, for deeper water.

Between the two castles, their headlands, she passes the invisible line that takes her from the keeping of the harbour to the keeping of the sea. The wind is a westerly, force two or three; the light is excellent, the coast visible for miles. She steers in a slow arc until she is more or less head to wind, then lashes the tiller and goes forward to hoist the main before running back to the cockpit, freeing the tiller and bringing the boat around until the green ribbon, tied now to the starboard shroud, blows at right angles to the deck. The boat heels. She turns off the engine, unfurls the jib, spends fifteen minutes shifting between the tiller and the winches, balancing the boat. Suddenly, there is nothing more to do, nothing but rest a hand on the curve of the tiller, narrow her eyes against the brilliance of the sea. She is sailing. She is alone. Ahead of her is the world's curve and beyond that, everything else. The known, the imagined, the imagined known.

Her most difficult moment is coming back to the mooring. She has not thought it through, not properly. Engine dead slow she passes the buoy, turns and comes up again hoping the tide will bring the boat to a gentle halt. It does, but by the time she has run to the bows the boat has drifted and the buoy is out of reach. She takes the boat around for a second try, then a third. This time she drops a weighted rope over the buoy, a lasso that draws tight as the boat is carried past on the stream. She's not sure if she's remembering this or if she is improvising. It doesn't matter. It is, evidently, the solution. She turns off the engine. The river's silence rises to meet her. Below, she scoops soup out of a tin into a saucepan, sits on the companionway steps to watch it heat. Everything is as it should be; nothing has gone wrong, or nothing serious. She took the boat out and she brought it back. There are skills to sailing alone that she will need to learn if sailing alone is to become a regular occurrence, and she makes a mental checklist of what she would need if she were to set sail not for a morning or a day but – say – for a week. She wonders how John Gosse managed, ghostly Gosse, who she and Tim have always imagined sailing on his own. Above all, she would need some sort of self-steering, a wind vane, an auto-helm. She will do some research. She will talk to people in the yard. To Robert Currey, perhaps.

Her phone is in a mesh pocket above the chart table. The little blue message light is blinking. She watches it. The call, she assumes, is from Tim, wanting to know when she'll be back, or if she can pick something up on the way home or to tell her something about Zoe. What does he want to tell her about Zoe? She turns off the gas under the soup, pours the soup into a cup and goes on deck. In future, she thinks, she might leave the phone in the car.

19

When Zoe is three and a half she gets chicken pox. Several other boys and girls in the playgroup have it. The illness does not distress her much and when she is better she seems to have moved into some new phase of life, to look out at the world with an alertness that wasn't there before, as if her infancy was being stripped from her, layer by layer.

She is strong, full of play, precociously musical. Tim buys her a pink ukelele. Because his own instruments are so valuable he will not let her do more than touch them, stroke the grain of the wood, the bright strings, with fingertips that have been carefully inspected for honey, chocolate, snot. All the guitars are at the cottage now, even the Lacôte from the treasure room at his parents' house. When not in use they are kept upstairs in the spare room in a locked cupboard.

She has lots of dolls, some beautiful ones from Ubu. She disciplines them harshly, smothers them with kisses. She pretends to be a kitten, a phase that lasts many weeks. She wants Maud to be a kitten with her. Tim, half hidden in the doorway to the kitchen, watches them, Maud on her hands and knees, a kitten that seems to have learnt its kitten nature out of a book. Nor can Maud make up stories, or only in the most laboured way. And asked to shake the hand of some invisible man or woman, someone newly sprung from her daughter's head, she is flummoxed. Was this how she was as a child? Tim thinks of the picture he stole from the cork board in her parents' house. Girl with brick wall, girl with white socks, girl unfathomed. When he asks her (gently, not wishing to appear to be probing her like some manner of therapist) she says she was like any other child. 'They're not all the same,' he says. 'I know,' she says. It's one of those discussions with Maud that goes nowhere.

He can see Maud in the set of the child's mouth, in the curls of her hair, the shape of her toes (Rathbone toes are very straight), but it's a long time before he sees any mannerism, any behaviours, that come distinctively, unarguably, from her mother. Then, one afternoon, just the two of them at home, he catches Zoe standing on the lawn watching nothing obvious with that same rooted calm, that uncanny stillness, he has witnessed so often in Maud. A switching off or a switching *in*. Something weirdly primitive about it; a posture, an expression, you might find painted on a piece of pottery buried with a Babylonian princess. He is not sure how much he likes to see it there, in his daughter's face.

A fortnight after this, stripping Zoe in the steam of her nightly bath, he sees black marks, black smudges, on the underside of her left forearm. He asks her to show him but she doesn't want to, holds her arm against her naked flank. When he asks again she does a little dance on the bathmat and as the last gesture of the dance presents him with her arm. He gets it then. The marks, a dozen loops and squiggles made with a felt-tip pen, are her version of her mother's tattoo, of *Sauve Qui Peut*. He tries to soap it off in the bath but she won't have it. It fades slowly. Thankfully, she does not attempt to renew it.

With Maud, there are discussions, at night mostly, sometimes in bed, about having another child.

'You were an only child,' he says. 'Wouldn't you like Zoe to have a brother or sister?'

'If you asked her she would say no.'

'If we asked her,' he says, 'she would have us sell the house to buy chocolate. She would certainly have us sell the boat.'

These discussions reach no conclusion. He does not attempt to insist; she does not say no, never. In the years since Zoe's birth they have used a variety of contraception (condoms; the pill; briefly, a diaphragm). Sometimes they go for weeks without touching each other. They are often tired. Her work, the long hours of travelling; his work caring for the child. By ten at night their appetite is more often for sleep than for each other, the physical labour of making love. And then the spell is broken. He notices her pulling her jumper over her head, the stretch of her girlish body. Or he says something that makes them both laugh and the tension between them, the almost unnoticeable tension, is instantly dissolved. They do it in the bedroom, once or twice in the bathroom under the shower, but it's better downstairs where they don't have to worry about the child waking. Maud is light enough to hold against a wall, her knees up by his shoulders. Or he has her sit astride him in the kitchen, her tights on the floor, her skirt up by her hips, her strong legs flexed, supper plates on the table still, the ticking of the kitchen clock, night pressed against the uncurtained window, a darkness thick as felt.

*   *   *

Their friends – their country friends – are Jack and Maggie, Chris and Bella, Lally and Tish. Friends, supper guests, fellow parents with children in the same toddler group as Zoe or with older children already at St Winifred's, the well-regarded local primary where, in September, Zoe will start. There is also childless Arnie, a friend of Tim's from prep school, working in estate management now, newly divorced and having 'the time of his life' but looking jowly and distracted and ten years older than he should.

All of them live within a dozen miles of the cottage, and with the exception of Tish, who has a Burmese mother, they are white, university educated and with money in the bank. Maud is the only one not to have been to public school (King's Bruton, Eton, Cheltenham Ladies' College, Roedean, Charterhouse); she is also the only one to have studied pure sciences. Sitting around each other's tables they talk about children, marriage, country living. They talk about politics (only Arnie unapologetically on the right); about the arts (the Royal Academy, the Edinburgh Fringe, HBO). Tish and Lally, who describe themselves as Dorset lesbian royalty, know all the local gossip. They know, for example, that the young vicar's wife has run away, that the young vicar is in disgrace, and that the old vicar – who is, reputedly, more interested in paleontology, in bone fragments and flint arrowheads than the forty-two articles of the Church of England – has been summoned out of retirement to keep the parish from drifting into Hinduism or devil worship.

'God, it's like Trollope!' says Jack and the others nod, all except Maud who has not picked up a novel since GCSEs and *Jude the Obscure* and to whom the name Trollope means nothing. She does not shine at these gatherings. She is friendly, speaks when spoken to, remembers to ask questions about the other children and has a small store of remarks about her own child, but she does not suddenly say, as Maggie does one day, that she is in love with the new plumber; does not, as Tish does, mimic the pompous blathering of a minister of state, does not (Lally) give a tearful defence of euthanasia, or tell (Bella) a risqué story about her year as an au pair girl in Rome.

'She's obviously incredibly bright,' says Chris, as he and Tim drive back from playing tennis on Jack and Maggie's grass court. 'Yes,' says Tim, 'she *is*,' but he's afraid something else has been meant, something more nuanced. Only Arnie seems to get her, or says he does. He appoints himself her champion, so that when Maggie – a night when Maud is late home from work and the party has begun without her – says how much she admires Maud, her quality of the *naïf*, he looks up from his plate (his place at the table with its gravy splashes, its spilt wine) and growls, 'Piss off, Maggie,' a moment that takes some smoothing over.

Tim hopes that one or other of the women will become Maud's particular friend. He thinks it will be good for her if she has such a friend. Who *are* her friends? Professor Kimber? The people at work? The moths? He thinks Tish might be a possibility, Bella at a push. He encourages her to accept the invitations that come. A girls' night out in Bath, a spa day at a local hotel, the inaugural meeting of a new book club. Finally, she goes. It's an evening at Chris and Bella's house, ladies only. She wears her dress of chocolate silk, the lighter jacket with its little burn. She's back by eleven-fifteen. When she comes in, Tim is sprawled on the sofa watching the end of *The Sopranos*. She watches it with him and when it's over he switches off the television and asks if she had a nice time. She says she did.

'What sort of nice time?'

'We saw a film. Then we had supper.'

'Sounds fun. What did you talk about at supper?'

'The film.'

'Just the film?'

'Other things too.'

'Come on, Maud. What sort of things?'

'They were talking about their dreams.'

'Did you tell them about yours?'

'What?'

'Your dreams. I know you have them because I hear you talking in your sleep. Quite often, in fact.'

She shakes her head. 'They asked me to explain what an enzyme is.'

'An enzyme?'

'Yes.'

'Let me get this right. They're talking about their dreams and they ask you to explain what an enzyme is?'

'Yes.'

'And did you?'

'Yes.'

'Do you think they understood?'

'I'm not sure,' she says, her jacket folded over her knees, 'but I don't think so.'

20

A fortnight before Zoe's first day at St Winifred's her parents have a row in the kitchen. 'Of *course* we must be there,' says Tim, waving a serving spoon. 'Her first day! We must *both* be there.'

Maud, sitting at the table, arms folded over her breasts, explains for the third time that she has a meeting at Southampton University at nine in the morning. A scheduled meeting. An important meeting.

'How can it be more important than *this*?' cries Tim.

'If you had a job,' she says, 'you'd know.'

'If I had a job,' he says, 'who would look after Zoe? You?'

She does not withdraw from the meeting (she is tabled to present the five-year follow-up results from the Kappa-opioids trial) but she tells them she will be late. When she tells them the reason they say that's fine, Maud, come when you can. This surprises her slightly. Perhaps the meeting was not as important as she thought.

* * *

The first day, the hush of early morning, the lamplit bedroom; Zoe, solemn queen, stands in her nightie and looks at her uniform laid out on the bottom of the bed. White vest, white pants, white shirt, grey tights, grey dress, scarlet cardigan, all of them clearly marked with her name, Zoe Rathbone. She can, of course, dress herself but this morning allows her parents to draw on her clothes. Her hair is brushed. She wears it much longer than her mother, too long perhaps, a mass of chestnut curls that Tim crushes in his fist then twists into a coloured band.

When breakfast is over they set off in Maud's Honda. The car, chilly when they first get into it, slowly warms up. The radio is on – warnings about congestion on roads many miles away. Maud turns it off. Behind them, the school bus swings out of a narrow turning, brushing rain from the hedgerows. It's a coach chartered from a local company. It looks too big for the lanes. 'One day, Zoe,' says Tim, sitting with her in the back of the car, 'you can go on the bus. All the coolest kids go on the bus. Did you go on the bus, Maud?'

'Sometimes,' she says.

Zoe sits upright in her booster chair, her cardigan buttoned, her new coat folded on the seat beside her. She has barely spoken since breakfast. Somehow she has surrounded herself with an atmosphere of sacrifice, as if the two people she most loves, most depends upon, have decided to sell her, and she – at barely five – must accept the inevitability of it.

It is not a long journey. At the school she walks between them, holds her mother's hand, her father's. The headmistress is waiting in the playground. The girls in their red cardigans, the boys in their red sweaters, are gathered around her. She smiles at each child and they look at her with awe. On the tarmac surface of the playground are the faintly chalked lines of old games.

The parents talk in quiet voices. Rain clouds pass overhead but no rain falls.

'Time to say our goodbyes,' says the headmistress, who has now been joined by her assistant, Miss Beazley. Zoe holds up her arms to her father. She embraces him then looks at her mother. Maud leans down and kisses her. 'Bye bye, Maud,' says the girl who has, this last summer, started addressing her mother by her name.

The parents are drifting away. Some children cling on, frantic. Miss Beazley is dispatched; she has the skills of separation. In they go, red and grey through the open doors behind the headmistress (who, at this distance, does not seem much bigger than a child herself). The parents wander back to their cars. Some are weeping. They cry, laugh at themselves, touch their chests as if to calm their troubled hearts.

Beside the Honda, Tim has his face against Maud's shoulder. Because he is so much taller than her there is something comical in the posture. He speaks into her shoulder, his hot breath, the trembling in his back. Bella appears. She has just dropped off the twins, who are in the year above Zoe. She tells Maud she'll take Tim home. She'll look after him. 'It's vile at first,' she says, 'an awful wrench. But by next week it will just be the new normal. Trust me.'

The driver of the school bus is standing by the open door of the coach, smoking, sucking his teeth. He winks at Maud. He's a young man who looks old or an old man who looks young. Maud gets into the car, checks her phone. As she drives out of the car park, Tim and Bella turn and wave to her.

It is, of course, as Bella said. Wise Bella! The first week, the second. The cottage has a new rhythm. Is it games today? Is it

Miss Beazley or Mrs Luckett this morning? Where are your shoes? Hey! It's ten past eight already! The smell of toast, the voices on the radio, the day still shadowed.

Sometimes Maud is with them but often she has left the house before the others are out of bed. Three, four hours of travelling, whole sections of motorway she can scroll across the shut lids of her eyes in the moments before sleep. She's a senior clinical research associate now. She earns just over thirty thousand a year, has her own cubicle on the top floor of the building in Reading. At the annual conference (Brighton last year, the hotel the IRA bombed) Josh Fenniman sees her sooner and for longer. She has proved her worth, her reliability, and though she is not one of those he has marked down, secretly, for high office, she is the type of employee he wishes to retain, and the management in Reading have been tasked with seeing she has enough to keep her interested. That tattoo still sounds alarm bells. What possessed her? But Josh Fenniman can recall moments from his own youth (he's still a youthful-seeming man), instances of exuberance before he saw the world for what it is. Someone should mention laser removal or that it might be wise to keep it covered up more, might certainly be a smart move to cover it up when she goes for a one-to-one with the CEO. It's not just the team player thing. Is she respectful? Is there some issue around respect? Henderson thinks she's on the spectrum but Henderson does not always see clearly, which is why his name, like Maud's, is not to be found on the list (the very short list) of those who will one day have the best things.

Sauve Qui Peut! Big indelible letters!

What *possessed* her?

21

They have Christmas at the Rathbones again. Gin, sloe gin, charades, midnight mass, a turkey so big Magnus tells the children it's an Alsatian. Zoe is swept up with her cousins, young teenagers now. Trails of gold foil from chocolate coins. Dogs held up on their hind legs and made to dance. On Boxing Day they walk over Rathbone land. Tussocky grass, the hills bled of their colour, the streams, shallow and broad, where the dogs lap their reflections. They have come out to see the hunt, and at last it comes, tiny figures working their way down the edge of a hill, then the ground reverberating, the pack spilling and reforming, the brute horses bullied on, Zoe on her father's back lost in a thrill of looking.

January, and welcome back children. Tim on the school run. Have you got *everything*? Then stopping to talk to Bella or one of the other mothers. Their names, the children's names – Sue who has Daniel and Zadie, Jenny who has Tamsin, Lu who has Maya and Rupert, Claire who has the little one whose name Tim can never remember, the one with the glasses and the red hair, the unfortunate limp.

Miss Beazley shutting the gates.

At home in the cottage he brews coffee and rolls a cigarette. There's a sheltered place by the back door and though sometimes it smells of fuel oil from the tank and is therefore probably not the safest place to smoke a cigarette, it has become a place of contemplation. Smoke, drink the coffee, try to think how it's all going (his life, his *relationship*), and when you cannot think any more or make it lie down, stop thinking and imagine music.

He is, at last, making progress with CYP2D6, the concerto he planned (and thought he would write in a month) when they were still in Bristol. He has a nice opening, a theme in common time, a minor key, the guitar a solo voice quietly establishing itself. Later movements will recycle the theme in new and unexpected guises – ragtime, for example, and then a slow movement like a stately, droll flamenco. He has his own computer, a slightly better one than Maud's, with software that rigs the screen with staves and offers orchestration at the press of a button. The dedication will read, 'For Zoe' or 'Zoe, with love'. Or just 'For Z'.

The mornings grow lighter. In the garden there are already spikes of new green and by the end of the month the rooks are busy in the bare trees opposite the cottage. On the drive to school a low sun slants across drenched fields. Sometimes there is ice, sometimes a steady green-seeming rain, the water from the road flung up onto the Lancia's windscreen, Tim leaning forward at the wheel.

In the cottage, blotchy paintings of houses or cats or smiling, schematic people, are Blu Tacked to doors or the kitchen cupboards. There are wands, there are pictures made from leaves, there are loo rolls rolled in glitter, there are jars with earth in them and twigs.

When Maud gets back to the cottage at night Zoe is often in bed. Tim says, 'Go up and look at her,' and so she goes, up the stairs in her work clothes to stand in the part-open doorway looking into the room's subtle blue and seeing the shadow of the bed then, after a moment, her eyes adjusting, the pale of her daughter's face on the pillow.

Sometimes Zoe is still awake, and in a whisper she calls to Maud and Maud sits on the bed while the child talks. They speak like prisoners, like escapees, or as if the night were sternly conducting its own strange music and must not be disturbed. She tells Maud urgent stories. There is something luxurious in her capacity to invent. All of it seems to mean something. She asks Maud where she has been and Maud tells her, her plain words accepted in silence. When they kiss goodnight they can hardly see each other's faces. Kiss an eye, kiss a nose, an eyebrow. Then the slow walking back to the door, the last goodnights, the very last a bare whisper like a sigh, the door pulled to but never shut.

Downstairs, Tim, angling a log into the stove or putting out a plate of reheated supper or listening to some programme on the radio about the burial practices of early humans (a grave in Vedbaek, Denmark, of a woman buried with a hundred and ninety teeth of red deer and wild boar around her head, and beside her, a child – hers, presumably – laid on a swan's wing, a flint dagger at her waist), asks Maud how Zoe was and Maud, sitting down to the reheated food or opening her laptop or just standing there, Maud style, looking at God knows, says, 'Zoe? Oh, she's fine.'

22

'Should we talk?'
  'If you want.'
  'It's not really about that, is it?'

Nights are like the bottom of somewhere, a kind of seabed. As for the days, they have a cunning of their own.

23

It's a morning in March, a month before the Easter holidays. Tim plays some of the new piece, twenty bars or so, for Bella. It's raw outside, damp and raw, and they are sitting in the warmth from the stove, their clothes unruly on the floor around them, the bell of the church tinkling the quarter-hour. It's an odd thing to play the guitar naked, the wood cool on your lap. And odd, too, to play for a naked woman who is sitting smiling in a half-lotus on the rug, her neck and cheeks still a little flushed from before. An odd thing but pleasant.

They've talked about it; they've gone into this with their eyes open. Bella will not be leaving her husband. Tim will not leave Maud. Nothing in the outward form of their lives needs to change. If Bella left Chris he would fall apart. He is, she explains, much more fragile than he looks. When his mother died he wouldn't get out of bed for a month. He became briefly incontinent. Regressed to an age somewhere around seven months.

As for Maud, what would become of her? Tim has – many

times – imagined himself telling her it's over, that he's leaving, taking Zoe with him. He is not sure when these thoughts began. He suspects the first time was probably about a month after the baby was born. The hard part is imagining Maud's reaction. Tears? Silence? Or would she wait until his back was turned then sink a boning knife between his shoulders?

There are moments when he believes that in the last six years he has learnt nothing important about her at all, nothing that *shows* her to him. More frequently now, much more frequently, are those occasions when he simply shakes his head and walks away, cannot be bothered to try to figure it out. Was his mother right about her? And smart-arse Magnus ('I can see why you wanted to fuck her, old boy. I just don't see the rest of it')?

But this is Maud, for Christ's sake! Maud who flew past him, lay dead on the ground then stood and walked. Who else has entered his life like that? Has entered his life with the force of myth?

'We take people on,' says Bella (Bella who *genuinely* likes Maud). 'It doesn't always make much sense. And then the children come along.'

Two or three times a week they are together. No great subterfuge is required, they just follow each other back from the school. The neighbours are both at work, there's no one else. If he said he felt guilty he'd be lying. He's put up with a lot; he deserves Bella. He is dazzled by her tallness (as tall as he is). He likes to arrange her limbs on the sofa as though he were going to sketch her. Once, when he was in her from behind, rooted in her, their four knees on the generous width of the sofa, her back hollowed, her backside tilted up a little, shining, he found himself looking out of the window and straight into the gaze of the old priest who was peering owlishly past the garden gate. He didn't tell Bella, didn't think the old man could see anything, though the thought that he *might* see, see life at work in the fucking of this long-armed woman, her streaming hair, did not displease him. Nor is his conscience much troubled by those occasions when a small deceit is needed for Maud – or possibly isn't needed, for who knows what she notices. Half the time she seems in a dream, the other half she looks at you and your skin is glass.

He tells himself he's a lizard but the thought only raises a moment of grim laughter. Less comfortable is the realization that driving his daughter to school is a sort of foreplay, so that he is aware of himself talking to her too much and too excitedly, sometimes wanting to tell her everything, to make her his little confidante. It also makes him drive faster than he should, the Lancia, the much-repaired Lancia, dancing through the lanes.

Then the holidays arrive and for three weeks he barely sees Bella. When he does it's with the children or with Chris or Maud. Between the lovers there's all the usual play of fleeting glances, the backs of their hands touching as they pass each other, the social kiss pressed a little harder than before. They have exchanged tokens. He gave her a silver moon on a silver chain; she gave him a ring bought years ago in Cairo that takes the form of twining snakes. He wears the ring on the first day of the new term, slips it on in the car, then drives past Bella in the school car park, his window down, his hand, the glinting ring, displayed.

They resume. The sofa, the stove. Sometimes music. The light is generous now, falls past the deep-set windows to find them in their innocence, their nakedness. One morning they have to hide from the postman. One morning the fuel-oil man comes and Tim has to drag on clothes and smooth his hair and banter with the man while the tank slowly fills. And one morning, the last week in May, her knees up by her chin, his body braced across her, braced like a gymnast, the phone rings, the answer phone comes on and the voice of Maud's mother fills the room saying Grandfather Ray is dead.

'We should stop,' says Bella. 'Timmy?'

But they don't stop. They keep going until they are done.

Zoe isn't with them at the crematorium. She only met Grandfather Ray twice, both times at The Poplars when he gave no sign of understanding who she was, and where she played contentedly with his Zimmer frame until it was time to kiss his bloodshot cheek and leave. Ubu has promised to take her up in his plane ('Don't fuss, Tim. It's a damn sight safer than a car').

The crematorium is new. From the road it looks like an inexpensive hotel or the clubhouse for a municipal golf course. Most of Swindon's dead come here now. In the car park, lines of hearses wait their turn in the shade of young trees.

Maud and Tim are in the front row of the chapel with Mr and Mrs Stamp. The row behind them has four people and the one behind that is empty. Across the aisle is a nurse from The Poplars and half a dozen old railwaymen in dark jackets.

When the coffin comes in, a young man with a top hat walks in front of it. None of the bearers seems to have a suit that fits them and this gives them, slightly, the look of clowns or exiles. The coffin is laid in the alcove. The young man takes off his hat and makes a solemn bow to the coffin. It is part of his work but the gesture carries with it something startling and profound. Who ever bowed to Grandfather Ray in life? Tim glances down the row, but if the moment has struck home there is no outward sign. Mrs Stamp has a ball of tissue in one hand but so far has had no use for it. Mr Stamp occasionally nods as if being secretly addressed, perhaps by the spirit of his dead father. They are invited to sit. On the order of service there is a roughly copied photograph of Grandfather Ray looking sixty, vigorous, a man cut out for work. A dependable man, a nice man.

The vicar is a woman. Is the cemetery a good posting? She makes a joke; the old men cough. There are no poems, nothing of that sort. A single hymn, a five-minute eulogy that the vicar has somehow constructed from two visits to The Poplars and a brief conversation with Mr and Mrs Stamp. There is a sentence about sailing with his beloved granddaughter (a smile here from the lectern to Maud). At the end, the curtains close with a curious jerking movement, like the end of a puppet show. The young man with the hat makes another deep bow and the doors of the hall are opened (not the way they came in, of course, where others will be waiting). The mourners shuffle out to the early summer air, a pathway next to raw beds of self-tending plants. Floral tributes have been laid out – one from the care home, one from the union. Over the low walls are views of the country, of sunlight on sheep-cropped hills.

The Stamps have invited people back to the house. There are sandwiches, biscuits, cups of tea, bottles of beer. The old men gather in the living room, stand together in a line as if on a platform in some hard wind, looking for a train that is already hopelessly delayed. Each in turn shakes Maud's hand and to each she speaks a few words before moving on to the next. Tim, sipping tea and keeping out of the way, feels his scalp prickle. What is she? The young Queen of the Night? Are they paying tribute to her? Renewing their allegiance?

When it's done and the crumbs have been hoovered and the glasses washed and put to dry on the rack and a mark like a hoof print, a mark made by one of the old men's boots, has been sponged from the carpet, Tim and Maud and Mr and Mrs Stamp sit in the kitchen. The wine in the garage has still not been found but there is beer left over from the wake and this is poured carefully into four tumblers. Tim asks questions about Grandfather Ray. He is hoping someone will tell a story about him but no one does. Quite casually, Mrs Stamp lets drop that Maud is to inherit everything, but then (in the next breath) that everything amounts to very little. Some savings, some of Grandmother Dot's old jewellery. Anything of real value was sold years ago, the money spent on care.

They eat supper – shepherd's pie in a pyrex dish – and afterwards sit in the living room for an hour drinking tea. No one says so but clearly it would not be appropriate to have the television on. At ten, Maud goes up to take a bath. Tim excuses himself and goes out to smoke in the street. He texts his mother: *How was the flight? Zoe OK?* He texts Bella: *I wish I was drunk. I wish I was with you. I'm a stranger here.*

From the houses opposite come small reports of life. Light spills from kitchen windows, from frosted bathroom windows. The parked cars give the impression of great patience. He tidies his cigarette into the gutter, goes into the house, pads up the narrow stairs. Maud is in her room sitting on the bed. She has a towel wrapped around her and is using another towel to dry her hair. White walls, a white MFI wardrobe, a small, frameless mirror. The room has only one picture, something cut long ago from a magazine, laminated on the laminating machine in the kitchen, and tacked to the wall at pillow height. A boat in heavy weather, a woman in yellow oilskins in the cockpit. He's seen it before and knows it's Clare Francis on her solo transatlantic run, mid-1970s.

'Quite a day,' he says. 'Eh?' He sits on the bed beside her, drops a kiss on her shoulder, then, when she looks at him, her bare face washed back to the brightness of bone, he leans, a little wildly, and kisses her mouth.

TWO

It is human nature to stand in the middle of a thing,
but you cannot stand in the middle of this . . .

Marianne Moore

1

Having eaten a sandwich upstairs in her cubicle, she has come down to spend half an hour in the animal room gentling rats and listening to the technician talk about the history of bluegrass – Bill Monroe, Earl Scruggs, 'the high lonesome style'. He talks softly. He doesn't ask questions. Now and then there are playful asides. Josh Fenniman he refers to as Uncle Jo. Trouble, he says, always starts on the ground floor – or better still, the basement.

She lifts the rats from their cages, picks them out by their tails and settles them on an arm folded across her chest. They're albino Sprague Dawley rats, bred for their easy natures, their docility. They push their heads into the crook of her arm. She strokes behind their ears, strokes their restless warmth, then lifts them back into the cage by the loose skin behind their necks.

It has been raining for days, perhaps for weeks. Slate-coloured November rain, the rivers suddenly muscular, old bridges over-whelmed. There are wild geese in the flooded fields. In cities the offices have their lights on at midday. Even in the windowless animal room you are aware of it, a background rattling, unlistened to but registered somewhere.

The history lesson has moved on. He's laying down the ancestry of a sound. Red Smiley, Don Reno, the Greenbriar Boys, the Country Gentlemen. Uncle Josh Graves from Tellico Plains, Tennessee. The names are like old shoes or old hats or old notebooks, notebooks with creased and marbled covers, the pages inside scrawled with dense handwriting you are never going to read.

Her phone rings. It's in the hip pocket of her lab coat. When she answers, there's a sound, a confusion of sounds. No one responds to her hello. She goes on listening. Someone who has her number in their phone has accidentally called her, someone out in the street or perhaps even standing by a television or a radio.

'Hello?' she says. 'Hello?'

Recitation. Song. As in a dream where some animal, a jaguar, rests its black head beside you on the pillow and speaks in a voice you know as well as your own.

She ends the call, looks at the phone, and after a moment puts the phone back in her pocket.

'Have they summoned you?' asks the technician. He's concentrating but quite at ease, an anaesthetized rat on the bench in front of him, a glass microcapillary tube angled to the back of one of its eyes.

Fifteen minutes after the call, a few minutes before the end of the lunch break, the woman from Human Resources comes in. She looks like herself yet also somehow strange, altered. Her beautiful shoes, her hair with the tawny highlights. She says, 'Can you come with me, Maud?' She holds out a hand to Maud. She has never done that before.

Between the animal room and the staff room are two flights of stairs. The woman is explaining to Maud that some people have come to see her. On the second flight it turns out that the people are from the police, that they are the police. A policeman and a policewoman. 'I'll stay with you,' she says, 'unless you want me to go.'

In the staff room the officers are standing with their hats in their hands.

'Hello,' says the policewoman. 'Are you Maud Rathbone?'

'She's Maud Stamp,' says the woman from Human Resources.

'But Henley Rathbone is your partner?'

'Tim,' says Maud. 'Yes.'

The policewoman nods. She manages a sort of smile at Maud, though her colleague looks mostly at the floor.

'Could you sit down for me please, Maud?' says the woman officer. She gestures to where four of the brightly coloured chairs have been arranged, two facing two, in a part of the room beside one of the tinted windows. The others wait until Maud is sitting before taking their own seats.

When they are finished – it doesn't take long – the woman from Human Resources goes to collect Maud's coat and work bag. Maud has already told them that she will drive herself to the hospital. This is not the usual way and some effort is made to change her mind, but she appears to be in control of herself, is quietly insistent, and it cannot be absolutely forbidden. She takes off her lab coat, takes the phone from the pocket, puts on her outdoor coat. The policewoman is watching her very closely. She and her colleague walk behind Maud as they leave the staff room. Anyone coming onto the corridor – a cleaner, Henderson even – might imagine at first that she was being arrested.

In the car park the woman from Human Resources holds an

umbrella over Maud's head. 'Have you got everything?' she asks. 'Are you sure?' Maud settles herself in the driving seat. The woman, leaning in under the umbrella, touches a brown half-curl of Maud's hair. Has the odd, immediately suppressed desire to kiss her.

Though it's not yet three o'clock the motorway is clogged. There are speed restrictions. Most cars have their lights on and as they pass they send up a wash of spray that lands brown and finely granulated on the windscreen. At the first service station after Swindon she stops, parks, and goes to the toilets. When she's finished she buys a pack of sandwiches and a bottle of water. In the car she drinks from the bottle, opens the sandwiches and puts them on the passenger seat. It takes another hour and a half to reach the turn-off for Bath. Twice during that time her phone rings but she makes no attempt to answer it. She follows the signs to the hospital, tries to leave the car in several small car parks in the hospital grounds before finding one with a space. She walks through the rain to A&E. When she speaks to the receptionist she is told that no one of that name has been admitted and then, with a little startled 'Ah!', the receptionist tells her that Mr Rathbone is in ICU and that he's there more as a precautionary measure really and someone will come out in a minute and take her to him. Have a seat.

She sits. Some of the people around her look calm and brave and some look frightened and brave and some just frightened. A young nurse comes and leans over her. 'Hello,' she says. 'Do you want to come with me?' She's younger than Maud, a young black woman, twenty-five or -six to Maud's thirty-four, but at some point on the walk to ICU she calls Maud 'sweetie'.

At the unit Maud is given into the care of a male nurse. The unit is hushed, heavily furnished with technology. There is no banter here, no attempt at homeliness. The temperature feels very similar to the animal room at Reading.

The male nurse leads Maud to Tim's bed. He is lying with his eyes shut, the side of one eye raw-looking, swollen, a small dressing in place. There's a canula in his left arm, a clear hose leading to a bag of fluid. His parents are sitting on chairs either side of the bed. His mother is holding his hand. His father is staring down at his own knees but glances up for a second to see who it is, then drops his gaze again. Tim's mother stands and comes over to Maud. There's a quick embrace, stiff-limbed, then – in the voice of someone who has decided that there must be at least one person who remains clear-headed – she explains the nature of her son's injuries. A concussion, two broken ribs, a fractured femur, a broken thumb, contusions. He has been examined, X-rayed, sedated. Tomorrow he will be moved to an observation ward and his leg will be put in a cast. He is not in any danger. They were worried about his eye but his eye will recover. They do not expect him to remain in the hospital longer than a week.

'Do you understand what I'm saying?'

'Yes,' says Maud. They look at each other. The older woman's face spasms. Her fingers tremble at her throat. Maud helps her back to her chair and stands beside her, looking down at Tim. At some point another nurse comes, a senior nurse in a dark blue dress. She has epaulettes. To Maud she says, 'Are you . . . ?'

And Tim's mother says, 'Yes, yes she is.'

The nurse smiles at Maud. 'Tim's doing very well,' she says. 'Shall we go down to the family room for a while? It's nice and quiet in there. We won't be disturbed.' She waits. Tim's father makes a noise in his throat. In other circumstances you might take it for laughter.

*   *   *

When she leaves the hospital the rain has stopped. It's a little surprising, and several people, emerging through the doors after long visits, peer up into the darkness suspiciously.

Her car smells of eggs. The open packet of uneaten sandwiches is still on the passenger seat. She looks for a bin, spends fifteen minutes wandering the grounds with the sandwiches in her hand before leaving them on top of some sort of metal junction box.

By the time she gets back to the cottage it feels late, the middle of the night, but it's not yet ten o'clock. The air is colder than in the city, apparently thinner. To the south, through breaking cloud, a dozen stars are visible. Sirius between two trees, and above it, the constellation of Orion.

She unlocks the cottage door, glides her fingers over the wall, feeling for the light switch. She has had some idea the cottage will be in chaos but of course it is not. Why would it be in chaos? She goes through to the kitchen. On the table are two unwashed cereal bowls and two spoons. She collects them, washes them, puts each thing away in its place then goes back into the living room. The room is cold and she thinks about lighting the stove. The phone rings. She watches it until it stops then takes off her coat and shoes and lies on the sofa, her coat pulled over her as a blanket. She is almost asleep when she sits up and rummages in her coat pocket for her phone. She opens it and scrolls through the log of recent calls until she finds the one she answered in the animal room. She does not expect to find a number and she doesn't. It's listed as unknown. An unknown caller.

2

In ICU the next morning they tell her Tim has already been moved, that she has just missed him. She sets off along broad corridors, the sick being wheeled in their beds, visitors frowning at signs. The usual smells, the predictable smells. When she finds him, a semi-private bay at the far end of the ward, his parents are with him again. They have stayed the night in a Bath hotel. Tim's mother says, 'You went home, I suppose.'

Tim is awake. He watches her approach the bed. When she leans down to kiss him he turns his face away. She waits. He will not look at her or speak to her. She leaves and walks around the hospital grounds. Sunlight glitters on every drenched surface. She decides to make a list of things she has to do – the dozen, the twenty urgent things she must attend to – but when she finds a pen in the glovebox of her car and smooths out the back of a Trial Volunteer Disclaimer form (TVD-1), she can think of nothing except calling her own parents, which she does, immediately, sitting in the car with the door open. They are both at work of course. It's a school day. She leaves a message asking them to call her, then goes back to the ward. Now there are three people by the bed. One of them is Bella. When she sees Maud she flinches, then recovers herself, smiles, begins to spill fresh tears, embraces Maud and whispers, 'Anything, anything at all. You only need to ask.'

It's another two days before Tim will speak to her and even then he will not meet her eyes. He tells her he will be discharged the day after tomorrow, that he'll have crutches and the use of a wheelchair. He says he'll stay with his parents. They will collect him and he'll stay with them.

'Where will you be?' he asks.

'At the cottage,' she says.

'Don't move anything,' he says.

'OK.'

'Nothing.'

'I won't.'

'Upstairs.'

'I haven't been there.'

'Nothing,' he says.

'No,' she says.

'Nothing.'

'I won't.'

'If you do . . .'

'I won't.'

Later the same day she's in the living room kneeling in front of the stove breaking kindling. She hears the garden gate and stands up in time to see a policewoman, plump and blonde, brushing droplets from her shoulders, raindrops that were strung on the thorns of the rose bush and which the shutting gate has shaken down on her.

Maud lets her in. She wipes her feet, looks at the wood in Maud's hand, the open mouth of the stove. 'I could help you with that,' she says. 'I've got one like that at home.'

Maud tells her the Rayburn has gone out and that the Rayburn runs the heating for the house. She thinks the oil tank is probably empty. She hasn't looked.

'Do you know how to get more oil?' asks the policewoman, and Maud says yes, she just has to call and the tanker will come.

'Good,' says the policewoman. 'It's important to stay warm.'

They sit. The policewoman has a plastic document wallet on her lap. She unzips it and takes out a thin sheaf of paper. She's from victim liaison and she starts by saying a few simple, kind things, then moves on to the papers and goes through them item by item, stopping after each to ask Maud if she has understood. The driver of the school coach has been arrested. His blood tests were negative but he has been charged under Section 1 of the Road Traffic Offenders Act. There will be an arraignment at the magistrates' court. There's no need for either Maud or Mr Rathbone to attend. At any future trial Mr Rathbone is likely to be called as a witness, though obviously not Maud. The coach itself is still being examined. Preliminary findings suggest it was mechanically sound, that there was, for example, nothing wrong with the brakes. Likewise, Mr Rathbone's car. Mechanically sound.

'You mean Tim,' says Maud. 'Tim's car.'

'Yes,' says the policewoman. 'I mean Tim.'

'Have you seen him?'

'A colleague has been to see him. To take a statement.'

Maud nods. The policewoman turns the page. There will be a

coroner's inquiry, she says. It's triggered automatically by a situation like this though if there's a trial the inquest may be adjourned until the verdict. 'Someone from the coroner's office will get in touch and talk you through it all. You will be invited to attend but you don't have to. It's up to you. Do you understand?'

She tells Maud that the children on the coach, the ones who were hurt, are back home now. One little boy has a broken arm and another a fractured cheekbone. The others just suffered bruising and shock. Counsellors will be going into the school next week. Experts.

She gives Maud her card and a sheet of paper with the numbers of various agencies and helplines. 'I'll let myself out,' she says, zipping up the wallet and standing. 'Don't forget to ring about the oil.'

Maud watches her through the window, sees her shake the raindrops onto her shoulders again. As if she had forgotten, or didn't care.

Magnus calls. Somehow he has been given the task of organizing things. He leaves businesslike messages. If there's something you want, he says, something particular, music for example, you need to let me know as soon as possible. If (the third message) I don't hear from you I'll assume you're content to let the family make the choices.

Then the vicar comes. It's the old vicar who replaced the young vicar whose wife ran away – who has presumably not come back, who is still running. He knocks softly, asks softly if he might come in for a moment. He's very tall. He has to bow his head to avoid the beams. Maud leads him through to the kitchen. There is still no oil for the Rayburn. For the last week she has been heating the room with a fan heater. For cooking she uses the microwave. Mostly she lives on cereal, toast, fruit.

She flicks on the kettle, squats to switch the heater on. The vicar watches her. The cuffs of his jacket are frayed. He is a scholar. He has a heart complaint that will not get better now. When she sits opposite him and passes him his mug he brings to bear fifty years of sitting in kitchens with men and women. It is, he thinks, a truth to be noted, how often the fire is out, the range unlit.

'I had a call from Father Wylie at the hospital. He's a Catholic of course, but in these situations we set such things aside. The differences, I mean. Is your husband here?'

'We're not married,' she says. 'He's at his parents' house.'

'Major Rathbone.'

'Yes.'

'Well, I'm sure he'll have all he needs there.'

He has seen rage, he has seen shock, he has seen derangement. Mostly he has seen bewilderment. This girl, this young woman looking into the steam of her tea, it's hard to say.

'You have been on your own then?'

'Yes.'

'Are your parents still with us?'

'What?'

'Might you also spend a little time with your family? As your, as Tim, is doing.'

'No,' she says.

'No?'

'No.'

He tries to draw her out, to make a space for her to pour herself into. He does not try to make any physical contact. Touch can be quite explosive in such circumstances but he has a half-dozen clean tissues folded in the right-hand pocket of his jacket and these, at the appropriate moment, he will offer. He sips his tea, noticing on the wall by the kitchen door a pattern of red hand-prints. Adult hands, a child's hands. He asks if she is sleeping, if she is eating. If he can help her with some practical matter? She is polite. She appears to be listening to him. Is she listening to him? Sometimes there is a noise in their heads they cannot hear past.

'Maud,' he says. 'Would you like me to say a prayer? We can stay just as we are. And it doesn't matter about being a churchgoer or even a believer – I mean whether or not you would describe yourself as a believer. We are all of us free to pray at any time. Any time we feel it might be helpful.'

'OK,' she says.

'Yes?'

'All right.'

He nods, smiles, shifts his gaze to the surface of the table, gathers his thoughts. His prayers have a noted conversational tone. His intention is to speak to her, the suffering woman, and speak to whatever may be with them in that place. He shuts his eyes; he assumes she has shut hers. He listens for a squeak, some catch in her breathing, but there's only the fan heater, the sound of a distant, apparently circling, helicopter, his own voice. 'Amen,' he says at last, 'amen,' and looks up to find her looking back at him with a gaze that predates his religion. He falters. He has not seen that for a long time. The hieroglyphic stare. The impression of a mind like a shaped and painted scapula, a mind like a horse's, moral as grass. The first time he saw it, it came from a girl of ten or so, looking down at him (a gangling schoolboy hurrying home) from the heaped rubble of a Bristol bomb site. The last time, ten years ago now, it was a man he was ministering to in the old jail at Shepton Mallet, one of those in whose presence you were not allowed to carry even a pencil for fear of what might be made out of it. It was not a theological matter. Why should we imagine we are all fruit of the same branch? We know so little of our own story. A few bones, artefacts. Something on the wall of a cave, misunderstood.

He smiles at her, a lopsided, apologetic smile. 'I've taken up enough of your time,' he says. 'More than enough.' He gets to his feet. She walks with him to the front door and he is thanking her for the tea and starting to think of the little reward he will give himself when he reaches home, when she says, 'On the day it happened I was at work. My phone rang and I heard her voice.'

'Oh?'

'The call was made afterwards. The time of the call.'

'Afterwards?'

'Yes.'

'You are sure?'

'Yes.'

'And since?'

She shakes her head. She has lost that unsettling dawn-of-the-world gaze now and her face, tilted up to him, is just a face, pale, plain as a dial, pretty in its way. He was, perhaps, mistaken in what he saw, what he thought he saw. Just an ordinary girl after all, a girl in trouble. He smooths the hair on the sides of his head. He would like to offer her the protection of a formal blessing but instead finds himself looking away into the garden, the black tangles of old growth like a kind of scribbling. 'It might be best to leave here for a while,' he says. 'Go somewhere you are less reminded. Where you feel safer. Can you think of such a place, my dear?'

3

The day itself then, a dozen moments beyond speaking of. The sense, among many, of something like indecency.

She sits with her parents. She sees Tim arrive in his wheelchair, his father pushing him, Tim's face like marble, his father's red, raw, scalded from the inside. As they move towards the front of the church hands settle on their shoulders and their backs, men's hands, women's, light as wings. These are noticed or not noticed, certainly they are not responded to. Behind them comes Mrs Rathbone, the twins, Magnus and his wife with their children, the girls in black velvet coats, the boys in the uniforms of their distant, expensive schools. Only Magnus notices Maud. He nods to her then busies himself with his family.

The church is in the town. Memorial plaques, thin pillars, thin November light through the windows. A lectern in the form of a bird, a tight screw of stone steps up to the pulpit. The vicar is not the old vicar who visited the cottage but a much younger man, someone known to the Rathbones. The church has a sound system, a loop of some sort, so that his voice comes untethered out of the middle air.

There are candles – everyone has been invited to hold a small candle. There is coughing, whispering. Now and then a noise, a groan, like something out of the lion house.

The little headmistress is there with her assistant, Miss Beazley, and some of the children from the class, a half-dozen selected from among the steadiest, the most reliable. When necessary, Miss Beazley touches a child to settle him, to bring him back.

Tish and Lally are four pews back on the Rathbone side. They have dressed in dark suits like men's suits but each wears a brightly coloured scarf, something out of Asia, something that pressed to the face would smell of sandalwood or attar of roses. In front of them are the twins who, in the last year, have become almost beautiful, their piled hair a lustrous, shadowed gold. Tim's mother holds Tim's hand. She keeps her back very straight. Tears run off her chin. The candle in her hand, the flame, is trembling.

The choir sings. A woman – a woman Maud has never seen before – reads a poem by Eleanor Farjeon.

Then the vicar invites Magnus Rathbone to come forward and speak on behalf of the family. He does it well. Three or four minutes, a graceful thanking of those who have shown their love and support, who have travelled long distances. The school, the choir. No trace of cynical, frivolous Magnus, Magnus who whipped off his bath towel to show himself to his brother's new girlfriend. He sits down and his wife leans to whisper something to him. There is not much more to be done. Maud's father has rolled up the order of service, holds it in his fist like a baton, taps the side of his knee. Mrs Stamp is taking care not to spill the wax from her candle onto her quilted coat. The simplest thing now, the simplest gesture, could burn the place to the ground. No one can move, no one can stay completely still. There is not enough air in the church. Soon, surely, someone will faint.

In the dying notes of the final piece of music, Tim's father lurches upwards and swings blindly out of the pew, smacking one of his heavy thighs against the woodwork. The vicar asks everybody to blow out their candles. One candle will be left burning on the altar and this, he explains, perhaps for the benefit of the children, is a symbol.

'Come on, Maudy,' says Maud's mother. 'Everybody's leaving.'

The children go first. They are ushered out by Miss Beazley and then collected and counted by the lychgate. A coach is waiting on the road, a coach from a different company. The driver, in jacket and tie, stands ready to guide the children on board.

By the church door (where yellow leaves have fallen in complicated patterns onto the dark of the wet path) the vicar is listening to something Tim's mother is saying. There is no sign of Tim's father. Slad – Slad who carried the great polished headboard up the stairs at the cottage – has been given the job of pushing Tim's chair. Each time Tim turns his head Slad pauses and Bella bobs down to hear what Tim has to say. When she straightens up it's the signal for Slad to go on with the pushing.

Maud is standing under a tree at the bottom of the yard, a chestnut crazed and magnificent with age. She is wearing one of her work outfits. Her head is bare. She has lost some weight, seven or eight pounds. Despite the cold she stands with her coat folded over her arm. She is waiting for her parents. She is not quite sure where they are, if she needs to go and look for them. People steal glances at her. Some of them murmur to her, words that are lost in the dampness of the air, absorbed by it. Someone, approaching from behind, touches her elbow. It's the policewoman, the blonde one who shook the rain onto her shoulders. She is not in uniform now.

'Mr Rathbone said it was all right to come,' she says. 'We sometimes do. Not always. I hope you don't mind?'

She waits for Maud to say something, then nods to her as if silence is as good an answer as any and perhaps the expected one.

'Why don't I wait with you?' she says. 'Until you're ready?'

4

Her parents drive back to Swindon the same day. They leave in the dark. Her mother has tidied the kitchen and her father has lit the stove for her, and this she understands as her parents working at the far range of what is possible for them. When they have gone she puts more wood in the stove and watches it for a while. She wonders if someone will come but no one does. In the kitchen she looks in the cupboards. She is not sure when she last ate anything. She thinks it was probably yesterday. She finds a tin of Morello cherries and she opens these and picks the cherries out of the syrup with her fingers. Tinker tailor soldier sailor. At midnight she listens to the shipping forecast.

A card from Josh Fenniman. It arrives with her bank statement, a charity mailshot, the parish magazine. The front of the card shows a boulder-strewn American landscape photographed at first light. Inside, in his own hand, there are expressions of sympathy, assurances of the company's support. The feeling behind the words is that he, Josh Fenniman, is someone who has known extremes of experience, that he has faced these and found the inner resources to master them. He signs himself *Joshua*. He includes his PA's direct line. Maud reads the card through once, quickly, then places it flat on the mantlepiece above the stove. In the afternoon she calls Reading and says she would like to come back to work the following week, or if that's not possible, the week after. It's not the woman from Human Resources she speaks to but someone in the same department, a woman with a Northern Irish accent she can't quite put a face to. It's clear from her voice, however, the tone of it, that she knows who Maud is and knows her story. Perhaps she even saw Maud that day leaving the building in the company of the police.

She shops in the supermarket in town. It's a place the Rathbones sometimes use but she doesn't see any of them. Before she unpacks her bags in the kitchen she takes from the big store cupboards above the worktop the animal pasta, the fruit bars, the lunchbox orange juice cartons, the peanut butter, the rice cakes, the little boxes, smaller than matchboxes, of California raisins. She moves it all to a cupboard at the other end of the kitchen where things rarely used or needed are kept on paper-lined shelves. She also finds various medicines – Calpol, junior disprin, syrup of figs. These she puts in a plastic bag and lowers the bag into the swing bin.

Three or four times a day the phone rings. A message from her mother saying the important thing is to eat nutritious food. A call from the police wanting to speak with Tim. A call from Arnie who, when the call was made, was clearly on his way to being drunk. He will come to her, he says, at a moment's notice.

Whatever she needs, anything at all, anything. And later, a second call, when he is fully drunk, saying there is obviously no God, that there are things she should know about, that she can call him in the middle of the night, it's not as if he's sleeping anyway and for God's sake she mustn't do anything stupid, mustn't, I don't know . . . Are we in control of our lives? Obviously not. And what then?

These messages from Arnie are the first she pays close attention to. A shout that carries above the noise of a shouting crowd. The unexpected value of incoherence.

The oil man comes. He whistles. He fills up the tank. He says it's usually her husband he sees. He says, 'We could all use a little sunshine, eh?'

One evening, walking in the lane, she sees an owl flying along the road in front of her. She assumes it's an owl. A large pale bird, silent and suddenly swerving into the dark of a field.

She thinks, as she walks home, she's about to come on. She's very regular, a day or two either way. In the downstairs toilet of the cottage she looks in her pants, touches herself. There's nothing. Nothing the next day or the next or the one after.

A visit from Slad. He has, he says, been asked to collect the picture, the little watercolour of the girl in the straw hat with the basket of cherries. He doesn't say why they want it back; it may have something to do with the insurance. He lifts it off its hook and puts it into a cloth bag he takes from one of his pockets. The bag is like those used to keep a pair of expensive shoes in, or that is pulled over the head of a man about to be hanged. He asks Maud if she wants him to take the hook out of the wall but she says he can leave it. There is nothing brusque or unfriendly in his behaviour. He spends a lot of his time around horses and his movements are measured, predictable.

At last the kitchen is properly warm. She sits at the table in lamplight drinking a glass of water. The night is wild and the wind is knocking a window somewhere upstairs, a window she should probably go up and secure.

There are flowers in the sink, white chrysanthemums she found on the doorstep with a card (*Deepest Sympathy*) signed by the neighbours, Sarah and Michael. White chrysanthemums, some greenery, cellophane, thin green ribbon. People know. All over the place people know. It may even be in the parish magazine. It doesn't matter. It's all right.

On the worktop between the bread bin and the toaster the child monitor is sitting in its base beside the plug socket. A red light shows that it's on, a green light that it's connected to the unit upstairs, that it's receiving. Sound is played through a speaker; it is also registered in a rippling fan of lights on the face of the monitor. She sips her water and watches the lights, the way they leap forward until almost the entire face is lit up then drop back for a moment before pulsing into life again. She watches. She drinks her water. She slowly drains the glass.

When she goes back to work the first person she sees is Kurt Henderson. Perhaps no one told him she was coming back. In his stare there is deep discomfort, a profound unreadiness. He says, hoarsely, 'I'm so sorry.' After a pause, he adds, 'Yeah.' He holds out the papers in his arms to indicate work, and shoulders his way into Meeting Room 2. *If you will tell me why the Fen appears impassable . . .*

She spends twenty minutes with the woman from Human Resources. It's agreed she will, for the time being, work a four-day week, that she will drop the Kappa-opioids project which is, anyway, pretty much running itself these days. She asks Maud how she is coping, how she and Tim are coping. She knows Maud well enough now not to expect much in return, much beyond some vague assurance, and when it comes she nods and smiles and says, 'Good, good.' She makes no mention of how Maud has been remembered in her prayers or how, at the church in Reading city centre where four or five services are held each Sunday, where there are bands and young faces wet with tears and the minister in jeans and a T-shirt struts the stage like a successful comedian, she has had Maud's name read out, thrown like a rose to the fluttering hands of the faithful.

Sweet Jesus Lord lay your healing hands on this woman!

Day two at work and she drives down to Croydon. There's a seminar, the latest in a series about the reporting of side-effects, a topic they can never quite get free of and that is starting to worry the team in Orlando. The assumption is that Fennidine/epibatidine is acting on the receptors for the chemical acetylcholine, but it's unclear what else it may be interacting with, what else is stimulated, released. On a screen they look at colour slides of positron emission brain scans. On one of these – image twelve, middle-aged female – there is a shadow shaped like a bird in flight.

During the coffee break a man strides over to Maud, leans over her and says, 'I hope Fenniman's aren't playing games with us. I hope they're serious about seeing this through. It would be a bloody disgrace if they don't see it through . . .'

He is interrupted, tapped on the elbow by a woman, a

colleague, and later, when he's been told, he is quiet, will not look at Maud, turns a pen through his fingers.

Mid-December: cold air descending from high latitudes. In the morning she scrapes ice off the windscreen then leaves the engine running while she goes in to make coffee. The kitchen is not untidy. She does not let the dishes pile up, does not forget now and then to sweep the floor. It is not untidy but it is different, like a ring no one wears any more or a path no one walks on, no one but her. She checks in her bag to see she has what she will need for the day. She looks, for perhaps a full minute, at the monitor on the worktop. One morning (ice on the tips of the grass, on the rosehips, on the stumps of cut maize, the steel bars of field gates) she passes a car that has come off the road, ridden up a bank and wedged itself in the hedgerow. She slows and sees a man standing beside the car with a scarf tied round his head. He's like a man from the year 1200. He grimaces, calls something she does not catch, waves her on.

It is at the end of this season, this three weeks of tumbling air that is written about in the newspapers, that she comes home to the cottage and finds the front door open. It's been dark for hours, no moon, no lights in the house. She calls then goes in and works her way through the house, visits almost every room. In the spare room she sees the guitar cupboard is open and empty. She goes downstairs. Someone is knocking on the door, a gentle but persistent knocking. It's the neighbours, Michael and Sarah. Michael has a torch. They are both wearing dark blue or black fleeces.

'Is everything all right?' asks Michael.

'We were very worried,' says Sarah.

'We didn't know what to do,' says Michael. 'We wanted to call someone but we didn't know who. We thought of calling the fire brigade.'

They wait, and when they see she has no idea what they are talking about, they begin to tell her, passing the story back and forth between them.

They had been off work for two days, the vomiting virus everybody has. At about half past three – they know the time because they were watching a programme on the television and it finishes at half past – they heard a car and a car door and looked out in time to see Tim going into the cottage. He was using a single crutch, he was on his own. They didn't think anything of it, not really, but then, from their kitchen window, they saw him go into the garden. He had a guitar with him and that *did* seem odd because it was cold and already starting to get dark and why would he want to go and play in the cold? But instead of playing he put the guitar on the grass and went back to the house and a few minutes later came out with another guitar, put that on the grass beside the first and went back to the house again. They had no idea what he was doing but they began to be anxious. Three or four guitars – and they knew he had good guitars, very good and very expensive – all just lying on the grass. The rest of it happened very quickly. He poured something on them, lit a match. It was like an explosion. It *was* an explosion. At first the flames were as tall as he was and he staggered back and nearly fell. Then he just stood there, watching until the fire was almost burnt out. Afterwards he went back into the house and a minute or two after that they heard the car again.

'We're not unsympathetic,' says Michael. 'We're just worried.'

'We're worried about fire,' says Sarah.

'The fire brigade,' says Michael, 'cannot be here in less than twenty minutes. More like half an hour.'

144

Maud has never heard them speak so much. They had seemed to be people of few words, people who moved about their lives almost silently. Now she sees this impression was wrong. They are full of words, words that were waiting for something to happen that would release them. She thanks them and closes the door. There's a torch on the kitchen windowsill. She turns it on and goes out to the passage between the kitchen and the oil tank. The back garden is small. A parcel of land with vegetable beds at the bottom, a low red-brick wall separating it from the neighbours' garden, a beech hedge on the lane side. The fire, what's left of it, is on the lawn close to the swing. There are embers still, a residual heat, the smell of an accelerant. She squats with the torch and lifts out the head of one of the guitars, wipes it with her thumb, sees the smutted inlay of diamonds and moons, feels how the wood is warm as a hand, then lays it back with the rest, the ashes, the heat-tangled wires, the blackened nuts and little cogs, the debris.

In the house the answer phone is flashing. A message from Tim's mother. 'Is Tim there, Maud? Have you seen him? He's taken one of the cars. It's the automatic so he can drive it. Will you please get in touch *immediately* if you see him?'

Then another message, weary. 'He's back. Will you kindly call when you get this? I think we should at least have a talk. We need to start making some sense of things. We need to find some way to go on with our lives.'

5

She does not warn them she is coming. Or she does not warn herself that she is going. It's a Saturday afternoon. She drives through patient country rain, parks in the courtyard. Dogs run out to greet her. They follow her through the rain to the door. There is an old stirrup bell here but no one ever rings it. She goes into the room with the waxed jackets, the cut-glass bowl with its shotgun cartridges. In the kitchen she finds Slad's wife, a heavy woman dicing meat, a bone-handled knife in one hand, its blade as long as Maud's forearm. She has never shown much friendliness to Maud, though Maud has never seen her show much friendliness to anyone other than Magnus, who treats her as a serf, a serf's chattel. Mrs Rathbone, she says, is lying down. Mr Rathbone is in his workshop and won't thank anyone for disturbing him.

'And Tim?'

'In his room,' she says.

'Upstairs?'

'How could he manage stairs?' says Mrs Slad. 'He's in the little room. Off the music room.'

Maud thanks her. She does not say that he managed the stairs at the cottage, managed them all right and carried things down. She goes out of the kitchen, through the morning room and along a short windowless passage to the music room. Rain-light on a faded carpet, on the scuffed black of violin cases, the glass face of a tall-clock. On the piano, the photographs are arranged in tilted rows like a solar farm. Children kneeling by a Christmas tree. Children in their school uniforms, hair neatly parted. Children with dogs, children on the knees of their parents. There are, she knows, at least three generations of them there, children smiling for the camera, or caught between one stride and the next, one gesture and the next, arms flung out, hands and fingers blurring into air.

To the left of the piano is another door. Through it, softly, a woman's voice.

She taps on the door and goes in. Tim is in bed, a single bed with wooden legs on casters, perhaps a child's bed. Bella is on a chair beside the bed, a book in her hand. She is wearing a turtle-neck dress of light grey cashmere, her hair scraped back and held with a clasp of muted silver.

'Hello, Maud,' she says. 'Would you like to speak to Tim? He's a bit drowsy, I'm afraid. A bad night last night.'

She too looks tired, a slight shadowing under her eyes as if, self-lessly, she shares the burden of bad nights. She stands, puts the book on the chair, and with a quick smile at Tim she leaves the room.

In the bed, Tim has the covers pulled up to his throat. He is not looking at Maud. Perhaps he is not looking at anything. On the small round table under the window are various medicines. She can see that one of these, from its trade name, is a benzodiazepine. She could, if she chose, tell him the drug's metabolizing enzymes. Could recite them to him like lines of poetry.

'The neighbours were scared,' she says. 'They're afraid you'll set fire to the house.'

'I thought about it,' he says.

'Did you burn them all?' she asks.

He nods.

'Even the Lacôte?'

'Yes.'

'Don't burn anything else,' she says.

'What do you want?' he says.

'Are you staying here?'

'Yes.'

'You're not coming back to the cottage?'

He moves his head on the pillow, rolls it in a narrow arc.

'Are you with Bella now?'

'For fuck's sake, Maud.'

'What?'

'Is that relevant? Who I'm with? Who you're with? Is it relevant?'

He shuts his eyes. He looks very like his mother. The book on the chair is *Vanity Fair*, a paperback with a creased spine, a man and woman on the cover, dancing formally.

There are things she was going to tell him. Things whose relevance she thinks he would not question. Now she sees that if she tells him these things he will start to scream.

In the music room Bella is sitting on the piano stool looking as if it is only a kind of politeness that keeps her from playing.

'Goodbye,' she says.

'Goodbye,' says Maud.

*   *   *

When she returns to the kitchen Mrs Slad has gone but Tim's father is there, leaning against the sink, arms folded, apparently studying the toes of his shoes. He looks up. 'Come through,' he says, and leads her to what the family call the small drawing room. There is no one else there. At one end of the room is a sideboard too large for the room, its shelves filled with porcelain dogs and more pictures of children. In the grate is the remnant of a morning fire. Tim's father leans down to it, prods it, then picks out from the wood basket a quarter log and lays it in the embers. All the wood comes from his own land.

'A drink?'

'No thanks.'

He goes to the table under the window, one of several about the house known as a 'drinks table'. Into two heavy glasses he pours two measures of Scotch.

'Never trust a man who doesn't drink,' he says. 'Applies to women too, I think.'

He grins at her. She takes the glass, touches it to her lips, feels the small burn where her lips have cracked.

'So you've been to see Tim.'

'Yes.'

'And how did you think he looked?'

She considers for a moment – the sallow face on the plumped-up pillow, the eyes that seemed, the moment before he shut them, to be pleading with her. 'Tired,' she says. 'Sad.'

'Sad?'

'Yes.'

'Sad. Mmm. Well, yes, we're all of us, over here Maud, a bit sad. You appear to be bearing up, however. I'm told you're back at work. Got the old lab coat on again.'

'Yes.'

'Good. Good for you.' He looks away from her. His face is flushed. When he speaks again it is with a voice that comes from somewhere much deeper inside of him, a voice he has been keeping hidden.

'Tim is not sad, Maud. Tim is devastated. My wife is devastated. I am devastated. Even bloody Magnus is devastated. Only you, you and perhaps your extraordinary parents, seem to be managing.'

He empties his glass, carries it over to the drinks table. With his back to her he says, 'I always rather admired you. The way you didn't try too hard to make people like you. Most people do, don't they?'

He pours another two fingers of Scotch into his glass, turns to her again. 'We used, in the family, to talk about you quite a lot. Does that surprise you? Two schools of thought, really. One, that you were a bright girl, a bit shy, a bit gauche, a bit unworldly but basically all right. The other school, quite a big one, had you down as cold-blooded, entirely self-absorbed and not really all right at all. One thing that both schools were agreed upon was that you hadn't the slightest interest in being a mother.'

'That's not true.'

'Oh, I think it is. I never saw the least evidence of any maternal instinct. I don't mean you were cruel. That would have taken a measure of engagement, some effort of imagination. No, no. In your own rather pathetic way you tried. But something was missing. Something fundamental. You reached for it and it simply wasn't there.'

He acts it out. The reaching, the clasping at air, the expression of open-mouthed surprise.

'Why are you saying this?' she asks.

150

'We saw you, Maud. I saw you. Everyone did. It wasn't difficult.'

He moves closer, close enough for her to smell his leathery aftershave, the whisky. He takes hold of her left hand, lifts her arm, slides up the sleeve of her sweater.

'Look at it,' he says. 'Who would want this on themselves? I'm sorry, but there's something very wrong with you and I wish to Christ Tim had never laid eyes on you. I wish none of us had.'

There are tears on his cheeks thick as varnish. He has given way to something, or something has given way inside him. She frees herself from his grasp, turns away from him towards the door.

'Don't you *dare*!' he shouts. 'Don't you . . .' He lunges at her. He is, in his fury, very strong. For half a second she is in pure flight, then her feet tangle with the end of the sofa and she slams into the base of the sideboard, lies there, dazed, while porcelain dogs and picture frames tumble onto the floor around her. Slowly, she gets to her knees. He reaches down for her and helps her to stand. He says he is sorry and sounds as if he means it. He draws her to him, holds her tightly, one hand smoothing the hair on the back of her head. His shoulders are heaving; his breath is very hot. 'Please,' he says, 'don't ever come back. Do you understand? Don't ever come here again.'

6

She spends Christmas with her parents in Swindon. As a present she is given a jumper, oatmeal-coloured; also the receipt in case she wishes to change it. No one comes round.

In January she is sick. A virus – perhaps the same one Michael and Sarah had. Acid in her throat, her nose. The impossibility of being warm. She keeps the stove going until she runs out of wood then lies thirty-six hours on the sofa wrapped in a heavy blanket. For part of this time there is a pain in her head and neck so intense she hardly dares to swallow. She doesn't bother with aspirin or ibuprofen. She takes one of the Fennidine from the box stamped FOR TRIAL USE ONLY. It's not the first she's taken. Several of the team involved with the trial have used them.

She sleeps or passes out, comes to in the cold room, in utter darkness. She has for a moment no idea where she is, then feels the rough weave of the cushion against her cheek and remembers. After a while she becomes aware of the sound of her own breathing and a few seconds later of something else, like the subtle echo of her breathing but an echo that does not stop when she holds her breath.

She turns her head. Whatever it is it seems to be coming from the stairs, the top of the stairs, and she frees her arms from the blanket and pushes herself, as quietly as she can, into a sitting position. She imagines a cat up there, crouched on the top step. She imagines a fox, aware of her, utterly still. Or a bird like the pale bird she saw flying low along the lane that night. At the same time she knows perfectly well there is no bird or fox or cat, nothing of that sort. She waits, listens, then climbs from the sofa and gropes her way towards the stairs, to the wall at the bottom of the stairs, the light switch. Half a minute of running her fingers over the wall to find the switch. The light changes everything, rocks her like a soft yet powerful blow to her chest. She screws shut her eyes and clutches the bannister. When she can open her eyes her view is the rise of carpeted steps, an angle of wall on the landing, the light itself in its red shade, which sways slightly in one of those currents of cool air that flow unstoppably about the cottage and are, perhaps, an integral part of how the building has survived. For two or three minutes she remains there, looking up the stairs. The temptation to speak a name, to loft a name into the lit air of the landing. Then she pads to the kitchen, drinks from the tap and sits on the floor, her back hard against the iron of the old Rayburn. When has she been this cold? She cannot think when she has ever been this cold.

It's another week before she's strong enough to go back to work. Even then she doesn't seem quite right, does not feel it or look it. On the day after St Valentine's, the woman from Human Resources comes to her cubicle, leans down by her ear and says, 'Can I borrow you for ten minutes?'

They go to her office. They sit opposite each other. The woman smiles. 'You're very pale,' she says.

'Am I?'

'Yes.'

'It's winter,' says Maud. 'And I was ill.'

'I know,' says the woman. 'But it's more than that, isn't it? You've been incredibly brave. Unbelievably brave. But it's all too soon. People are worried about you, Maud. People here, people at Croydon. They're worried. Concerned. They don't think you should be back, not yet. And I have to think of them too. Of their needs. The truth is a lot of them are uncomfortable. They want to support you as a colleague but they don't know how. Do you see what I'm saying? Does it make sense? I've been in touch with Orlando. The view there is that you should take more time. What they'd like is for you to finish the week and then begin a period of leave until the end of the summer. September, say. That will enable us to offer at least six months to your replacement. You'll be on full pay for the first three months and a sliding percentage thereafter. I'll get in touch with you in July and see how you're doing. See what you're feeling ready for. Now how does that sound, as a package? Does it sound fair to you? Maud?'

So she sits at home; her work clothes in the wardrobe; her laptop on the kitchen table, shut; her work bag, mostly empty, against the wall by the front door. In a shoebox in the kitchen, beneath scraps of paper with tradesmen's phone numbers and various oddments such as a postcard from Tish and Lally (Buenos Aires) and a small photograph of herself as a schoolgirl standing against the wall at the back of the house in Swindon (a photograph Tim must have asked her parents for), she finds some of Tim's tobacco and cigarette papers. She hasn't smoked since she was fifteen, when the man whose children she used to babysit for gave her cigarettes from his pack after what he called *sessions*. The tobacco is dry and hard to roll but by concentrating and trying several times she ends up with something like a cigarette. She smokes half of it, drops the rest into the dregs of her tea.

She receives a letter from Arnie. It describes, over several pages, the descent of his life, his struggle with weakness and mystery, his ailments, his insomnia, his stab at poetry. It is written on office notepaper. It is, apparently, a love letter.

On the same day that the letter comes she drags the heavy furniture to the edges of the living room to vacuum the floor. Under the sofa she finds a red marble and a green one. She also finds the torn and empty envelope of a condom, the type *ribbed for mutual pleasure*. She examines it, turns the little silvery envelope through her fingers; would perhaps have put it on the stove if the stove were lit. At what point would she have minded this? She's not sure. It feels mostly like old news. Old news about Tim and Bella. Old news about herself. Old news about the race, the species. Very briefly, and in an almost academic way, she imagines breaking one of Bella's very white and beautiful wrists. Then she reaches up and places the envelope beside Josh Fenniman's card on the mantlepiece. She goes on with the vacuuming.

For a long time she does not go upstairs other than to fetch clothes or use the bathroom. She sleeps on the sofa and then, one evening, as if for a moment she has forgotten everything, she goes upstairs and sleeps in the bedroom, in the bed with the walnut headboard. Some of Tim's clothes are folded over a chair by the window. A book he was reading is on the floor by his side of the bed. She hears mice run across the roof spaces above the bedroom ceiling.

She thinks of them chewing the insulation from the wiring, thinks she should buy traps for them, poison, but knows she won't, not now.

Whole days are passed either sitting in the kitchen or sitting on the sofa or sitting on the stairs or standing somewhere between these places. She could not account for these days, could not begin to.

When she needs to, she drives into town to buy things. She has a glimpse of Slad's wife in the supermarket looking through packs of meat. She thinks she sees the blonde policewoman go past in a car but may have imagined it. She sees Arnie talking on a street corner to an older man in a tweed suit and the man saying something and Arnie laughing as if he hadn't a care in the world.

Some nights, rather than go to bed, she watches the television, often with the sound turned down. The oddest programmes on at three in the morning. Sales channels selling a kind of mock jewellery. Detective shows, ten or twenty years old. Educational shows about daily life in Lima, the formation of valleys, beginners' Gaelic. On one of these shows – the Gaelic primer? – there's a woman about her own age, with rosy cheeks and short blonde hair. She's wearing a black swimsuit of the kind that comes down to mid-thigh like a pair of cycling shorts. She's standing on the deck of a boat, a big old wooden boat, anchored in some northern sea. It's quite obvious how cold everything is – the air, the woman, the green water. She seems to be speaking to someone behind the camera. Now and then she breaks off to look, a little apprehensively, at the sea, and all the while she is edging towards the side of the boat until at last she's standing on the wooden gunnels, supporting herself by holding the ratlines. For a good fifteen seconds she stands there in her black swimsuit, the camera settled on her back, her strong legs, her shoulders reddening in the wind.

Then she lets go of the ratlines, balances, sways forward a little, bends her knees and launches herself into a brief arc in which her heavy body is suddenly graceful. She breaks the water. The camera watches. The water settles. There is no sign of the woman.

That same night, when at last Maud climbs into the old bed, falls into it with that strange exhaustion that comes from doing nothing, she has a dream that feels as if it is a continuation of the dive, though there is no sea, or wooden deck or shyly smiling woman. Instead, she is in the presence of a very old man. He is turned away from her, his head, what she can see of it, like a bag of damaged plush in which a metal ball is kept, an iron ball. She is explaining to him what has happened to her. She doesn't miss anything out. Among other things she tells him about the phone call in the animal room, about the lights on the monitor in the kitchen, about the night she felt herself observed from the top of the stairs. When she has finished telling him these things he turns to her and she sees that it's Rawlins the judo instructor, Rawlins old, ancient, perhaps dead.

She sleeps until nearly midday, wakes with the sense of his having said something to her, something she should have taken note of and cannot now remember, but standing in the bathroom, stripping for a shower, she catches sight of her arm, of *Sauve Qui Peut*, and wonders if that is what he said. That.

She showers, pulls on clothes, goes downstairs. She makes coffee, rolls a cigarette and goes into the garden. On the lawn, a black circle on the grass from the fire. Unexpected sunlight, unexpected warmth. She smokes and sips her coffee, looks up at the windows at the back of the house. When she has finished her coffee she goes back into the house, leaves her mug on the kitchen table, goes up the stairs and opens the door of the nursery or what, half jokingly and right at the start when they were painting it, they called the nursery. She strips the bed, bundles the sheets, the duvet cover. The pink ukelele is lying in the middle of the floor. She had forgotten about the ukelele, that it existed. She leans it against a wall then changes her mind and lays it on the stripped bed before changing her mind again and leaning it against the wall. She shuts the not quite perfectly shut window. She folds the scattered clothes. She takes the bedding down to the kitchen, puts it in the washing machine, sets the programme, starts it.

The way the drum swings one way and then, after a pause, swings the other.

How one moment you are not ready and the next, somehow, you are.

In the bedroom she puts the big holdall at the end of the bed, starts with a layer of pants, bras, tights, vests. Then jeans, shirts, shorts, a pair of black cotton culottes that Tim called her coolie trousers. A jumper of oiled wool she has had for years that smells like rope treated with Scandinavian tar. The soft blue jumper, a little moth-eaten, she bought the winter she was pregnant. Thermals. Salopettes, rolled tight. Helly Hansen jacket rolled tight. Every pair of thick socks she can find. Deck shoes. Musto half-length sea boots. A red travel towel. A striped beanie, finger-less gloves. From the bathroom her toothbrush, toothpaste and a half-box of tampons, though she still hasn't come on, not for months, a fact she has shared with no one, not even the dreamed head of old Rawlins.

A tube of SPF 25 face protector. Nail clippers, deodorant. She zips the bag, heaves it, lets it slide down the stairs ahead of her. Back in the bathroom she takes off her top and uses a pair of heavy dressmaking scissors (she who has never made a dress) to cut her hair. Cuts it so close you could hold the back of her head in your hand like the shell of something. Here and there the skin shows through. In one place, by the crown, she has nicked herself.

She carries the holdall out to the car then goes back to the kitchen, moves the washing to the dryer, sets it to run for an hour. She unplugs the monitor, locks the back door, puts her phone and charger in her pocket, shuts and locks the front door. It's the middle of the day. Other than birds provoked to song by the warmer weather, she cannot hear a sound. She walks on the path, the old seabed. The gate swings shut behind her. She does not look back.

THREE

And so, into our darkness life seeps,
keeping its part of the bargain.

John Ashbery

1

Through his window (where pictures of boats are displayed on boards, pictures with curling edges yellowed by the light) the broker is looking at an imagined building. The owners of the yard – men who always arrive in convoys of 4x4s, like a shooting party – have plans to build a marina hotel, something with two hundred bedrooms, a spa, a gym, a couple of restaurants (one to be called The Olde Yard and to have a theme of boat-building and be decorated with parts of boats and boat-builders' tools). He has seen the architect's model in the marina office, the clever trees, the people sized like grains of rice. His own office will go, of course. Everything improvised, everything merely makeshift, will go. On the model he has gone already.

He opens the tin of cigarillos, takes one out and taps the end of it on the desk. The air today is heavy with rain waiting to fall. The river, the boats on their moorings, the hazed green of the far bank, all of it held in that stillness that comes just before or just after the event.

At two o'clock – the schedule! – he has an old boat to see, a big ketch, ex-charter, beautiful and impossible, a boat that will devour time and money and must be sold to someone who knows exactly what he's doing, or to some romantic, some moneyed fool, who will pin a picture of it to a wall in his house and sigh over it.

Next high tide is 16.15. Low tide at 21.15. Where are we now? Springs? Just past springs? He tries to recall if he saw the moon last night, tries to reconstruct some fugitive moment of the night, himself in T-shirt and boxers standing over the toilet bowl (light off because he cannot bear the light on at such a moment, the mind softened from sleep) and thinks he *did* see it, a moon with a bite out of it sliding towards the hills between the town and the cliffs (those fields where careless farmers occasionally drive their tractors into thin air), and he's nodding at this, pleased to have recovered something that would otherwise have been entirely lost, nodding and holding up the unlit cigarillo like a conductor's baton, when the door of his office is pushed open and without a single measurable instant of hesitation, he meets her eyes, smiles at her and says, 'Your season starting already?'

The boat is in the yard, on its legs of chocked wood. It has been there since the previous September when it was hauled out after a summer of four or five weekend sails. This, as the broker knows, is the common fate of boats. Bought, loved, sailed. Then loved less, sailed less. Because there is always money to be spent – mooring fees, yard fees, endless repairs, refits – the boat becomes a burden. Finally, someone makes a decision they refer to as 'sensible'. They come to the broker's office. They smile sadly. They look a little ashamed.

Between them – Maud at the front – they carry a ladder. *Lodestar* looks tired, a boat not entirely convincing any more. If it were a car you might consider stripping it for its parts.

'A dab of paint,' says the broker. 'A scrape down. Always look a bit sorry for themselves at the end of the winter.'

She knows all this, of course. He's talking for the sake of talking. She goes up the ladder. Legs, backside, steps over the rail.

'Everything OK up there?'

She is already undoing the tarpaulin. From the nearside shroud a scrap of ribbon lifts to the breeze.

'Rob's around somewhere. Or at least his car's here. Nice to have you back, Maud. Please be careful up there.'

She has, he thinks, walking back to his office, cut her hair with blunt shears, a bread knife. Something like that. Or it fell out? She's had chemo and has spent the winter sitting in a ward with a drip in her arm, a view of the incinerator chimney. Yet she doesn't look frail, sickly. She looks like a woman it would be a serious mistake to force into a corner. Does he like her? Trust her? He has, he imagines, seen her type before (or perhaps just read about them). Women who step out of a burning town and who, later, turn out to be the reason the town was burning. One of those wide-eyed girls who carry a kind of wreckage in their wake.

The boat's cabin is a shell, a skin, a form blown in glass, slightly unreal. She sits on one of the benches, the Moroccan red upholstery that has not lasted well, that already looks to have absorbed too much weather. There is so much to do – so much! – but after sitting a while doing nothing there seems less. She goes through to the forward cabin, begins to look through lockers, reach into sail bags. She touches the coiled anchor chain, the anchor, the spare. In the saloon she finds things left behind from the previous summer and the one before that. An almost empty tube of sun cream, a sun hat, a crumpled T-shirt. It's all her stuff, or hers and John Gosse's. His books are still behind the fiddle rails, *Sailing Alone Around the World, The Dhammapada*. Also the picture, the boat at sunset or sunrise, the frame screwed to the bulkhead.

On deck she picks her way up to the pulpit rail, checks the rail, the forestay, the plate, the bow roller, cleats, fairleads, walks slowly backwards, touching everything as she comes to it, testing it. It is at first just an impersonation of purpose but by degrees becomes what it mimicked. At the mast she looks up, following the ascent of ropes to where they disappear into the sheaves like streams into the earth. Spreaders, reflector, the masthead light. She moves to the cockpit and uses her fingers to dig out leaf rot, dig out God knows what from the cockpit drains. She opens the left-hand seat locker and connects up the gas bottle for the galley stove. She stands by the tiller. The boat, lifted, is on course for the upper boughs of oak trees. She has hardly noticed that it's raining, gusts of it crossing the river, beading her hair, the whole valley swallowed in a cloud.

Below her, the yard looks deserted. She wipes the water from her face, steps through the companionway, shuts the hatch and lies down on one of the benches, cold hands between her thighs.

When she wakes it's late afternoon. Through the delicate crazing of the saloon window she watches the reinvention of colour, the low sun flooding the valley, the oddness of a day that grows brighter rather than darker at its close. A figure in red is crossing the yard towards her. She watches him then pushes back the hatch and steps into the coolness of the rain-cleaned air. He waves to her, and when he's closer, standing at the foot of the ladder squinting up at her, he says, 'Chris told me you were here. Want me to run a cable up?'

'Yes,' she says. 'Please.'

'Tomorrow morning OK?'

'Yes.'

'So you're down for a while?'

'Yes.'

'When do you want to get her in the water?'

'I'm not sure. A week?'

'Well, you're ahead of the crowd. That shouldn't be a problem.'

Silence.

'I'll see you in the morning then.'

'Yes. OK.'

He waves again and turns back towards the boat shed. On the far side of the river the sun is dropping behind the hills. There are patches of gold on the bank behind her but the yard and the river are already being sifted into the first blue of twilight. She will need to find things before it's dark – the lantern, the torch, the sleeping bag that has overwintered in the quarter berth. People are not supposed to sleep on the cradled boats but she has made no other arrangement. She can use the sink and toilets at the marina. There's tinned food on board, a bottle of water in her bag. She will not be noticed. Other than the broker and Robert Currey, there's not a living soul who knows she is here.

Twice during the night she comes to in the dark with all her senses alert. The first time she does not know where she is, can feel only the constriction of the bag, the nearness of unlit walls. It is the boat's smell and the dank odour of the unaired sleeping bag that bring her back. Then again, hours later, opening her eyes to a glassy light and the sketched clutter of the cabin, the barometer's brass edge like a setting moon. In between – between one waking and the next – hours of dreamless sleep and a rest truer than she has known in months.

At seven-thirty she's in the cockpit dismantling a winch that does not, perhaps, really need dismantling. Robert Currey arrives waving a thermos and a white paper bag that turns out to have a bacon sandwich in it.

She comes down the ladder to him. The sandwich smells delicious. As soon as he passes it to her she takes it out of the bag and starts to eat.

'I guessed you were going to sleep up there,' he says. 'No skin off my nose but it's against the rules. And you don't have a great record for knowing where the edge of a boat is.'

'That was once,' she says, her mouth full of bread and bacon.

By quarter past nine she has power cable and a plan of work. By ten she's wearing overalls and goggles and using the jet spray to sluice the bottom of the boat. What she can't clean off with the spray she scrapes off with the edge of a palette knife then rubs down with wet-and-dry. The sun comes out and she steps from under the shadow of the boat, holds her face up to the warmth of it.

After lunch she begins to patch-prime the gel-coat, then crosses to the town on the chain ferry to buy anti-foul. The ferry has only four cars on it and a recycling truck, a few foot passengers. The money is collected by a man with a leather saddlebag. The crossing takes seven minutes and everything he does, the little conversations, the handing out of change, the stroll to the ferry gates, is timed to perfection. He cannot help it.

In the town the cafes and seafront kiosks are mostly shut, their flyers still announcing the previous summer's fishing trips, the motor-boat rentals whose prices will go up by a pound or two this year. A man on a stepladder paints the woodwork of his souvenir shop. A traffic warden sits on a bollard looking at the water.

The chandlery is smaller than the chip shop next door to it, but inside, over two floors (and on the edges of the stairs) is almost everything a boat, a boat-owner, even a boat-builder, might have need of. Snap shackles, ratchet blocks, battery boxes, hand flares, sea boots, fenders, tidal atlases, bilge pumps. Drums of coloured polyester braid, shock cord, PVC hose by the metre. Skin fittings, cable glands, grapnel anchors. The woman who works there – sometimes there is a girl too but the woman is always there – knows what you need better than you know it yourself, yet she looks as if she has no particular interest in boats, does not sail, does not perhaps much care for the sea. She points Maud towards the shelves of paint along the back wall then watches her from the end of the aisle, this young woman she has, she thinks, seen before. Quite what is wrong with her – and something is – she cannot say. Tempting to imagine she's on the drink – boat people often are. But her skin looked clear, her eyes. Nor, when she comes back to the counter, does she smell of drink. She pays with a card, carries the paint, a pot in each hand, towards the door, but stops beside the charts, puts the paint down and stays for nearly forty minutes, her fingers walking to and fro across the tops of the plastic envelopes. With another customer, a different sort of customer, the woman might have offered some assistance, but this one either knows exactly what she's doing or she hasn't a clue. When she comes to the counter again she has Admiralty charts 4011 and 4012. 'And these,' she says, a little burr to her voice, not Devon though. The woman puts them in a bag. The North Atlantic Northern Part and North Atlantic Southern Part, respectively. It all seems clear enough now, and when she leaves the shop, steps into the street where two gulls are scrapping over a chip in the gutter, the woman leans by the window to watch her go and thinks *we won't be seeing you again*, and this thought strikes her like a prophesy, so that for several minutes she does not know whether to make more tea or rearrange the footwear display on the first floor. And this is not like her. It is not like her at all.

2

The next morning Maud pulls on her overalls over jeans and jumper, brews coffee, eats a banana, eats a square of chocolate and goes on deck. She sits on the coach-house roof, looking up river to where the water and the light meet. She rolls a cigarette from a pouch bought in the town. She is becoming better at rolling, better at smoking.

When she has finished her cigarette she goes down the ladder with one of the tins of anti-foul. Yesterday, in the late afternoon, she taped the boat's waterline. Now she walks slowly around the hull, checking her work. When she is satisfied, she opens the tin and pours some paint into a tray, coats the mohair roller and begins to paint. She's been at it for an hour, her eyes starting to smart, when Robert Currey comes over with a box of disposable gloves and a pair of plastic goggles.

'There's a reason it keeps stuff off the bottom of boats,' he says.

In one of his pockets he finds a rag, finds a corner cleaner than the others and wipes a splash of anti-foul from the back of her right hand. It takes only a few seconds and during those seconds neither of them speak.

By lunchtime she has the first coat finished and steps away from the boat to get the smell of it out of her mouth. The yard is busier today though most boats still look unattended. On the slipway, Robert Currey and another yardsman are working on a pleasure boat, a converted survey boat once called *Skagen*, now called *Tinkerbelle* and strung with bunting. Robert Currey, disappearing down a hatchway, stops to wave and Maud waves back.

The second coat of paint goes on the following day. According to the instructions the paint should have the thickness of a business card, like those cards, mostly unused, she has in a box in the car – Maud Stamp, Senior Clinical Associate.

By mid-afternoon the paint is dry enough to peel off the tape. It's not a perfect job but it's good enough. She touches up, wipes away any unevenness with a rag dipped in solvent. She is booked in with the launching crane for next Monday. That gives her two more days to do whatever must be done in the dry. What is not done, what is missed, will have to stay that way. This she has already decided. On Monday the boat will go into the water and she will go into the boat. There are no alternatives, certainly none she can think of. Go back to the cottage? Go back to those things she spoke of to the dreamed head of Rawlins? Behind her the way has closed. She has closed it herself or something beyond her closed it. It hardly matters. She cannot wait any longer. The one thing that feels genuinely dangerous is stillness.

The night before the launch she goes down to the marina toilet block with her towel and wash bag. It's late and there's no one else in the block, no one she can hear. She undresses, puts her clothes in a locker, steps into the cubicle, puts a pound coin in the slot, turns on the shower. The water's cold. It shocks her. Then it starts to heat up and the cubicle fills with steam and her skin glows pink. She looks at herself through the steam. A blackened thumbnail; three little bruises on each shin, a long graze high on her left thigh from some forgotten collision, perhaps with the edge of the saloon table while she manoeuvred in the dark. The timer ticks. The water slides in sheets of light over her breasts and belly and thighs. She remembers Camille showing her her tattoo, saying it meant fuck me until I cry and making a face like a girl crying. She has not had a single sexual thought in four months. Neither, in four months, has she bled. Are these things connected? She touches herself, very lightly, a ringless ring finger in the dark hair between her thighs, presses at the lips of her sex then lets the tip of her finger slide into the heat inside her. She leans against the wall of the cubicle, hooks her finger a little deeper, a little deeper. She's not a fool; she's not naive; she knows that desire, memory and grief are wound together like strands in a wire. What she does not know is what she should do about it. She slides her finger out. The ticking of the timer grows louder, then stops. She does not have another coin. She dries herself quickly, pulls on clothes over skin still clammy. When she comes out into the washroom she sees that she is not alone, though she heard no one come in. A woman is at one of the sinks, a woman of sixty or more, stripped to the waist and soaping herself under her arms. On the woman's back, either side of her spine and running down from her shoulder blades, are two lines of scar tissue. The mirror shows a weathered face and eyes of narrowed gold. For a few seconds she studies Maud in the glass as if trying to decide whether or not she knows her. Then she nods and smiles. It might be taken for approval. It might be taken for 'Keep going!'

3

The crane driver is a young man basking in the last of his youth. He has red-blond hair that will be blond entirely by midsummer, a face that is starting to talk about him, to give him away, though looked at casually he can still be whatever you want him to be. He lounges by the ladder to his cab watching Robert Currey and Maud make last-minute preparations for the lift. The morning's rain has blown through. In a painted box outside the marina office a half-dozen awkward daffodils are dotted with the rain. On the road down to the yard one shade of green is slowly moving through another.

Chris Totten comes out to watch. Over the next few weeks many of the boats in the yard, those that are not forgotten, will find their way back into the water, but *Lodestar* is one of the first and he never tires, not quite, of that moment when a boat is settled onto its reflection. He makes remarks to Maud, compliments her on how the boat is looking (would, perhaps, like to compliment her on how *she* is looking, which is slightly better than she did when she arrived), then goes over to smoke with the crane driver. 'Your busy time now,' he says, and the crane driver nods.

On the boat's topside Robert Currey is bolting shut the sling. He hangs off the shackle, swings off it, then calls, 'All right. She's yours!' The crane driver climbs into his cab. He puts on sunglasses. All his movements are confident. He takes up the slack in the wire and for an instant the weight of the boat and the force of the crane are perfectly balanced. Then the boat lifts free and the sling creaks and everybody is perfectly still.

When it's in the water and free of the gear, Maud goes on board to take it round to a visitor's berth on the pontoon. This is where she will do the next phase of the work, but when she turns the ignition key there's a belch of smoke, a brief thudding of pistons, then silence. She slides below, lifts off the companionway steps and looks at the colour of the fuel in the separator. Not clear red, not even amber. She drains the bowl, finds a spare filter in the locker of spare and useful things under the starboard berth in the forecabin, fits the filter, slacks off the bleed screw, works the fuel pump, tightens the screw, clambers up into the cockpit and turns the key again. The engine starts. She casts off and brings the boat round to the pontoon. Robert Currey takes her lines.

'You're good with that engine,' he says.

'I should have checked it before,' she says.

'Even so, you sorted it. And no one checks everything.'

She steps onto the pontoon, fusses with a bow spring. When she has it as she wants it she stands and says, 'I need some things.'

'Oh yes?'

'A self-steering vane.'

'OK.' He walks to the stern of the boat, examines it for a

moment. 'No problem getting a vane on there,' he says. 'Want me to source one for you?'

She nods. 'And lazy jacks for reefing. And a new mainsail halyard.'

'You'll want a rigger then. Unless you fancy trying it yourself? I'll give Mal a call. When he's sober he's about the best you'll find on this piece of coast. What else?'

'I'm going to take the guard rail off. Fit more U bolts.'

'Clip on,' he says, 'rather than wait for the rail to catch you nicely behind the knees. OK. And what about a jackstay?'

'Yes,' she says. 'Down the centre line.'

'Wire or rope?'

'I don't know.'

'Wire will be noisy. You can get plastic-sheathed stuff but then you can't see if there's a problem with the wire.'

'Rope.'

'Rope it is.'

'I can do a lot of it,' she says.

'I know that.'

'I don't have all the tools.'

He nods. 'You're going out on your own.'

'I've done it before.'

'But you're going further this time.'

She shrugs. 'I don't know.' Then, 'yes.'

'Can I ask you something? What's the furthest you've been on your own?'

'Cowes.'

'The Isle of Wight?'

'Yes.'

'Have you sailed at night on your own?'

'No.'

He nods again, looks up river to where the tide is sliding from the mud flats. There are a few dinghies out, the usual comings and goings around the foreshore.

'I'm no sailor,' he says. 'I can build most of a boat but that's about it. The boats here, Maud, all these boats here, they're basically sound. They're not going to suddenly open up. They won't go to the bottom the first time a wave breaks over the deck. The question is always who's sailing them. And sailing alone, well, it's a frame-of-mind thing, isn't it?'

He waits, gives her a chance to reply, to reassure him. A chance even to tell him to keep his nose out, to back off. When she says nothing, just stands there on the slats of the pontoon looking at him in a way that makes it impossible to know if she has understood him, he says, 'Can you be ready to start at seven tomorrow morning? I can do a couple of hours with you before I have to go back to *Tinkerbelle*. Maybe we can do some more in the evenings. There's plenty of light now.'

'I'll pay you the proper rate,' she says.

'Let's worry about that later,' he says.

'I haven't lost my job,' she says. 'I'm on leave.'

'On leave?'

'Yes.'

'That's all right then,' he says.

4

With Robert Currey beside her, nothing in the work feels too difficult, nothing overwhelms. The canvas tool bag – the pantomime fish – always seems to have what they need. Several times during these mornings and evenings with Currey she remembers working with Grandfather Ray, the pair of them in his garage with the pre-cut parts of the dinghy, the smell of glue and resin, the Calor gas from the heater. Her hair in a plait then, her small hands passing out the tools. The radio on. The old man quietly whistling. Some slung lamp on a flex they worked beneath.

She does not mention any of this to Robert Currey. When they talk it's about the boat, the work in hand. They fit a new bow roller, a new samson post. They fit the U bolts – one either side of the cockpit, low down, so that she could, in theory, clip on before leaving the cabin; two each side going forward, all of them with steel backing plates and lock nuts.

The rigger comes. He's sweating cider. He has eyes like a frightened horse. Robert Currey speaks to him, calms him as though he were indeed a frightened horse. The rigger gets to work, hauls himself to the top of the mast, rope coiled over his shoulder. He takes half a day, and when the job is done he seems returned to some less disastrous version of himself. He accepts a mug of tea from Maud. He grins and shows the remnants of his teeth.

Day by day the weather sweetens. Maud works in T-shirt and jeans, her feet bare when she's on the boat. A van delivers the wind vane – a three-year-old Hydrovane from a yard in Chichester. With its parts laid out along the pontoon it looks at first like the wreckage of a small plane that has flown into the side of a building. At half five, Robert Currey crosses the yard from *Tinkerbelle*. He puts the tender in the water at *Lodestar*'s stern, measures up, then drills the fibreglass while Maud, leaning through the pushpit tails, holds the mounting brackets in place. Ten minutes in the boat shed produces six three-quarter-inch backing plates. By twenty to eight, after wrestling with a seized bolt at the base of the drive unit, and a moment of vexation when it appeared the nylon vane cover was too small, the system is in place.

'This will be your new best friend,' says Robert Currey, tilting the vane on its axis and watching it swing back to its centre line. 'Most people give them names. You got a name in mind?'

'For the vane?'

He laughs at her, her expression. 'You don't have to give it a name,' he says, 'but we should drink a toast to it. That would be a nautical thing to do. Got any drink on board?'

She goes below and comes up a moment later with a bottle of dark liquor and two plastic glasses.

'Navy rum,' says Currey, squinting at the bottle. 'I wouldn't have put you down for that.'

'Tim bought it,' she says.

'Right,' says Robert Currey. 'For emergency uses.'

'He thought it was something the boat should have.'

'He was probably right.'

'Yes,' she says.

He holds the glasses and she pours a measure of rum into each. 'Thank you,' she says.

'You're welcome,' he says. Across the water a light comes on in a house on the side of the hill, a farmhouse perhaps, a light that leaps like a spark from the darkness.

Two days later she takes the boat out into the bay. Ten knots of wind, an April sky fretted with high cloud, the headlands gleaming. When she has the boat balanced she secures the tiller, removes the vane lock-pin and angles the leading edge of the vane into the wind. She wedges herself into a corner of the cockpit and stares at it, the delicate tilting and twitching of the vane in its orange nylon cover. She checks the compass, looks at the boat's wake. It's working but it's over-correcting, the boat crossing and recrossing its heading. She goes back and adjusts the angle of the vane, leans it away from the vertical. This is better, steadier, but it takes another three adjustments before she has it as she wants it. She's on a close reach doing five knots, the sea ribbed and sparkling, a gull flying at deck height off her port side. Improbable as it seems, *Lodestar* is holding a course and the gear bolted to the transom is steering it. She is free! Free to do whatever she needs. Trim a sail, keep watch. Go below to make coffee. Go below to sleep.

With the control lines she moves the vane's leading edge and the boat arcs gently away from the wind. She lets out the jib a little, feels the boat settle again. She is lost in it, this new game in which she mediates between the wind and the gear. Her role on the boat has changed. It already seems strange that she managed on her own before, scurrying between one task and the next like a figure in a silent film. Now she is a type of technician. No more lunging for a winch as the boat comes around. No more running forward to free a line only to find the boat immediately starting to luff. She reaches into the cabin for her tobacco pouch and squats on the cockpit sole to roll a cigarette out of the wind, then sits up wondering where the vane's weak points are, what a big wave might buckle, how she might repair it in the middle of the night. Everything can break; she knows that. Everything will break in the end; she knows that too, for what it's worth. But the vane – all that calibrated simplicity – has the look of something that will go on for a long time. She even likes the bright orange cover. It is a flag, a banner. She finds it comforting, and for that, if nothing else, she is grateful.

She has four more days before her pontoon booking expires. After that she must either renew or move to the swinging moorings in mid-river. Working with Robert Currey – sometimes so late they must wear head torches to see what they're doing – the boat is fitted with tubular steel 'goalposts' over the head of the vane, and onto the crossbar they mount a pair of fifty-watt rigid solar panels. This should answer most of her electrical needs – it will at least mean significantly less time running the engine. Currey promises to fit an AC inverter for her. 'You'll be able to plug stuff in,' he says. 'CD player, hairdryer, power tools. You can charge your phone.' Apparently, there's someone he knows who might have a spare Victron out in a shed. Someone who might part with it for beer money.

She fills up with water and lays in some food. On the morning of the fifth day she casts herself off from the pontoon and motors out to the old mooring. When the boat's secure, the bows parting the incoming tide, she goes below and pushes all the sail bags out through the forward hatch, then sits under the mast passing canvas through her hands looking for tears, loose stitching, signs of chaffing. Her mainsail and the furling jib she is not worried about. The others came with the boat, or all except the red spinnaker she has hardly used, that she does not quite trust herself to manage on her own. There's a genoa she could hank onto the spare forestay (this extra stay an innovation from the days of John Gosse). Another foresail, already much repaired around the tack; and a little storm jib, suitably stiff and battered, though with no obvious signs of weakness.

She bags them and drops them back through the hatch into the forecabin. It's mid-afternoon. She cooks eggs, eats them sitting on the companionway steps looking into the cabin. To her right is the VHF, the new battery monitor, the charge controller for the solar panels. Below these, the Navtex, the GPS, the radar, the chart table itself, chartless at the moment, just a coffee mug, an ashtray, the Breton plotter and a pair of brass dividers. In the deep shelf at the back of the table is a *Reeds Almanac*, a book of ocean landfalls, John Gosse's old Channel pilot. Above, in the mesh pocket, is a Garmin handheld GPS, a pair of lighters, her phone (off), a pair of sunglasses, her pass for the hospital in Croydon. The Zeiss binoculars are in the wooden cubby beside her cheek, a torch in the same cubby, another torch somewhere among her bedding in the quarter berth. Behind her, in the cockpit lockers, she has parachute flares and handheld flares (she saw Robert Currey checking the dates on them). Also fenders and spare warps in there. Harnesses, foghorn, a canvas bucket of decent size, big enough perhaps to be used as a sea anchor.

Some items – the sail thread, the fishing line – are already lost or have somehow become absent from the plan of the boat she carries in her head. Others – a soldering iron, a measuring jug, a spare wristwatch, writing paper, a swimsuit (though she has shorts and T-shirts and these, surely, will serve) – she simply does not have. But if her lines were cut in the night and she woke at sea, she has enough, more than enough, to survive, to keep going. The boat is ready. It is ready, and there is nothing now except to decide what it has all been for.

She is a woman alone on a boat. What is strange about that? Yet it feels as if she has taken her place in the heart of the impossible, and for the space of four or five breaths an immense physical weakness overwhelms her. The thought of hauling on ropes, of doing the thousand things the most ordinary day at sea will demand of her, is intolerable. Also, weirdly remote, as if she were thinking of things she will never do.

She pushes herself away from the steps and puts her plate in the steel sink. She kneels on the cabin sole, opens a locker under the port-side bench, rummages there a while and pulls out a green backpack. She unzips it, looks inside, sniffs it, then starts to collect things from various parts of the boat, laying them first on the red bench before packing them carefully into the bag. This will be the crash bag, kept at hand to be snatched up when all else is lost – the bag of last resorts. She will not need breast pads or a spare nightie for this one. She will need a hand compass, a pair of smoke flares, a signalling mirror, a good knife. She will need, if she can only find it, the fishing line. The line, the hooks and lures . . .

5

I n Chris Totten's office it's the hour he laughingly refers to as closing time. No one has been in all day. In the late morning he spoke on the phone to a broker in Brixham. He has sent three emails. He has eaten a ham sandwich he prepared in his kitchen at home while listening to the early morning news on the radio (swine flu, fifty dead Taliban, an earthquake in Cumbria). And now it's closing time and he is standing from his desk and starting to stretch when Robert Currey taps on the window and a moment later, comes through the door.

They were not at school together, and neither would remember the first time they met because to neither would the occasion have felt important. They live in different areas of the town but the town is small and each is dimly aware of the other's life, sees the other in a bar or a convenience store or in the street. And each of them lives alone and so can guess at something of the other's private routine because it must, in some way, be like his own; a thought that might, perhaps, be comforting, but isn't.

'Chris.'

'Rob.'

'What's new in here, then?'

'Well, this is not a good time to sell boats.'

'The rich are still rich, aren't they? Recession or no.'

'I tend not to sell to the rich. I sell to the moderately well-off.'

'And they're holding on to their pennies, are they?'

'I was thinking I should get myself a little day boat. Go out in the mornings and catch a few mackerel.'

'Become a fisherman?'

'Or take tourists out to the castle.'

'You'll find there's a bit of competition for that.'

'Maybe I'll get something at the new hotel. Park people's cars.'

'You'll be all right.'

'We're going to have to reinvent ourselves a bit. Even you, Rob.'

The yardsman nods though it's hard to say if he's listening. He's looking through the office window towards the river. Without turning he says, 'What's she up to, do you think? On *Lodestar*?'

'Maud? You'd know better than me.'

'Would I?'

'You spend time with her.'

'I spend time with the boat.'

'She's on the boat.'

'Something's not right. Where's the husband? Where's the child?'

'As you say,' says the broker, 'something's amiss.'

'So you don't know what she's got planned, then?'

'I don't know she's got anything planned.'

'She's got something planned. Just spent the best part of three and a half grand on the boat. Self-steering. Solar panels.'

'You didn't ask her?'

'You know what she's like.'

'Cards close to her chest.'

'It's like it doesn't occur to her anyone might want to know.'

'And you want to know.'

'Nothing wrong with that, is there?'

'Nothing at all.'

'You know what she told me? The furthest she's sailed on her own is the Isle of Wight.'

'She looks the part, though. Don't you think? Looks handy.'

'I don't know.'

'You're worried about her.'

'I wouldn't say that.'

'Come on.'

'I'd say she's a good sailor. I'd also say she'd be a fool to head off into blue water in the state she's in now.'

'Isn't that what sailors have always done?'

'What?'

'Cut and run.'

'Bollocks.'

'You're worried about her.'

'You saw what she looked like when she came down here.'

'Not good.'

'No.'

'Cut her hair with a penknife.'

'God knows.'

'Like Joan of Arc.'

'What are you on about?'

'Joan of Arc. You know.'

'And what's his name isn't coming down, is he?'

'She ever mention him?'

'Not really.'

'Tim.'

'Yes. Tim.'

'I don't think he's coming down.'

'She's on her own.'

'She looked on her own even when he was with her.'

'She's on her own now.'

'And you're worried about her.'

'I don't want to read in the paper about a boat on the rocks or a boat found drifting.'

'You want to help her.'

'Help her?'

'Rescue her.'

For a few seconds the yardsman says nothing. He seems to be considering it. Then he steps to the office door, pauses and looks back. 'You've got a dirty mind, Christopher Totten,' he says. He opens the door and goes out, crossing at a measured stride to where his car is parked. The broker stays where he is. His office is full of shadow, and to the shadowed floor, almost inaudibly, he says, 'Not.'

6

On the boat the masthead light looks frail, as if a small white flame were burning there, unpredictably. Another light, broader, shows at the cabin's uncurtained windows and forms a restless slick on the water below. Maud, leaning over the chart table, a thin cigarette in one hand (the last of her tobacco), is walking the brass dividers over the outspread chart of the Atlantic Ocean, west, then south, then west again. At the edges of the table she has her books of pilotage open at the relevant pages. Photographs of headlands, lighthouses, diagrams of channels, leading marks, transits and light sectors. Back and forwards go the points of the dividers. She makes notes on a pad, pulls on the cigarette, brushes ash away, carefully, from the Azores. The brass-bound clock says five past eleven. She looks about herself, reaches to drop the end of the cigarette into the dregs of a mug of tea in the sink, rubs her eyes, stretches, looks back for long minutes at the chart, then breaks off suddenly, goes to the heads, cleans her teeth, spits out into the toilet bowl, urinates, pumps out the bowl.

In the saloon she takes off her jeans, climbs up into the quarter berth, wriggles into the bag and reaches up to put off the light. Within minutes she is asleep (her face, her posture, like those drawings of people sleeping in the Underground during the London Blitz) but minutes later she is awake again, all drowsiness fled, every sense straining. Someone is on the boat. Someone's feet are walking over the deck above her. In one movement she swings herself out of the berth. Her hand, from memory or luck, falls onto the dividers. She listens, waits. The sound of movement has stopped but out of the silence comes the noise of breathing, the gentle rasp of breathing on the other side of the washboards.

A tap on the wood of the boards. As if someone had tapped on her chest, her ribs.

'Who is it?' she asks. Her voice is steady.

He gives a name but she doesn't recognize it. 'The crane driver,' he says. 'From the yard?'

After a pause she says, 'What do you want?' and after another pause he replies, 'I was passing. Thought I might stop and say hello. I've got a bottle.'

'A bottle?'

'It's Saturday night,' he says. 'I'll go if you want.'

Is this how it always is? A man tapping on wood; a woman trying to catch her thoughts in flight? She turns on the chart table light, pulls on her jeans. 'It's not locked,' she says.

The hatch slides back. The crane driver's head is there. All the angles are odd. He grins and holds up his bottle. He lifts out the top washboard and slides down into the cabin.

'Where's your boat?' she asks.

He nods towards the bow. 'No guard rail makes it nice and easy to get up. It's snug in here, though. Lovely.'

She does not know if he is drunk and if he is, how drunk. There is the smell of drink on his breath but rowing in the dark will have sobered him a little. He puts the bottle on the folding table. He has a windproof jacket on, the round neck of a T-shirt underneath.

'Shall I get us some glasses?' he says.

'I'll get them,' she says.

'I saw your light,' he says. 'Then it went out. But it seemed a shame to turn back.' He opens the bottle, a screw-top bottle of red wine, and when she puts the plastic tumblers on the table he fills each to within half an inch of the brim.

'Love and life,' he says. He drinks his wine with two big swallows. 'There's quite a tide running,' he says. 'It's thirsty work.'

The light on his cheeks, on the red threads of his hair, his eyelashes. He doesn't remind her of anybody. She leans her back against the edge of the chart table. 'Have you got any tobacco?' she asks.

He looks pleased at this, immediately delves into pockets. 'Want me to roll it for you?'

She shakes her head. He watches her, is ready with his lighter. 'I half expected to find Rob on board.'

'Who?'

'Rob Currey. I thought you were friends.'

'He works on the boat.'

'It's nothing to do with me,' he says. He laughs. 'You mind if I have a poke about?'

'OK,' she says.

He moves down the saloon, looking along the shelves. He leans into the heads, the unlit forecabin with its ghostly sail bags. He looks at the framed photograph of the boat at sunset or sunrise, then comes back up the other side of the table, looks at the charts on the chart table, at the quarter berth, the electronics. He is standing very close to her. His jacket makes a rustling sound with each small movement.

'You going far?' he asks, tapping the chart, but he doesn't wait for an answer. His eye has been caught by a white card box among the pencils and spare fuses in a small open drawer at the back of the chart table. 'Trial use only,' he says, reading the label on the box. When he looks inside, one of the blister sheets is empty and the other has two of the small green capsules missing. He looks at her.

'It's called Fennidine,' she says.

'Nice,' he says. 'Fennidine. Should I take one?'

'They're for pain,' she says.

'Then I should definitely take one.' He laughs, pushes the blister sheets back in the box and puts it back where he found it. He pours them each another glass of wine. 'You get a lot of head-aches? Or is it the curse?'

'I'm a scientist,' she says. 'I work for a company that develops medicines.'

'And you take them.'

'They like us to,' she says.

'Terms and conditions,' he says.

'No one tells us to,' she says.

'What's it like, then? Aspirin?'

'It has a structure like nicotine.'

He nods. 'I don't see you going to the office much.'

'I'm on leave,' she says.

'On leave.'

'Yes.'

'Should I believe all this?' he says.

'Why not?' she says.

'For a start you've got a tat,' he says. 'I've never met a scientist with a tat before.'

'Do you know any scientists?' she asks.

'At school,' he says. 'But they weren't like you.'

'What were they like?'

'Not like you.'

She nods.

'Have you got anything else to drink?' he asks. 'I don't really like wine.'

'I've got rum.'

'Perfecto.'

She turns from him to reach into the cupboard where the rum is kept and where she replaced it after drinking the toast to the new vane. The crane driver steps across the distance between them and settles his hands on her shoulders. She does not move. The weight of his hands on her shoulders, his breath on the back of her head. When she turns he takes the bottle from her and puts it on the folding table. 'We're just two lonely people,' he says, 'in a lonely old world.' He kisses her brow. He strokes her thigh. 'This is nice,' he says. He shifts his hand from her thigh to the unbuttoned steel button of her jeans, tugs at the opening until the zip unfastens. He flattens the palm of his hand against her belly, slides his hand beneath the waistband of her jeans and her pants, his middle finger settling into the groove over her sex and moving there, quite gently, until he can slide a finger inside her. He does this for perhaps a minute, working his finger inside her then drawing it out a little and pressing it back in. They don't speak. When he takes his hand out of her pants they shuffle across to the companionway steps. She sits on the middle step and takes off her jeans and pants though not her T-shirt or bra. He takes off his jacket and drops it on the sole. He doesn't take off his trousers but pushes them down to mid-thigh. His arms hook under her knees, his hands on her upper arms. For a moment it feels like she has closed against him, sealed herself over. He's pressing and getting nowhere. Then, as if her skin has opened at the bidding of a thought – hers rather than his – he's inside her, his weight forcing her against the step. She pushes back at him and he feels the strength of her legs, her belly, the strange restlessness of that strength. He knows he won't last long. It's not going to be like that – controlled, patient. He grunts, rhythmically, like a man doing bench presses. Now and then she looks at him and when she does the plainness of that look makes him turn his head away. He's fucking her, this woman he first saw with her husband when the boat was new to them, he's fucking her, but he begins to worry that he's losing his hardness. He wants a sex picture but this is not quite a sex picture. Should he have rowed home when he saw her light go off? Should he have rowed back to the landing steps, the parade with its friendly flags? He shuts his eyes and concentrates. He thinks of other girls, girls as enthusiastic, as indifferent as he was himself. He imagines her as a prostitute; he imagines rape; he imagines love. At last he feels himself starting to come and is pulling out of her when she says, quietly, but quite clearly, 'You can come inside me.'

Women – he knows full well – cannot be trusted, but the moment is upon him, and it's like those creatures, God knows, whose organs lock for the duration. He cries out, 'Christ fuck!' He grabs at her clumpy hair, takes what he can of it in his fists. Three big spasms, his stuff flying into her. Then ten more thrusts to end it all and at last the longed-for stillness, the pair of them panting like runners, the first brief kiss, the last.

They separate. They pull on their clothes. She asks for a cigarette and he says, 'I'll roll you a couple so you've got one for the morning.' They smoke together. There seems some agreement between them to pretend that what has just happened has not just happened. It's not shame exactly. Perhaps just the knowledge that it was one of those events whose awkwardness will not be lessened by time, that time cannot make beautiful. They do not touch again. He puts on his jacket and zips it to the neck.

She goes on deck with him, stands there while he slithers down into his inflatable, settles himself, finds the oars. She undoes his line and throws it to him. 'Cheers,' he says, and nothing more. She can hardly see him. The little boat is carried by the current. She hears the quick rhythm of the oars as he shapes a course, then a steadier rhythm as he pulls away.

Below again, she feels cold. She washes out one of the glasses they used, fills it with water and drinks it. She puts the washboards in, draws shut the hatch, bolts it, takes off her jeans again and climbs up into the quarter berth. There's clean underwear, five or six pairs in one of the lockers, but she can't be bothered, it doesn't matter. She puts out the chart table light and lies on her back in the dark, the sleeping bag pulled up to her chin. She's shivering a little, she hurts a little, mostly in her lower back, the back of her hips. As she warms, so the shivering eases and becomes almost pleasant. Perhaps half an hour has passed since he left her and she is nearly asleep, drifting in a tangle of after-images, aftershocks, when she hears for the second time the sound of movement above her, but softer this time, softer and lighter. Light feet along the deck. Light feet stepping onto the cabin roof. Light feet moving along the roof and stopping at a place she guesses to be exactly above her face. It could be a bird, of course. But a bird landing on the deck in the dark? She reaches up and touches the bulkhead, rests her fingers there.

7

Though it is a Sunday and he has no official business there, Robert Currey parks in the yard in his usual place and walks down to where the yard abruptly ends in a short drop to the water. Over the river the fog is so thick you could spin a coin and lose sight of it before it came into your palm again. On the road along the headland he was able to look over the top of it, the table-smooth upper surface of the fog, and on either side, like things finished while the rest was still dreamed, the green of woodland and high fields.

He does not think it will last much longer now. Everyone who lives along this coastline knows these fogs well. Sometimes they linger half a day but once you can see them thinning, once the sun gets into them, they burn off in an hour.

He steps away from the water's edge (too much staring into the fog starts to do odd things to you) and goes back to lean against the side of his car. On the back seat, in an orange Sainsbury's bag, he has a Victron inverter that he will, when it's clear, take out to

Lodestar. His friend brought it round last night and the yardsman paid him from the petty cash he keeps in a plastic wallet in the fridge. It will not take him long to fit it. He has already pictured in his mind where it should go. And while he is fitting it he will talk to her and find out her plans (if she has any, which he is starting to doubt). He will speak plainly to her in the way he has earned. He will press her and hear the truth from her.

Away from the fog it's already warm. He rubs his neck and throat. He has shaved this morning and cannot think of the last time he shaved on a Sunday morning. He even came close to putting on a few drops of aftershave from the bottle with dusty glass shoulders on the shelf above the sink, but the thought of being in the confines of the cabin and everywhere smelling himself, unable to escape the smell of himself, made him leave the bottle where it was. It has a foolish name. He finds it slightly odd that he ever bought it.

The masts of the yachts along the nearest pontoon are clear now to the upper spreaders. This is how it goes, from the upper air down to the water where the last of it will drift for a few minutes like wisps of smoke. He opens the car door, takes out the Sainsbury's bag, looks in at the inverter, fetches a cordless drill from the boot of the car and strolls to the gate leading to the pontoons. He taps in the four-digit code and walks down the sloping duckboards to where they keep the yard tender, a small black rib with a two-stroke outboard. The rowing boat that's usually tethered to the rib isn't there this morning, which is a little surprising, though such boats have a way of coming and going, of being viewed as a kind of public property. It's not his problem, certainly not this morning. He stands on the pontoon watching the fog dissolve. All the yachts on the pontoons are in the sunlight now, and the river to twenty yards out is bright as spring water.

In the middle of the river the fog is at its most stubborn. He shades his eyes, bides his time. A bird lifts out of the fog, and taking the sun on its wings seems for a second to blaze with silver flames.

He can make out the mast of the boat at the town end of the swinging moorings now – a nice little sloop called *Aphelion*. Along from her there's *Black Witch* and then, still ghostly, a motor sailer called *Jacqui*. *Lodestar* is astern of *Jacqui* but the fog hasn't given her up yet. He waits, turns away to get his bearings, looks back, counts off the boats again. He can see *Lodestar*'s mooring buoy, a grey ball becoming a pink ball. There is no sign of *Lodestar*. He stays there, unmoving, until he can see down as far as the fuel barge and up to where the river curves and the tower of a church stands out faintly from the land behind it. There is no confusion. Nor, he finds, is he much surprised. With one hand and with the bobbing of his head he makes a small courteous gesture to the water, then he picks up his bag, the cordless drill, and starts back to the car.

FOUR

This is the Hour of Lead –
Remembered, if outlived . . .

Emily Dickinson

1

She spends the night in Fowey, a visitors' mooring opposite the town quay. The next morning, with the VHF turned up to catch warnings from the gunnery ranges off Dodman Point, she follows the coast, counts off headlands, finds herself at three in the afternoon riding the swell in Falmouth Bay, the lighthouse looking freshly painted, cliffs of siltstone, slate, tumbled sandstone, rising to grazed fields and slow-moving cloud. She drops the sails and starts the engine, follows another yacht past the eastern breakwater to the inner harbour and on to the marina. Two men, idling on the pontoons, take her lines. They compliment her on the boat, try to engage her in conversation, then, seeing there will be none, wander off, unoffended.

She puts the boat in order, checks her fenders, tightens the mooring lines, runs a cable to the mains socket on the pontoon. When she has finished she cooks pasta and stirs in a tin of tuna with its oil, sits in the cockpit to eat it. A woman from the marina office comes by. She's sorry to disturb her. 'How long do you think you'll be staying?'

'A night,' says Maud, her lips and chin slicked with oil.

When the woman has gone, Maud washes the pot and plate in water warmed by the engine on the run in. She is tired but tiredness does not signify; she will, she knows, be more tired later, much more. She goes into the town just as she is, in her shorts and summer sweater, the trainers she has had for years, size 4. Now and then she sees herself in the windows of the shops she's passing but feels no strong ownership of that shadow. Once, as though walking on unmarked ways through a forest, she stops and glances behind her, suddenly anxious she will not know her route to the boat again. It's only a moment, then a bare slim shoulder, some teenage girl on her phone, jostles her on the narrow pavement and she goes on.

At the supermarket she takes two trolleys, pulls one and pushes the other. She has not written out a list but there is a list in her head. Dry food, tinned food, twenty packets of boil-in-the-bag rice, all varieties. Vacuum-packed bread, vacuum-packed bacon. Rye crackers, rice cakes. Coffee, tea, chocolate. Powdered milk. Three dozen eggs. Twenty oranges and twenty lemons. Potatoes, carrots, spring greens, onions, cabbages.

People passing her, women passing her, must imagine she has a family of six at home, six at least, and has been left (poor love, poor fool) to do this on her own, a husband dawdling by the magazines, the kids larking in the aisles.

Four packs of tobacco. A dozen packets of Rizlas, the ones with the cut corners in the green packs. It's what Tim had. It's what she's become used to.

Torch batteries, batteries for the radio. Various items from the pharmacy.

At the checkout she pays with her card and wonders if there will be some problem, if Fenniman's have remembered to pay her, their absent employee. She asks for her bags to be delivered to the marina, gives her name and the name of the boat. The supermarket is used to making deliveries to the marina, and because she has spent a good sum of money the delivery will be free. They give her a discount voucher for her next visit. She looks at it a moment, then folds it and slides it into the back pocket of her shorts.

On board again she listens to the six o'clock shipping forecast. Winds from the south-east, three or four, rain for a time in the morning, then showers. On the boat beside her – a wooden boat, a cutter with a name like one of the heroines in those old novels she has not read – a party is starting. Two men with glossy beards, two women with braided hair, a boy squatting like a buddha on a varnished hatch, the pop of a cork, a voice pretending to scold, then laughing. The women's movements are languorous. The men touch things with the confidence of ownership. The boy is mysterious, beautiful, his glances quick as light on water. One of the women, carrying a plate of food, notices Maud, seems on the verge of saying something, then looks away.

She's asleep on one of the saloon cabin benches when her shopping arrives. The deliveryman is cooing to her from the pontoon. He has a dunnage trolley loaded with orange carrier bags. He offers to carry the bags below but Maud says it's OK. He hands her the bags two at a time and she arranges them along the sides of the cockpit and the top of the coach-house roof, then signs the electronic pad, her name a spider's web on the machine's glass.

'I used to sail a bit myself,' he says, putting away his machine, nodding to the boat. 'Then life came along.'

It's dark before she has packed away the last of it. She has endeavoured to be methodical but many items are simply squeezed in wherever they will fit. When stowing anything on a boat you should consider the boat turned upside down. What will come away? What will fly and shatter? She looks about herself, the little space – four steps to the saloon bulkhead, four steps back to the companionway – and knows that a great deal would fly, that the air would be full of it.

She rolls a cigarette, leans at the chart table – that cluttered shelf – leans over 4011, North Atlantic Ocean, Northern Part, and beneath it, 4012, North Atlantic Ocean, Southern Part. It is not possible to memorize an entire chart but she could make a passable sketch of certain coastlines, could mark in a dozen soundings, the locations of certain features – Craggan Rocks, Vrogue Rock, the Longships Lighthouse.

Her plan is to quit Falmouth three hours before high water (Dover) and reach the Lizard an hour later. From the Lizard she will turn south-west and ride the ebbing tide across the shipping lanes. She has a waypoint in mind, a buoy, ODAS Brittany, a hundred and fifty miles off the French coast at Brest. Two days' sailing – less if the conditions are favourable – though time on such a passage hardly matters. She is not expected anywhere.

In the morning she will top up with water and diesel then leave the marina at half twelve to be clear of the harbour a little after one. All this is plain enough. It is plain and sensible and readily understood. At the same time it feels whimsical and fatally private, a plan that will disappear like a shout and leave no trace of itself.

She goes on deck with a torch to check her lines. The party on the cutter is over or they have moved it ashore. She steps onto the pontoon, reties one of the springs, steps back on board, switches off the torch and gazes at the clustered lights of the town – then turns seawards, investigates the shadows, the silvered channel, the lit buoys that mark the way out. This is all she needs for now. It's a readiness of sorts, and she stands there a long while meeting it all in silence, her breath like a feather laid along her tongue.

In the morning, she rises to the sound of the promised rain, boils two eggs (from her great supply), makes coffee, makes more coffee, pulls out the washboards and leans against the companionway steps under the shelter of the hatch, blowing tobacco smoke towards the town.

By ten, the rain has softened and lies in the wind, drifts with it. She busies herself with twice-done jobs and notices – four seconds of peering at herself in the little mirror screwed to the back of the door in the heads – that her hair has grown long enough to begin to curl.

At eleven she no longer knows how to distract herself. She pulls on her coastal jacket, steps down onto the pontoon, unplugs herself from the electrics, goes to the marina office to settle up, then comes back and begins to loosen her lines. In the textbooks of sailing, particularly the textbooks of short-handed sailing, the leaving of moorings – marinas, pontoons, harbour walls – is listed among those evolutions most likely to cause trouble. State of the wind, state of the tide, and all around her, packed tight, other people's boats, some of them – most, perhaps – worth a great deal more than *Lodestar*. She frees all lines except the bow warp and the stern spring, puts both of these on a slip. She starts the engine, then goes forward and begins to pay out the bow warp. One of the men from the cutter calls, 'Want a hand?' but it's too late for that. She slips the bow warp, hurries to the cockpit to put the engine in gear, slips the back spring, hauls it in and drops it in crazy loops round her feet.

'Where're you headed?' calls the man, leaning over the stern rail of his beautiful boat.

'West,' calls Maud in return, and the man, if he has heard her at all, simply nods, raises an arm in farewell and turns away.

By the time the light is failing she's mid-Channel and beating into wind and tide. She switches on the navigation lights; the Hydrovane is steering, the needle in the lit bowl of the binnacle floating over 235, 239, 237, 235.

During the first hours, moving south from the Lizard, the shipping was heavy; now it is quieter and her course should take her well clear of the lane around Ushant. Off her port bow a freighter is heading up channel; to starboard, a pair of fishing boats are rolling in the swell fifty yards from each other. She is not sure if they are fishing, can see no black cones hoisted and they have not put on their lights yet. She watches them; she has been watching everything – seabirds, flotsam, the shifting light. Watching the boat, too; watching and listening.

Before it is properly dark she decides to go below and eat, use the heads, put on more clothes, prepare for the night. She has not, since her eggs at breakfast, eaten more than a few oatcakes. Her stomach is tender, her appetite less than it should be. It would be wise now to make a proper meal but she settles for a cereal bar, a mug of black tea, a couple of Kwells (less sleep-inducing than Stugeron).

Sitting on the leeward bench she strips down to her T-shirt then layers up, pulling clothes from the lockers beneath her. She puts on her salopettes, her coastal jacket, her sea boots. It is May and the wind is temperate but at some point in the night she will be cold. Fatigue will see to that.

A last mouthful of tea, then she goes to the companionway

steps, pauses, reaches over and takes her phone from the mesh pocket above the chart table. It is not clear what has prompted this other than a fleeting thought about whether or not to wear her beanie and hearing in that thought something of Tim's voice. She does not question it. Her hand reaching out is argument enough.

On deck she looks for shipping, checks the compass, the Hydrovane, then fits herself into the angle between the cabin and the edge of the cockpit and switches on the phone. The battery is down to about thirty per cent, and as Robert Currey did not install the inverter she will not be able to charge the phone at sea. There are two missed calls, both more than a week old. One number she recognizes immediately as the office in Reading; the other she has seen before but is less certain of. She thinks it is probably the police, perhaps the woman officer who came to the cottage, who waited with her in the churchyard.

There is only a single bar of reception – it flickers at the top of the screen like a faltering pulse – but she types in the number, listens to several seconds of hissing, then a ring tone that sounds unfamiliar, as if the call is being routed through a foreign exchange.

'Tim's phone,' says a woman's voice, brightly, and then, after a short pause, 'Hello?' and after a second pause, during which each perhaps can hear the other's breathing, 'Maud?'

Maud ends the call, powers down the phone, slides it into one of the deep pockets of her jacket. She had thought some auto-mated voice might tell her she was out of range, that the number she was calling was unreachable. As for what she would have said if Tim had answered rather than Bella, she had nothing prepared. Told him where she was? How the boat was handling? That the green ribbon was still tied to the starboard shroud though the weather had washed and bleached it almost white? Or she could have simply held the phone out to the sea – even tossed it over the side to let him listen for a few seconds to whatever that sounded like, a phone sinking.

She imagines him asking Bella who it was, who called, and Bella saying, 'I think it was Maud,' and when asked what she had said, answering, '*Nothing*,' and Tim saying, 'Yes, that sounds like her.'

One of the steadiest patterns of their time together – in place from their earliest days – was a kind of call and response whereby Tim would ask her questions and she would answer them. As time went by her answers became less and less satisfactory to him. He had an expression that told her this – the unsmiling mouth, the eyes briefly widened. And certain phrases: 'That's it?' 'Yes . . . ?' Even (something a teacher might have said to him at his school) 'I'm waiting . . .'

He said to her once, 'Men complain all the time about women talking all the time. But I have the original silent woman.'

He described – more than once and each time with different emphasis – a cartoon he had seen in a magazine, or that someone had seen, Magnus perhaps: a caveman on the phone to his friend, the caveman's wife standing in the background. 'I'm thinking of teaching her to speak,' says the caveman. 'That can't do any harm, can it?'

She thinks of the last time she saw him, his head on the pillow, his eyes turned away from her, his medicines on the table, the open book, the sound of the rain, the willows by the stream. And she remembers – it's the stream itself that joins the two thoughts – the Boxing Day morning they all went out in boots and scarves to watch the hunt ride through, how they spotted them, still half a mile off, and watched them work their way down past the black hedges then zig-zag through empty fields until they were suddenly there, a hundred yards away, fifty yards, the horses big as cavalry horses, the master at the front in his faded coat, his face like bronze, raising the bone handle of his whip in salute . . .

The memory of it laid down in the moment like a rune in the soft matter of her brain.

On the VHF, after a burst of static, the Falmouth coastguard invites all mariners to switch to channel 79. She ducks her head below the hatch, dials in the new channel and hangs there, waiting.

Sunrise has no fanfare, just a cautious brightening, a hairline crack of gold bright enough to leave a line across the eye as you turn from it. The sea, that all night has simply been a sound, becomes again a particular set of distances, a thing she can study, that scatters under her gaze, that is both patterned and shapeless. She wonders if she has, for much of the last hour, been sleeping. The night, her memory of it, is not coherent. Lights that did not approach. The noise of a plane heading for France or some destination beyond. A shower of rain that lasted no more than a few minutes, that made the skin of her hands shine. A little later, the night unbroken still, the cautious calling of birds. Twice she went below to brew tea, roll a cigarette, use the heads, squint at the GPS. And there was a moment – before her last visit below? Afterwards? – when she felt she was falling and reached out urgently for something to hold on to only to find she was sitting, perfectly safe, in her wedge of cockpit, the boat riding forwards in easy sequences.

And now the dawn drifting towards her, small waves rising blue and silver out of the grey. She scans the horizon, climbs stiffly down the companionway steps, unzips her jacket and drops it on the leeward bench. The latest forecast from the Navtex is for force four, five by nightfall. No gale warnings, sea state moderate. She takes off her boots, her salopettes. She sets her alarm clock for thirty minutes, gets up into the berth. She's on a port tack and the heel of the boat rolls her against the skin of the hull, the water's infinite rhythms. She has never slept at sea before – not as a solo sailor – and for a while she fights it, the recklessness of it. Then sleep swallows her in the skip between instants, leaves her dreaming she is a woman alone on a boat too anxious to sleep. As if her sleeping head could think of nothing more fantastic.

When she opens her eyes again she knows from the light that the morning is well advanced and sits up so suddenly she hits her head and cries out, the first time she has heard her voice since speaking to the man on the cutter.

She goes on deck in her socks as though the seconds it would take to put on her boots might be the time she needed to avert a collision with the bow of a super-tanker, but when she stands in the cockpit the only vessel she can see, a good mile off her starboard beam, looks like a tall ship, a sail trainer perhaps, all sails set and heading west into the deep Atlantic.

For over two hours *Lodestar* has sailed unattended. Nothing has gone wrong. The course is good still, the sails sweetly curved, the boat balanced and making the best part of six knots through a low swell. There is even a hint of warmth in the wind, some promise of the light and air of the south.

Below again, she reads off her co-ordinates from the GPS, finds herself on the chart, then puts the kettle on the gimbaled burner and discovers her appetite is back. She scrambles three eggs, eats them on ham and bread, rolls a cigarette, smokes it in the cockpit, coils rope and sluices out the cockpit sole with a bucket of sea water. Then she goes forward to inspect the rigging, to look up the mast, to test the lashings on the little Bombard inflatable, check shackles, touch the sails. She kneels at the pulpit rail and looks down at the boat's stem smashing the green tiles of the sea. She has been underway for not quite twenty-four hours but already a sense of pattern is emerging. The unspectacular doing of the necessary, the looking out, the tending, the slow ceasing of expectation. A hermit in her floating cell, a pilgrim, an exile, a woman out of a Book of Hours who works her life like a garden, who suffers in it if necessary, who rarely looks up.

In the late afternoon, clouds descend. For hours the world is grey and she has the company of silent grey birds. The sea is muffled. It's not raining but somehow she still gets wet.

At ten, she fries up cabbage and caraway seeds, eats it out of the pan standing in the space between the galley stove and the companionway steps, the boat humming under her boots. She catnaps in the cockpit, her head lolling onto her chest, each short sleep with its brief luminous dream, each dream immediately forgotten as she wakes to the sound of wind and water.

At three in the morning she reaches the continental shelf, its contour lit by the lights of fishing boats, a great curve of them she cannot see the end of, a line running south and east towards Bilbao, north towards the coast of Ireland. She hears the fishermen's voices on the VHF, alters course to sail between two of their boats, bracing herself to feel *Lodestar* caught suddenly in the hatchwork of a net. As she passes them, as she leaves them behind, the depth gauge in the cockpit shifts from a hundred metres to three hundred to five hundred then, going beyond what it can measure or display, the screen is suddenly blank.

When she can pick out the first signs of day she goes down to sleep, not in her berth – she is afraid she will not wake up – but on the leeward bench, her head on one of the little velvety cushions embroidered with the boat's name that Tim's mother gave them as a Christmas present the year after they bought the boat together. She sleeps for an hour, gets up to check the course, goes on deck to tack, comes down and sleeps a second hour on the other bench, the matching cushion.

The middle of the day is given over to repacking some of her store cupboards. The fresh food has already taken on a smell of boats, the inside of a boat. The radio is on, a test match at the Oval, the commentators passing sly remarks about each other's clothes. Then a few minutes after six she sights her way marker, ODAS Brittany, spots it first with the naked eye – a black stick in the distance off the boat's starboard shoulder – then finds it with the Zeiss, a black and yellow buoy with a ring of lights on top, the sea beyond it swept with shadow.

She marks her position on the chart – a dot within a circle. She makes a sandwich, makes coffee, puts a splash of rum in the coffee. The rum is to mark the relief she feels, the slight astonishment that she has found it, a buoy no bigger than a family car, upturned and tethered out here at the top of a cliff of green water. She carries her coffee up to the cockpit. The taste of the rum brings back the touch of the crane driver, the scent of him, certain things he said (Perfecto, Cheers, Christ fuck). Brings back, too, how that night on the swinging mooring had become uncontainable, how (almost invisible to herself on the deck) she crept out of the harbour through the forming fog, and halfway to Fowey, below for a moment using the heads, found his sperm in the crease of her pants, the crease of herself, and thought *what if?* while deciding immediately and with whatever certainty she could muster in the face of such recklessness, that nothing of his would grow in her, could grow in her.

She is due to come on next week but won't – the absence of those secret tides she hardly noticed until they were gone. She will be dry again, dry as stone, and this is another kind of silence, something in her like those shocked clocks found at the scene of a disaster, the hands stopped at the instant.

(The first time she bled her mother left at the end of her bed a roll of those bags you find in budget hotels and the toilets of aeroplanes for the disposal of what cannot be flushed. Also a newspaper article, laminated, about teenage girls getting pregnant, a picture of them sitting with their babies in some kind of day centre, smiling like those Flemish Madonnas in the old paintings where the frames are decorated with wildflowers.)

She sets a new course, a little to the west of the old one. Her next waypoint is a patch of water twenty nautical miles off the coast of Terceira in the Azores. She will only stop there – Terceira or Faial – if she needs to, if there's some problem with the boat. Otherwise she will keep sailing, drop down to somewhere on a line with Senegal, then across to wherever it is she is heading, her destination . . .

To the man on the cutter she said simply 'west' but everything, approached, becomes specific, like it or not, and sooner or later west must take on a name, a set of co-ordinates. All those evenings at the yard and on the mooring, when she stayed up late with the charts walking the dividers across the sea like dowsing rods until, each time, they hesitated somewhere in the mid-Atlantic. She has ruled out the United States – she has no entry visa and does not want to try to explain herself to the Department of Homeland Security. Several times she has travelled to Fenniman HQ in Orlando and knows the US customs force is made up of young men fierce for category and that nothing she could say about her situation would fit between the narrow lines of any form they possessed (how many others like her? How many at any given time had purposes and business only really explicable through a medium like song?).

Cuba is possible, Cuba via Bermuda. Then work her way south to the Windward Islands. Or Mexico? She has not rejected Mexico. In the drawer at the back of the chart table she has the *Book of Landfalls* (a book as thick and heavy as her old textbooks of biology). She will find somewhere. She will not sail off the edge of the world. Cayo Largo, Île-à-Vache, Montego Bay. She is most tempted by those places she fails most completely to imagine. For example, a place called Progreso on the Yucatán coastline where nothing else seems to exist, nothing the Admiralty thought worth depicting. A dot on the mustard yellow the chart uses to distinguish the land from the sea. A dot, and beside it a blot of purple to indicate a light. Some manner of settlement off the waters of the Campeche Bank. A place whose ambition for itself she could not begin to guess at.

Day after day, the tasks she allots to herself, the little cleaning jobs, the meals taken standing up by the galley. Nights under the waxing moon, silver wake, green phosphorescence. Sleeping for an hour, for half an hour, waking to the same scene her eyes closed to.

She wears shorts and a shirt now, bare feet growing brown and bruised. Hair lightening, face darkening. Little cracks, salt-sores, on the skin of her hands.

In the early hours of her tenth night at sea the boat wakes her with a new angle, a new noise. There's a front passing overhead and she goes on deck, one hand fumbling with the zip of her jacket, one hand clutching at the shadows around her. In the cockpit she pulls up her hood only to have it immediately blown down again.

There is no sense of the boat struggling, but after watching it a while, the bows thudding into the swell, her face becoming streaked with drifts of sea water, she furls the jib to roughly half its full surface then struggles into her harness, clips on, and goes to the mast to free the main halyard and drops two reefs' worth of mainsail into the lazy jacks. The boat slows, quietens. In daylight she might have left it to sail hard but it's half four in the morning and she wants to get below again.

There are no lights visible other than her own. She has not seen a ship for forty-eight hours. As she passes the depth gauge she flashes her torch beam at it, wipes away the moisture with her thumb. It's blank, of course, but she knows from the chart there's more than five thousand metres of water beneath her.

She is sailing an average of ninety nautical miles a day, noon to noon. When she closes her eyes she sees only the sea, its ceaseless motion, neither rough nor quiet, neither away from nor towards, a view unburdened with anything resembling meaning.

Forty degrees north, twenty-four west. She is, she judges, a day and a half from the island of Terceira. In the late morning she is sitting, smoking in the lee of the mast, when a plume of feathering water rises, thirty, forty metres from the boat. A slick back appears, a fin, then just a patch of seething water, settling. She stands, one hand gripping the mast, her gaze sweeping the surface of the sea. And there it is again! Ten metres closer, a noise like the steam whistle of a drowned factory, the high plume dispersing, the great back rolling. Two of them, she thinks, two at least. If one rises under the boat then the boat is finished. She glances at the life raft in its orange canister, pictures the crash bag beside her berth. Do they know she's here? Can they hear the boat, see it?

She waits. She is ready for them, but still gasps the next time one surfaces. A clear view of the flexing blow-hole, a mottled fin, detailed and living. An eye? Does she see an eye? And if she sees it, is it blank, remote? A plaque of shone metal, a green stone washed and washed? Or a thing that glances at her, that is full of kinship?

Another plume – but further off, further ahead. They are passing her, finished with their investigation of her, if that's what it was. It is understood of course that such creatures are on a journey, their tonnage in constant purposeful flight, but when they have gone she misses them with an intensity she could not have anticipated. She stands on the coach-house roof, damp from the mist of their breath. Her cigarette is out and unsmokeable. Their breath had no strong smell to it, was not, as she might have imagined it, like the puddles on a fish dock. In its temperature, it seemed to carry the warmth of their blood, their four-chambered hearts.

All day the wind is southerly. She's sailing close-hauled on a short sea, jib and main winched tight. The knocking makes her ribs ache or her ribs were aching anyway. Her longest sleep since leaving England is three and a half hours. She is tired; she supposes she is tired. Sometimes she looks at the chart or the GPS or the battery monitor and there's a moment, no more than a second or two, when she doesn't know what she's looking at.

The fourteenth night, drowsing in the cockpit (her life rising and dipping with the rising and dipping of the boat), she wakes with the sense of having been touched, caressed, and looks out to see a light on her port bow like the light you might see from an aeroplane, the first spark of the sun on some huge, sluggish river thirty-five thousand feet below. She watches it double and dance in the lenses of the binoculars, watches it slowly fade with the hushed blue rising of the day, then sees in its place the unmistakeable smudge of an island.

All day she sails towards it. With each hour some new detail appears. The shocking green of trees, of vegetation. Every time she goes below then comes on deck again, she stares at it with an impatience she has been free from for many days. A ship comes out from the port, a coaster, a supply ship. It passes her in a long curve, a red ship, or a white ship red with rust, a dozen figures leaning over the rail. One of them – brown arm, white singlet – waves to her, and after a moment she remembers to wave back.

By mid-afternoon she can pick out the white tower of a church, white houses straggling up from the port into the green volcanic hills. She tacks to put herself on course to round the island's eastern end. The port is there, tucked away from the long weather of open sea. She is almost in thrall to the place, an island green as Dorset – greener – and crowding the eye after so many days of emptiness, grey sea.

It's evening before she's passing the breakwater. She sees the first lights come on (the lighthouse flashing red in sequences of four) then the lights along the front, the headlights of a car climbing into the hills. For several minutes, the thought of being tied up in port, of going below and sleeping eight hours, sleeping without setting the radar alarm, without some part of her seeming to be on deck still, watching for ships, for weather, for some rope or wire to wear through and stream along the wind, it tempts her. It's not too late. Just start the engine, drop the sails, put the boat about. But there was a cost involved in getting this journey started (she doesn't know what it was, perhaps it was almost everything) and to break the rhythm of her movement even for a night puts it all at risk. She's thirty-nine degrees above the equator. Below thirty-five – thirty for sure – she should find the trades, and once she's in the trades she can pole out the sails and have the wind behind her all the way to Havana, to Progreso, to wherever.

She looks at the island – whale-backed, spangled – looks and turns away. Ahead of her each rising lip of water carries the light of the setting sun. Stars rise. A planet on the old moon's shoulder.

(To sailors, the night sky turns about the earth, a shell of glass around a globe.)

2

Two days south of the island, two days of good sailing, the wind dies and the boat drifts over a sea clear as tap water. (She should of course have gone via the Canaries or the Cape Verde Islands, but this is the route Nicolette Milnes Walker took on her way to becoming the first woman to cross single-handed, and Maud, who was given the book of the voyage on her twelfth birthday – a picture on the cover of Milnes Walker taking a sun-sight in a bikini – has never forgotten it.)

Shoals of little fish gather around the boat, eating the weed from the boat's hull. The sails hang. She leaves them up because they offer her some shade. She moves about the boat in shorts and a T-shirt, then in shorts, then in nothing but a hat. She has a choice of hats – her own blue cotton baseball cap and a straw hat she found long ago in one of the lockers in the forecabin, a battered type of Panama, the straw watermarked and fraying but still serviceable. Was it Gosse's hat? It fits her well and is cooler to wear than the cap.

She stretches (she remembers some of Tim's yoga). She smokes with her back against the metal of the mast and when the mast is too hot, against the canister of the life raft. An event is the vapour trail of a plane, graze pink in the light of the evening sun. Or a bird almost indistinguishable from its element.

She could start the engine – a whole tank of diesel – but the silence hangs sheer and the engine would shatter it.

She thinks of swimming, and once the thought has occurred to her – such benign and cool-looking water – it grows into an appetite, a kind of thirst. The boat is travelling on a current at about the speed of an old man walking with a child, but in the water she will travel on the same current. She can see no risk.

From the stern of the boat she trails a length of buoyant rope then goes forward until she is standing by the pulpit rail. She lays her hat on the deck – feels nude beyond the mere stripping off of clothes – and for half a minute observes the faded green ribbon on the shroud for some sign of a breeze but the ribbon, though it trembles, hangs slack. She shuffles forwards, curls her toes over the edge of the deck. She is thinking of the woman she watched on the television, small hours of the morning, standing as she now stands, at an edge, a divide, her back flushed with the cold as Maud's is reddened by the sun. Fellow feeling – not exactly sisterly, but something, a recognition, the awareness of lines like surgeon's thread sewn through the hearts of strangers and now and then drawn taut. She looks to the horizon, teeters, slightly giddy in the midst of so much light, then leans into her dive, her head breaking the water into pieces of gold.

When she surfaces and looks up at the weird brightness of her own boat the first thing she sees is the green ribbon lifted from the shroud and floating in a curve like the sine wave on the screen of an oscillator. The sails draw breath, the boat tilts away from her. She cannot, from the water, see the rope she trailed. She kicks out. The water is cold and the boat is two hundred yards from her before the ribbon lies down again and the sails empty themselves and hang slack. She finds the rope, pulls herself along its length, then grapples herself aboard beside the Hydrovane. She sits in the cockpit streaming water. She is shaking a little (adrenaline that prepares the body for a wound, that anticipates the wound), and when she tries to roll a cigarette in the church gloom of the cabin her hands are unsteady and the tobacco spills onto the cabin floor.

That night she sleeps on deck and watches satellites. The boat drifts. The sound of the sails is like the sound of someone turning restlessly in their sleep. She's in the bag, her head on a folded jumper, the sea blue one she wore in the flat in Bristol that winter she was first pregnant, the flat smelling of toast, of dust scorched by the elements of the heaters.

She sleeps for twenty minutes, ten minutes, forty minutes. Each time she wakes she feels a hand on her thigh, a hand against her cheek, sees through slitted eyes the stars heaped up on the horizon.

Things pass her by, creatures of some sort. She hears one of them circle the boat twice, quite slowly, before moving off. Other sounds play from below through the muffle of her jumper. They are an effect of the water perhaps, of the cabin's bundled acoustics, the way the whole boat has always been a type of instrument. Tempting, though, to free herself from the sleeping bag and run on light feet to the cockpit, thrust her head under the hatch and *see*.

(See what?)

In the morning, sweating in the bag from the heat of the sun, she wakes out of a dream of slow trains passing to find the boat in the middle of an island of light bulbs. There are thousands of them, and at every touch of the boat each glass shell rocks against its neighbours and sounds them. Gently, she stirs them with the boat hook. Some are broken, their filaments open to the air, but most are whole and seem – their glass skins signalling the light of the sun – to be switched on.

How long have they been in the sea? How far have they drifted together? With her bucket she scoops some out and examines them. General Electric. Sixty watts. Clear glass. Bayonet fittings starting to crust with salt, to react. She keeps one and lowers the others back into the water.

It's like glass spawn.

By midday the wind is back, a breeze from the south-east, a bare breeze, but enough to make headway. The bulbs rattle past the hull, then she is free of them and the sea is darker and she puts on clothes again. She is businesslike, she works the boat. She has come, by the log, one thousand four hundred and eighty nautical miles since Falmouth. Below her, marked on the chart, a submerged mountain called Atlantis.

3

It might have gone on like this forever, her parish a thirty-two-foot boat, her days both empty and purposeful, her nights as the lonely caretaker of a vast, unlit theatre. So much of the journey has gone as she might have wished it to – no gross difficulty, nothing beyond her reach – that when she is woken (three-fifteen in the morning, her twentieth night at sea) by the crazed insect-call of the radar alarm and swings out of her berth to find herself ankle deep in water, the moment feels due; feels, in truth, long awaited.

She climbs – runs – through the open hatchway, jumps down into the cockpit, misjudges something – the heel of the boat, her own velocity – and only avoids going over the side by snatching at one of the steel goalposts at the stern. A sudden heat in her left hand, felt and dismissed. She steadies herself, wraps an arm around the post, stares out into the darkness around the boat. Sees nothing, hears nothing.

Whatever triggered the alarm has come and gone. Sometimes a wave can do it. Dolphins. A whale.

She goes below again, puts on the red nightlight and tastes the water to be sure it's salt and not coming from some breach in the fresh-water tank. It's salt – salt mired with diesel and whatever debris accumulates in the hidden places of the boat, now carried up.

She tries to judge if the boat is sinking. She does not think it is. The boat is still sailing. It has not appreciably slowed, it is not wallowing. If the water is rising inside it's rising slowly.

She reaches for the torch, flashes its beam at the crash bag then follows its light into the forecabin. Her black bin-bag of empty tins and cartons is moving in the water as if it contained something living. She goes to the anchor locker. If one of the anchors has worked loose it might have done some damage, but other than the usual slick of moisture the locker is dry. She works her way back, throws everything from the cabin sole onto the berths. She needs to pull up the floor but when the fingers of her left hand touch the brass pull ring she shouts with pain, turns the light onto her own hand and sees how the tip of her third finger is bent backwards, an angle of fifteen, twenty degrees. She wedges the torch into the V of the bunks and uses her right hand. She has not lifted these panels in a long time. They feel jammed, sucked in – then the first comes away so abruptly she topples backwards into the water on the saloon floor. She writhes there a moment, finds her feet, slings the panel through the folded door of the heads and kneels by what she has opened up. Plenty of water here. One of the through-hulls gone? Which one? The log? She reaches deeper, up to her elbow, up to her shoulder. By stretching out her fingers she can touch a jagged crown of plastic, the water pouring through it like the bubbling of a secret spring.

And there is something else down there, a small, shaped piece of metal or plastic she assumes is part of the broken fitting but which, when she pulls it out and holds it to the light of the torch, turns out to be a little heart-shaped hair clip of painted tin, and for several seconds, squatting barelegged in the half-dark, in the pooling water, the hurt boat, she simply stares at it.

A hair clip painted with red enamel and little white flowers.

She does not know where to put it – she almost puts it in her mouth – then she reaches up, slides it into her hair and snaps it shut.

With the torch she walks backwards into the saloon. She hauls up the next panel and slings it beside the first. She knows what she needs but she is not sure where to find it. She starts to dig things out of cupboards, pulls them out and drops them any-where. She protects her left hand. She pauses to think, to think hard, then crosses quickly to the other side of the boat, opens a compartment by the galley, rummages, and comes out with a shaped, softwood plug. She kneels by the bilges, gropes for the broken fitting, pushes in the plug, strikes it with the flat of her palm, then hammers it home with the waterlogged mallet of Captain Slocum's journal.

She's working well now or that's her impression. Who's to judge it? Old Rawlins? From the cockpit locker she fetches the two-foot-long anodized steel bilge-pump handle (a good-sized pump for a boat like this), slots it into its socket between the companionway steps and the quarter berth and pumps, hard, for twenty minutes, rests for half a minute, then pumps for another fifteen, rests and manages another ten minutes before the burning in her back, the nausea of it, forces her to stop. The bilges are still full but the water has dropped to below the level of the sole. She checks on the wooden plug, drinks from the galley tap and goes back to pumping. Day is breaking before she is shifting more air than water. She drags herself up into the cockpit. The morning is faultless – crystal blue with a dozen small clouds like the smoke from silent guns. She holds her damaged hand in her lap, feels out the joint, seizes it, pulls, twists, pulls again, then leans over the side of the boat to dry-vomit. When she has recovered, when the two or three big shudders are over, she goes below to the deranged cabin, finds a roll of electrician's tape and binds the reset finger to the finger beside it. In the daylight she can inspect the plug more thoroughly. The wood, saturated, has darkened and swelled (as it is intended to swell) and pressed itself into the pattern of the broken fitting. If water is coming in it's coming at the rate of a dripping tap. For now, at least, the boat is secure. No reason to turn back for the Azores. Certainly no reason to send out any kind of distress call.

She takes off her wet clothes, finds dry clothes, sits heavily on the starboard saloon bench, feels for the hair clip, slides it out of her hair and stares at it as if to make sure – she's drunk with tiredness – that it's not some figment, some invention out of the night's emergency.

For a few wild seconds she imagines fetching her phone from the pocket of her coastal jacket and calling the old priest, imagines it being possible, and her telling him what she has found and hearing him sigh (sitting up alone, not in the nice old vicarage in the village but a brick box on an estate in the town) and say, 'My dear, my dear, is there somewhere safer you could go?'

She sits there. She does not look pretty; she does not look easy to like. She's afraid, of course, but fear does not consume her. She spends a while trying to think of some plausible explanation as to how the clip came to be there, tucked away in the boat's flooded lungs. All she can come up with by way of an answer is her own foolishness in imagining she could sail free of anything. Isn't that one of the rules of running away? Never to assume that what you're running from isn't somehow ahead of you?

Someone like you comes to a bad end, said Henderson that night at the hotel, the wadded toilet paper against his cut head. What do people know in such moments? What do they see? Anything? And she remembers something else he said – not then, but during her interview for Fenniman's – a little phrase that must have been related to her work with Professor Kimber in Bristol. The wound's journey.

The wound's journey.

She sighs – sighs like an old woman who, in the dead of night, has started searching for something she cannot remember the name of, will never remember the name of. Then she sweeps everything from the bench onto the cabin sole and lies down, just as she is, the hair clip clutched to her chest, a fist that even in sleep does not soften.

4

The plug, the bung, is holding. Strange that something so simple – so cheap! – should work so well, but it does.

The boat sails on a broad reach, six knots according to the GPS screen, sometimes seven. In darkness, she cuts the line forty degrees west – a line that followed northwards would take her to the coast of Greenland. Followed south it would land her a few hundred miles from the mouth of the Amazon.

Her twenty-ninth night – a field of dry lightning in the sky ahead. It is miles away but she finds the handheld GPS and puts it in the oven in case the boat is hit. A boat hit by lightning can lose all its electrics but an oven is supposed to function as a Faraday cage. A boat hit by lightning can also lose its keel bolts. About that there is nothing to be done.

The tap and press of water, the rustling of the sails, the boat's ceaseless small adjustments, her own movements, her own breath, her own thoughts, the voice of those thoughts.

The wind creeps up; she takes in sail. The boat is flying – a hundred and twenty, a hundred and thirty miles in a day.

Through the binoculars, a ship ploughing eastwards. Hard to see at first what kind of ship it is. Two smaller ships are following. They are slim and shadowy and fast. The bigger ship, she realizes, is an aircraft carrier. They are soon gone, and the sea is empty again. Perfectly empty.

Her reset finger is acutely sensitive. She seems to catch it with everything she does – cooking, washing, using a winch, coiling a rope, adjusting the Hydrovane. She makes a splint by splitting off the edge of a wooden ruler and taping it into place, a job that takes her half the morning. Rolling cigarettes requires a new technique (she rolls them on the chart table and leans down to lick the gum).

When the pain is troublesome or if it keeps her from sleeping, she cuts a tab of Fennidine in half, swallows it with tea or water. Sometimes a sip of rum.

The weather is becoming hard to guess. The Navtex is out of range; the long-wave radio does not offer reports for the mid-Atlantic. If she sees a ship she could call on the VHF for a forecast but other than the aircraft carrier and its escort she has not seen anything in nearly a week. She should have an SSB on board or a satellite phone, but she has her barometer, her book of clouds, her eyes. She tells herself that others have managed before her and that she too will manage. She recalls to herself sometimes the fact that people have rowed across the Atlantic in open boats.

*   *   *

On deck, making her rounds, dead centre of the night, she grips the starboard shroud and looks up at high cloud scudding across a hazy moon. The next morning, a fine slanting rain begins, light but relentless. She is glad of it at first and stands bareheaded to have it wash the salt out of her hair. Then it starts to bother her, to make her restless. It goes on all day, patient and unceasing. In the night, two hours into sleep, she's roused by the sound of something flogging on the deck and goes up with the torch. As soon as she is outside she's aware of how the wind has strengthened. It's getting under the inflatable on the foredeck, lifting it and dropping it down. She spends forty minutes redoing the lashings. She could have done it in half the time but she's using one hand and her teeth. Only when she has finished does she realize she's not wearing her harness, is not clipped on.

Below deck she wipes her face dry with a tea cloth. The barometer is down a point and she decides to tidy things away, put things in their proper places, secure the lockers, clear the galley. Instead she sits down and reads two pages of the *Dhammapada*, sees a note in the margin, presumably written by Gosse, and spends several minutes trying to decide if it says *Doctrinal* or *Doctor's at 1*. Then she puts the book down and goes out to do what she should have done the last time. She furls the jib to something like a fifth of its full size, takes in two reefs' worth of the mainsail, does it all clearly, cleanly, robotically, then slithers back into the cabin, glistening with the wet and making, with each action, a little grunt of effort. She lifts a panel from the cabin sole to inspect the bung, replaces the panel, and is glancing round for her tobacco when the boat lurches and she ends on her back in a comical tangle between the saloon table and the port-side bench. She's not hurt; bruised perhaps but not hurt. She gets her boots off, hangs her jacket to drip in the heads, gets up into the quarter berth and is asleep within seconds.

For an hour the sea rolls her but cannot wake her. When she does wake there's a grey light in the cabin. White water and darker water are swirling past the port-side windows. She can read the anemometer from where she is lying. Thirty knots, gusting thirty-five. She gets up and goes in a series of short, staggered vectors to look at the barometer. It's down to a thousand millibars. She taps it, hard, but the reading is steady. She puts on her salopettes, her jacket, her boots, her harness, and gets out through the hatch. The rising sun is unobscured but to the north there is a wall of cloud that appears to grow directly out of the sea – brown, purple, at its base a luminous soaked black.

Statistically, this should not be happening. In September perhaps, the height of the storm season, but not in June.

The swell is shorter, steeper. Much steeper. At each crest she has a view that stretches for miles; in the troughs she is hemmed in by water. She needs to make a decision but puts it off for an hour, sitting below smoking and nibbling biscuits, then comes up to see the port-side toe rail under the water, water streaming along the deck like molten glass, and decides to run south, have the sea behind her, the sea, the wind and whatever the wind is bringing.

She disengages the Hydrovane and takes the tiller. She brings the bows down to 110. She is worried the boat will gybe but she has the mainsheet in tight – the boom would not have much of an arc to swing through. The jib, in the shadow of the main, starts to flap. She ignores it.

Now that she is running, the movement is easier. She is pitching rather than yawing, the seas plunging under her stern, accelerating her, then leaving her to slide into the trough. She helms for an hour then reconnects the Hydrovane, spends twenty minutes playing with the angle of the vane before she decides she can trust it. She goes below. Out of the wind, out of the worst of the noise, she stands on braced legs at the chart table, stares at the chart, the GPS, shuts her eyes and sleeps for several seconds before waking to the sound of water shooting through the ventilation slats in the washboard.

She's trying to remember everything she knows about riding out a gale. She has, at least, no shortage of sea room – better to face this out here than in the whipping tides of the English Channel, some lee shore becoming invisible in the haze. She tries the radio, picks up, very faintly, an orchestra playing music she would guess was either Korean or Chinese, Indian perhaps. Then a voice in a language she thinks belongs to some ex-Soviet state, a woman's voice speaking with great sobriety as if announcing the demise of the president, the fall of a city. She switches it off and kneels on the cabin floor, groping in a food locker. The kettle launches itself from the galley and bounces off the table by her head before disappearing through the opening to the forecabin. She finds a can of baked beans, peels off the lid, gets a spoon and eats them cold, the whole can, tomato sauce on her fingers, her chin, her jacket. She's briefly nauseous, then better. She would like something hot to drink but it is not safe now to have boiling water down here and she would need first to find the kettle. She spends quarter of an hour rolling a cigarette then sits at the bottom of the steps to smoke it, one booted foot against the chart table to keep herself in place. There is no restful space. As the boat is struck by the seas, so she is struck by the boat.

A new unpredictability has entered the boat's movements. It is, she realizes, starting to surf, and a boat that surfs is not under control. She turns up the collar of her jacket (it is not the most expensive model, not the one she needs now), tapes shut the Velcro bindings and climbs the companionway steps. The moment her head is above the hatch the wind opens her mouth, pushes at the lids of her eyes. She clips on, squirms her way into the cockpit, draws the hatch tight shut and stands with her back against the washboards squinting through the tunnel of her hands at the cloud wall behind her, the storm wall that has blotted out half the sky and is now closing on her at a rate she cannot possibly outrun.

She turns to the sails; the boat is over-canvassed, that much is obvious. Somehow she must find a balance between maintaining steerage and keeping the boat from overreaching itself. She wants the storm jib up. The storm jib is a good strong sail but it's stowed in the forecabin and she cannot risk opening the forehatch and having the sea plunge through it. She will have to bring it out through the cockpit, take it forwards. She stands there a moment, gathering the wherewithal, then unclips herself, drops back through the hatchway – waits – feels the movement of the boat, runs down through the saloon and arrives in the forecabin in time to brace against the impact at the base of the wave. The storm jib bag is small but heavy. Getting it out through the cockpit hatchway, dragging it, thrusting it ahead of herself, the cabin rearing around her, is a dumb-show of gross effort.

In the cockpit she clips to the central jackstay and works her way forward a yard at a time until she is sitting on the foredeck, her boots by the pulpit rail. She starts to pull the sail from its bag. A kindly hand has written in black indelible marker which corner of the sail is which. She shackles the tack to the base of the spare stay then hanks on until she reaches the head. Every thirty seconds the sea sweeps over her legs. Water forces itself up the inside of her salopettes, forces itself under her jacket, down the back of her salopettes. She crawls to the mast, drops the remains of the mainsail, binds it with bungees, then bangs her shoulders against the mast while she finds a halyard for the storm jib. She uncleats the halyard, slithers back to the jib, undoes the halyard shackle with the marlinspike she once gave to Tim as a present but which later, somehow, became her marlinspike. She attaches the head of the jib, frees the sheets from the furling jib, reties the bowlins through the clew of the storm jib, hoists the jib from the mast, regains the cockpit, sheets in the jib, cleats it, and sits on the grid of the cockpit sole, her chest heaving, her clothes soaked through.

She's cold; she needs dry clothes, but the thought of trying to undress and dress in the confusion below makes her hang on in a blood warm, blood cold huddle. Thoughts arrive; none of them are about boats and the sea. When at last she moves, her limbs are stiff, slow to react to the boat's bucking. A dozen times on her way down she is thrown against some unforgiving edge but she makes no sound or nothing you might hear above the wind. When she tries to get out of her clothes they cling to her. She scrapes them from herself, leaves them where they fall, tugs dry clothes from the holdall in the locker under the chart table, climbs into them while clinging to whatever will take her weight, puts on her salopettes again, her heavy jacket. She looks for her hat, her beanie, wants it very much and spends a crazed quarter-hour searching for it and fending off the cabin before remembering the hat is in the pocket of her jacket.

The light outside is a dusk light, though it is the storm's dark rather than the day's. She clips on and looks down the length of the boat. She watches the bows. With each descent they dig a little deeper, and each time they rise the whole boat shudders with the weight of the water. How far, how deep would the bows have to go before they could not struggle back and the whole boat sailed itself under the sea? This is not a fantasy; there are records of such things.

234

She disengages the Hydrovane and takes the tiller. At the crest of the next wave she puts the tiller over to come down the face of it at an angle. At the bottom she straightens up, takes the sea under the stern. She's never had to do this before – it's pure theory – but the bows are drier and the boat feels a little safer. As for how long she can keep it up she doesn't know. It means timing things carefully; it means staying alert, watching for the wave that comes from a different angle. The wind shoves at her continually. She needs both hands around the tiller, and she cannot sit – she must see what is happening, must look down the long field of the wave, use all the strength of her belly to hold the rudder against its force.

She manages for the best part of two hours then gives it up – she has no choice. Her eyes are raw from salt and wind. Nor can she trust what she is seeing, not now when the difference between the last of the light and the first of the dark is so small. She will lash the tiller amidships, let the boat find its own angle to the wind, its own luck. And she has ducked down, searching in the shadows around her legs for a rope to lash with, when she hears her name, quite clearly shouted, and because it seems to come from behind her she unbends and looks back to see a wave bigger than any she has ever seen, a grey wall with a grey crest crumbling down its face like masonry, the whole thing apparently at right angles to the wind. She turns from it, flings her arms around the boom, locks her hands to her wrists. Three seconds later it comes aboard (this thing that carries its own unanswerable truth), smashes the air from her lungs, breaks her grip, lifts her, accelerates her, whips her against the wire of the starboard shroud and flings her into the sea.

The sea. The sea is ready for her. It spins her, rakes at her clothes, pushes at her mouth. She has no idea which way is up.

Her brain is lit with an entirely new light, pinkish, as if she were looking out through the meninges of her own skull. Then her line comes taut, she's hauled briefly into air, and as the boat heels towards her, the sea – those five square yards she's thrashing in – lifts her with strange exactness and she arches herself, extends herself like a dancer, hooks three fingers of her good hand through a grab rail and is raised up as the boat rights itself.

For a time – a bare minute perhaps – she clings to the ledge of deck, her face, the smacked flower of her mouth, pressed against one of the coach-house windows. Misjudge her next move and she will be in the sea again; she cannot hope to be so lucky a second time. She tries to guess from its movement how the boat is lying to the sea, decides it's beam on or thereabouts, waits for her side of the deck to swing up, then breaks cover and scrambles head first into the cockpit.

There's a foot of water in the cockpit, though as it must have been brimful after the wave it's evident the drain holes are clear and working.

She is sitting on rope. She gathers it, makes one end fast to a cleat on the side of the cockpit, puts the tiller amidships, takes three turns around it with the rope, and makes it off to the cleat on the far side. She gets to her knees, to her feet, looks forward. The mast is still there; what else is there or not there she cannot tell.

She pushes back the hatch and drops through it with black water following, closes the hatch and bolts it.

The temptation to creep into her berth, to go there just as she is in her layers of soaked gear, is almost overwhelming. Instead, she switches on the nightlight and starts to pump, bends herself blindly to it, the pain in her ribs – the wound she sustained going over the side – making her cry as she cried that time she caught her hand between the trailer and the dinghy, and Grandfather Ray hovered around her not knowing what to say or how to comfort such a creature, a hunched girl in her anorak getting her crying out of the way before standing, smudge-eyed, and wanting to get onto the water.

If nothing else, the pump is something to hold on to, and if she can keep the boat dry, if she can keep whatever water is inside it to manageable levels, then there is hope of coming through. She remembers what Robert Currey said, how all the boats were basically sound, that they would not suddenly go down, would not open up like the old wooden ships in the stories (some of which must be true) seam by rotten seam. But how many had been tested like this? On the anemometer the wind speed is moving between fifty-four and fifty-eight knots. She knows her Beaufort. Storm force ten, violent storm eleven.

How long can a storm last? It can last for days.

She stops pumping; and there is only a little water over the sole. She sits on the nearest bench, undresses with one hand. When she gets below her T-shirt she sees the rhubarb-coloured welts across her ribs, touches them, then pulls on what might be her last dry top, puts on the sea-blue jumper above it, puts on a pair of track-suit trousers, then the salopettes. One of her sea boots was left in the sea. She takes off the other and wedges her damp feet into her trainers.

As for food, there's food on the floor, an apple among other things that has been cannoning towards her, cannoning away, for the last ten minutes. She picks it up and bites it. It's salty, tastes of bruises, has grit on its skin. She eats it to a slender core, tosses the core towards the galley sink, misses. Also on the floor, the white box, TRIAL USE ONLY, its cardboard sodden but still somehow intact. She swallows two of the capsules with her own spit. (She has never taken two before but it was a dose they some-times discussed, and one Josh Fenniman himself was said to look favourably upon, a subject referred to in Reading as the 'high-end' question.)

The quarter berth is too wet to lie in. Water must have come down when the cockpit was flooded; the lockers must have flooded too, and leaked. She works her way back to the nearest bench. Under the seat is a triangular canvas lee-cloth. She pulls it out, hooks its eyes over the fittings on the cabin ceiling. The canvas smells ancient, smells like a scrap of sail from a ship-of-the-line in Admiral Shovell's time. With one hand gripping the handhold at the edge of the chart table, she climbs behind the cloth and onto the bench. The instant she is in she is thrown against the canvas so that her whole weight is on it. It does not split, the eyes do not unravel. A moment later she is being forced against the padded back of the seat.

It should not be possible to sleep with such violence but she shuts her eyes and for minutes together there is something very like sleep. The storm does not abate. The storm has resources beyond imagining. An hour after lying down she feels the wind veering and knows that out there in the dark a hammer is swinging.

Get up?

Do what?

She could trail warps.

She could put down oil (but she is not carrying enough oil).

She could start the engine, increase manoeuvrability, take the helm.

She is sick with tiredness. More tired than when the baby was born, infinitely more, but she cannot leave the boat to struggle on its own, cannot hide away down here in its belly. She starts to scrabble free of the bench, the lee-cloth – it's like Lazarus climbing

238

from his grave – and she is crouching by the side of the bench, waiting for her moment to cross to the companionway when she hears a noise she might have taken for the roaring of surf if she didn't know there was three thousand metres of water below her, the nearest land a thousand miles away. She waits but does not need to wait for long. The boat is struck on its starboard side, overwhelmed and flattened to the water. Maud somersaults across the table to the port-side bench, on top of her a rain of clothes, charts, books. The brass dividers like a throwing knife. They miss her, just.

At ninety degrees, the mast in the water, the boat pauses as if to play out some subtle reckoning of the forces, then goes on with its roll. The speed of its turning is like the sweep of a second hand on a clock: not fast, not slow. She is tipped onto the cabin ceiling, falls with everything that is free to fall with her. At one-eighty the boat stops again, keel to the sky (and what does *that* look like? To see it, even in a dream . . .). She fights her way upwards but up has become a confusing place and among those objects lying on her is the top of the saloon table that has freed itself from its gear and landed – three hinged leaves of oak – across her chest. She knows what's happening but knowing does not help. Nothing she does or does not do now will make the slightest difference. The boat begins to move again. It gives out some frantic sound of its own effort, slides from one-eighty to two hundred, snags again (Maud and all else spilling down the starboard bulkhead) then swings up and rears out of the sea as if revolted by its former state. This last quarter of the wheel is the most violent, the most difficult to defend against. Before, she was falling; now she is dropped, flung down. Her forehead misses the edge of the lower companionway step by perhaps two inches. The tabletop lands across her ankles. Her face is in a swill of water. When she can stand she is in the kind of darkness the eye immediately sketches shapes onto, outlines, faces, things that cannot be there. She finds the pump handle, clutches it with one hand and reaches around herself with the other. How much of the boat is still there? Cabin window. Cabin roof. The washboards, miraculously; the hatch apparently (though she can't quite reach it). If she could find the torch she could see what else is there, but the torch has taken flight with the rest and she is not sure she wants to see what it would show her. There is no glow from the VHF, no comforting light from any screen or dial.

She touches herself, frisks herself; she does not seem to have broken a limb, to be bleeding from anywhere obvious. Though she can see nothing, she can hear everything, but the sound she attends to above all others is the thudding on the hull, a noise like a giant fist beating drunkenly at the side of the boat not far from where she is standing. She knows what it is, or she can guess. She needs the bolt-cutters and the bolt-cutters are in the forepeak. She starts to grope her way through the saloon, something primitive and crazed in her movements, something insect-like in the way each time she is thrown off her path she immediately returns. And she has some luck. The heavy tools are where they should be and it is not difficult to feel out the cutters. Four, five times on her way back to the companionway she falls. She does not know what she's falling over, cannot see it. It doesn't matter. All that matters now is getting on deck.

She drags back the hatch but leaves in the washboards, slithers over them like an otter. In the cockpit she clips on, shuts the hatch, and on hands and knees makes her way along the deck. The mast has gone, or part of it has – she cannot see how much – but whatever was torn away is now hanging from the rigging and beating, with each roll of the boat, against a layer of fibreglass half the width of her thumbnail. Wire, rope, anything holding it to the boat must be cut through. It takes twenty minutes; it takes forever. Most of the work must be done lying down, her feet lodged against whatever she can find that still feels solid, the water breaking over her head again and again, her eyes burning from the salt. She cuts; she creeps forward. A last piece of wire – the starboard shroud? – and then she knows it's gone, feels it go, feels the sea suck it away.

She rises up: two quick strides put her back in the cockpit. She cowers there until the boat, lifting on the back of a wave, has a motion that is briefly predictable, then she opens the hatch, climbs down into the greater darkness, and shuts the hatch behind her. At the bottom of the steps she kicks away whatever is beneath her. She widens her stance, takes hold of the pump handle with both hands, and with a steady, an irrepressible rhythm, she starts to work it.

(Strength is weakness rearranged, a rope plaited from grass.)

5

For another fourteen hours the storm is undiminished. It drives the boat south, scatters it south like a leaf down an alley. All day she hides in the cabin waiting for something to give. She crouches, she clings on, she even sleeps a little. At dusk she goes on deck. To get the hatch open is an immense and exhausting struggle but she gets it open. The first thing she sees is that half of the mast and all of the standing rigging has gone. The boom has sheared off at the neck, the inflatable is gone, the life-raft canister. When she looks sternwards there is no sign of the steel goalposts with the solar panels, the aerials. The Hydrovane too, all of it, gone without a trace.

The wind is no more than a five now, a stiff breeze, but the seas are still big, each wave, if it came aboard, if it broke over the boat, capable of doing more damage, of finishing it perhaps. Somehow the boat is riding them – the stubbornness of form, the clever lines, the clever men who built her.

She goes below, closes the hatch. She drinks from the galley tap, staggers about scavenging for food, finds shattered jars, burst containers, floating vegetables. There's a Dundee cake wedged behind the stove chimney. She breaks off a fistful and eats it. She thinks of the life raft and whether, torn from the deck, it inflated, as it should have. Whether it is out there now, already many miles away, a life raft traceable to the boat. Empty.

She sleeps behind the lee-cloth. When she comes to, the light through the salt-greasy windows illuminates a disorder that can only be thought of as total. Even the little fridge is face down at the far end of the cabin.

On deck the sun is high, blinding. She is dressed in her heavy-weather gear still. She sits on the cockpit seat like an actor who has wandered off the set to smoke a cigarette. The movement of the sea has changed, the swell, in foaming green fractals, slower and more regular. She is hot from the sun, hot from fever too perhaps. She gets her jacket off. The clothes below have dried onto her, or almost dried. She strips down until her top half is bare to the wind and sun, her lower half still swathed in Neoprene. The skin of her arms, breasts and belly is dead white. There are fewer bruises than she expected. The worst is around her ribs – her whole flank starting to flower. She puts her T-shirt on, pulls up the braces on her salopettes. She already knows the main GPS is dead, has tried it twenty times and got nothing, but the hand-held is down there somewhere and she goes below to search for it. During the search she finds other things that are useful – the tin opener, her Green River knife, a pouch of tobacco still in its cellophane – but the handheld has disappeared and she is wondering, in her fevered state, if it could somehow have fallen out of the cabin and over the side, when she opens the door of the oven and finds it where she left it the night she saw the lightning.

Hard to believe it could still function after the battering it must have taken but when she turns it on it vibrates in her hand, lights up. She takes it to the cockpit, shades the screen, peers at it and reads off the co-ordinates, reads them aloud.

'North zero five one. West zero zero two.'

She switches it off, switches it on again, reads off the same figures. North zero five one. West zero zero two. She knows those co-ordinates, she doesn't need to look on any chart. If she plotted them the dot would sit over the cottage in Dorset. Some sort of reset? Did she test it once at the cottage? Did Tim? She reboots it, several times; nothing changes. She turns it off, puts it in the thigh pocket of her salopettes, looks up with narrowed eyes at the perfect wilderness around her. At least the binnacle compass seems trustworthy (not much in there to break – inch-thick glass, a card, some manner of alcohol). It shows a heading just west of south. Since the storm's beginning she may have travelled several hundred miles in that direction. She tries the engine. The starter battery is flat. She tries wiring in one of the other batteries but in the capsize they were flung from their mountings and have, apparently, discharged in the water on the cabin floor. One of them produces a flicker of light in the ignition indicator but the engine remains silent. And even if she could get the charge she needs, the engine itself must be full of water, the fuel lines clogged with sediment from the tank.

For a long time she tries to puzzle out how to jury-rig a sail. Has someone explained it to her? Has she read about it? One of those ingenious Frenchmen for example, part engineer, part poet, who, in the dead centre of the Pacific, rebuilds his boat out of its own ruins . . .

She has twelve feet of mast, possibly more. The first thing is to secure it with some rigging and she starts to collect, out of the sail locker, the cockpit lockers, whatever she has left in the way of sheets and halyards and spare blocks. The deck is far from steady but she judges it steady enough to work on. She does not bother with a harness and line though it is not many days since these saved her life.

With a pencil, on the back flyleaf of the *Dhammapada*, she makes a sketch of what she needs to do, then she goes to the mast, rope slung like a bandolier across her shoulder. She secures the mooring steps (they're metal, lightweight, telescopic) to the base of the mast and goes up until she can reach the top of the stump. First she makes the backstays with a pair of red Dyneema sheets, running them back to the cockpit and taking up the slack on the winches. Next, she ties on a brand new thirty-metre rope and leads it forward and under the through-pin of the samson post, sweats it until it's as taut as her weight and strength can make it, makes it off on the post, goes back to the cockpit to take another turn on the winches.

The sun is reddening the back of her neck. She loses herself for a moment, sways, recovers, and goes up the mooring steps with a block, attaches it to the top of the stump with wire lashed in place with shock cord and an entire roll of two-inch-wide plastic tape. She threads a polyester halyard through the block, secures one end to the cleat at the base of the mast. The other end has a Wichard snap shackle spliced into it. This will take the head of the sail.

From its locker she drags out Gosse's old number four jib, thrusts it out through the forehatch, cannot, in her condition, haul herself out after it, and goes out through the main hatch. She attaches the shackle, ties on a sheet at the clew, raises the sail and makes it off at the big wooden cleat behind the tiller. The wind is light – the storm's echo, ghost winds. The sail is her attempt at a trysail. It looks, she thinks, like the laundry of the poor, but it fills, briefly, and the boat slides forward. If the wind stays light then the rig is feasible; if it strengthens then the number four jib will join the other debris she has left across an arc of ocean. All this is the work of many hours. It is the best she can do. It is all she can do.

Four or five times a day, she pumps the bilges. Everything, even survival – especially survival – has its routines.

The wooden bung in the broken fitting is still secure, but water is seeping in from somewhere else, probably from several places. She should, ideally, work the pump once an hour, and would do if she had the strength. She makes herself eat but cannot always keep the food down. To do more than lie for hours in the shade of the sail requires a doggedness that each time is a little harder to summon.

In the sea during the day, clumps of sargasso weed, the blue shadows of dorados, triggerfish. In the sea at night, globes of drifting light like the wax in a lava lamp. Dinoflagellates, cope-pods. Struck by the boat they break, swirl past, reform.

She uses stars, dead reckoning and the colour of the sea to esti-mate her position. She is close to the equator, perhaps south of it already. She has seen the Southern Cross but can still see northern stars.

The chart, stained, frayed, beginning to split apart, is folded to show an area of ocean and land that includes Suriname, French Guiana, the shoulder of Brazil. At the centre of her square is the Vema Fracture Zone. She is, she believes, somewhere on that square.

*　　*　　*

The things the sea carries to her. An object off her port bow she thought at first must be a creature of some sort, something sleeping in the water, a dolphin, a pilot whale. She even thinks of the seals she has seen sleeping in the mouths of certain bays, at the edges of loughs. It turns out to be a suitcase, and though she might have guessed herself to be beyond curiosity, the effort of it, she catches the case's handle with the boat hook (the boat hook that has survived everything), hauls it into the cockpit and sits, hugging her ribs, panting, and looking at it, a suitcase, bronze-coloured, quite new and not, it seems, much damaged by the sea. It has an Air France label on it and a name, illegible other than for the initial R.

She assumes the case will be locked but it isn't. She assumes the contents will be heavy with water but that too turns out to be wrong. She leans over it, the open case with its quilted, silvery lining, reaches down to touch a white shirt still neatly folded. There's a hesitancy to her touching, as if the shirt were not merely a stranger's possession but the stranger himself (she who has no history of making the first move). A white shirt, only slightly damp, and beneath it two more, then a black jacket with black satin lapels, black trousers, a man's underwear, several pairs of thin black socks.

There's a wash bag of fake leather with half a dozen disposable razors inside, a brand of toothpaste called *Sorriso*, a condom, a tube of cream that, from its listed contents, is for the treatment of a chronic skin condition.

A phrase book, French to Portuguese.

Two novels, one in English, the other in Spanish, though after a moment she realizes it's the same novel – *The Last Adventure of Sanchez Coello, Conquistador/La última aventura del conquistador Sanchez Coello.*

247

Tucked beside the books is a box of *Garoto* chocolates; also a copy of the *International Herald Tribune*, the date of the paper the day after she sailed from England ('76 Feared Dead in South African Goldmine').

One of the hip pockets of the jacket has a small religious medal in it and three used tickets for the Paris Metro. The other pocket is full of red petals from some large, possibly tropical flower. She holds the petals in her hand, dazzled by their colour, and when she pours them back into the pocket (its opening dark and moist as a mouth) they leave a faint red stain on her palm.

During the night the boat passes more cases – big ones, small ones, some with stout buckles, some wrapped entirely in layers of plastic film. She does not see them. She is asleep, splayed to the cooler air, her split lips parted, dreaming of someone called Sanchez Coello, conquistador in a tuxedo, dragging the petals from the heads of flowers as he passes them . . .

She has been at sea for forty days. She does not go below more than she needs to; below is hotter than above, and below the shadows loll, heap up in a nook or hang suggestively in the narrow places. She goes down to drink water from the galley, to forage in the lockers for unspoiled food, to pump the bilges. In the mornings there's always an inch or two of sea water over the cabin sole. She is almost used to it, the water pearly dark and cool around her bare feet.

She notes the sharpness of her joints, the rising bone, her breasts like a twelve-year-old's, the thin brown hardness of her thighs. It does not alarm her. She has been alive long enough to know that women's bodies are endlessly plastic, can remember herself in her third trimester, a ripeness that had a kind of violence at the back of it. And now she is turning into wood like one of those nymphs Tim told her about, daughters of river gods running for their lives through the forest. She does not remember their names. The stories were as dense and strange as anything she ever told him about eukaryotic genes, monoclonal antibodies, catalysis. When she asked him if such stories had a purpose, he said yes, yes of course, but he could not tell her what it was. Just grinned. Wanted to kiss her.

Forty-third day. The water tank is empty. Yesterday a flow, a lace of water, today nothing. She counts the bottles of water. Several burst their skins in the capsize. There are six left, each containing a litre and a half. She wraps each one in a piece of clothing, stores them in a locker where no sharp edge can find them.

In the night a flying fish lands on the deck. She hears it floundering about in the cockpit. She gets up and kills it. In the morning she cuts off its wings, guts it and cuts two pink-white fillets from it. Though she has gas she does not trust the connections and does not want to blow up the boat. She makes sashimi, throws the remains over the side where some larger fish, a small shark perhaps, immediately seizes it. To finish her meal she eats some of the sweets from the yellow box in the suitcase. There are various kinds. Her favourite is called *Serenida de Amor*. Of the others, she likes one that tastes of hazelnuts and is called *Surreal*.

Half an hour after eating all this she throws up over the stern.

How everything is terribly fragile. A girl at school, for example, who came off her push bike and knocked her head, a bruise no bigger than a primrose, no blood. She lay a month in a coma then died.

How everything is insanely strong. Those men and women she has come across in her work, children too, who lie on their beds or sit on their tall chairs with eyes wide and wild as if receiving unbearable news from distant galaxies. And that film she was shown in the Radcliffe – something made in the 1960s when science had not entirely given up on the freak show – a man whose skin was so sensitive to any impression, any touch, the technician could make him writhe with the gliding tip of a feather. But such people survive. They cut up their food and live for years.

Forty-sixth day. She wakes in the late afternoon from a long drowsing on the foredeck to find herself looking at distant clouds. The clouds are new. A line of them, white, blue white, stretching down the western horizon. She looks at them with that all-her-life animal talent for looking, that composed and hunkered gazing that seems to be the nub of her, the thing she is burning back to. Then she makes herself look down. When she looks up the clouds are still there. Three hours of this – a sort of game. Looking, turning away. Then the clouds flush red, ignite, fade to blue. Night falls with that suddenness she is not yet accustomed to. No moon rises. The boat creeps forward, the water hisses. She lays her head on a pillow of rope and is woken hours later by a breeze crackling the sail. She turns to the sky. Rain, like the sudden spilling of small coins. She strips off. She opens her mouth. In two minutes the rain is over but her grey shadow glistens and her mouth tastes of something miraculous. She sits up. She is almost cold and relishes it. By instinct she turns to the west again. There is a light there now, a spark at the edge of the night, a light trembling with distance.

A setting star? But she knows at once it is not a star.

A ship? Then why does the bearing not change?

If the light is on land then there are certain calculations to be made. Height of observer above the water; height of the light observed. She does not know the height of the light. On the shore? The top of a cliff? In the end it is nothing but a guess. The light, she decides, is twenty miles away. Twenty nautical miles or less. At the speed she is making (the speed she thinks she is making) that's ten hours of sailing, of drifting.

Long before sunrise she loses the light, but by the middle of the morning the clouds are back and two hours later she sees through the Zeiss an uneven black line beneath the clouds, the kind of line a young child might draw across a sheet of paper spread out on the floor, the beginning of something but not something yet, just a line heading out, its tip a point containing everything.

She lowers the binoculars, closes her eyes. 'Where have you brought me?' she asks, her voice a rasp. She feels no heavier than a blade of grass; a puff of wind could send her spinning over the water. She creeps below, opens the last can of fruit, sits in the dark of the cabin with it, water swilling over her feet. When she's finished with the can she simply drops it.

She could take the tiller now but the current and a south-east breeze is slowly bringing her in. Sooner or later a coaster will appear, a fishing boat, a Customs launch. Perhaps they have seen her already, the good people of Progreso, of Île-à-Vache, but when she scans the shore she can make out no houses or boats, no smoke, no glitter of glass.

By late afternoon she is heading towards a scatter of small steep islands half a mile from the mainland. She does not want to be among those islands in darkness. She fetches the crash bag, brings it up on deck, checks on the flares, the Lumica light sticks, the torch. She has, at most, another three hours of daylight.

Through the binoculars she watches birds wheeling about the peaks of the islands, how they slide from the sheer edges of the rock in silent avalanches, fall towards the surface of the sea then, with two or three powerful beats of their wings, rise again.

The smell of land! Like putting down your window on the motorway at night after rain. Breathing in, deeply.

She passes the islands, slides past close enough to hear the birds, their endless calling. Under the hull a network of local currents is edging her ever nearer to the shore. The water is green and perfectly clear. She lies on the foredeck and stares down, sees the shadows of fish, the shadows of small rocks. The boat has a draft of just under six feet. She waits for the first touch. When it comes – this boat, this keel that has sailed above canyons – it is very gentle. A slight checking of its motion, then afloat again, then a second contact, more certain. The bows swing; the boat dips towards the shore. She drops the plough anchor over the leeward side, lets go all the chain she has. From below she fetches her phone, a few clothes, a half-full packet of raisins, her passport, her wallet. The little hair clip, the heart of tin, which she has kept safely in a zipped pouch in the wallet, she threads onto a length of shock cord and ties the cord with a double knot around her neck.

In the cockpit she steps over the stranger's suitcase (it's bone dry now and dull like a pebble brought home from the beach). She lowers the makeshift sail, bundles it. The day is settling into its short twilight; the boat's keel growls on the sand. She puts on her trainers, ties one of the straps of the crash bag to her wrist, looks about herself as if, surely, she has forgotten something, then sits in her shorts and T-shirt, feet dangling a little way above the water. She remains there for several minutes staring at the shore, the low bluff of red rock, the curtain of trees above it. No one appears. There is nothing, to the naked eye, to suggest anyone has ever set foot there before. She eases herself down into the water. It is awkward to swim with the bag, with the pain in her ribs, but soon she can feel the ridged sand below her and she wades ashore, spilling the sea from her shoulders, then her belly, then her knees, until she is standing on the beach in the land's shadow, the water behind her lit like coals, the boat crouched like a thing at prayer.

FIVE

I hope you will forgive me if I use the word 'truth'. The moment I say 'truth' I expect people to ask 'what is truth?' 'Does truth exist?'. Let us imagine that it exists. The word exists, therefore the feeling exists.

Hélène Cixous

1

She climbs the scarp – red rock and shadow. She is not steady on her feet. The land has no give in it, cannot be trodden upon as the sea could.

At the top she sits to catch her breath. In fifteen minutes she has walked further than she has in weeks. The air is warm, the moon rising out of the sea with a face of finely meshed gold, a soft and intricate moon, but bright enough for her to make out a landscape of bare grey trees, darker bushes, the suggestion of low hills in the distance. With the binoculars she scans for a light, perhaps the one she saw from the boat, but there is nothing, and nothing to tell her the direction she should take – no path, no signs, only the scarp and the grey trees, the moon creeping out of the sea.

She decides to keep to the coast if she can, and as the way looks slightly clearer in one direction than the other she turns left – south – and walks the fringe of open ground at the top of the scarp until the trees press her to the edge and she is forced to turn inland. The moon is higher now and in its light the tops of the grey trees have become silver, the ground below them bare, dark, uneven. Often she has to shift her route where the scrub rises up in a black fence directly ahead of her, and once, brushing against the edge of one of these thickets, she feels something slice the skin of her arm with the ease of a razor. After this she is more careful.

She hears the singing of insects, though the place where she is moving is always quieter, the singing always at a distance. She's land sick, heavy on her feet, but keeps up a steady pace, her shadow crossing bones of moonlight, then lost for a moment in something darker than herself, then out into moonlight again.

She startles a bird. It passes close in front of her face with an angry beating of wings and she stumbles backwards, loses her balance and falls. When she gets up she is unsure of her bearings. Which way is the coast? Which way was she headed? She digs out the compass from her pack. The luminous tip of the needle wavers delicately. She finds herself, heads off again, swimming between the silver trees, following paths more imagined than real, the trees and the light laying themselves down in patterns on her brain, a game of minimal differences, a kaleidoscope of moonlit branches that ends with such abruptness she teeters and rocks on her heels as if at the edge of a precipice. In fact, she's standing at the edge of a road, or if not a road then a track of packed earth but certainly wide enough to take a car. She finds her torch, shines it both ways, then shines it by her feet, looking for tyre prints, and thinks she can see some though it's hard to be sure. Again, she must decide on a direction. Again she chooses left.

On the track she goes more quickly, feels safer, more certain of finding help, and soon. Either side of her is the same scrub and bare trees she walked through from the scarp but ahead of her, surely, even if she has to walk all night, there will be a farm, a settlement, the edge of a city perhaps, and she pictures herself (she's half asleep in the monotony, the rhythm of her walking) passing suburban gardens, silent roundabouts, traffic lights signalling to no one.

The moon is overhead now, its light pixellating the air, the uncertain distance. She pauses to drink some of her water, to eat some of the raisins, then puts the pack on and sets off, last woman on earth, first woman on earth, her shadow rippling over the dust of the track, her feet in her trainers making a dull sound, a soft sound, surprisingly soft. Another hour of this, then another, burrowing into the silence of the night, the night's outrageous amplitude, her nose full of the scent of whatever is growing at the side of the track. Slowly – or she is slow to notice it – the land to her right is altering. The silver trees are thinning out; then they have gone entirely and in their place there are palm trees, very tall, gently curved, their heads sparked with moonlight, the ground below them splashed with each tree's starburst of shadow.

She wanders into the midst of them; it's difficult not to. Are they coconut palms or some other kind? Does someone harvest them? They do not look to have grown randomly but to stand in rows. She takes out the torch again, shines it around her, the beam breaking on the trunks of the trees. When she puts it off she's blind. She considers letting off a flare – she has two in her bag and someone might see. Instead, she squats at the base of the nearest tree. The air is still warm. The blood thuds in her head and seems to mimic the beat of her walking. She drinks some water then lies down, pillowing her head on the pack. The ground smells like a spice but when she shuts her eyes it is the sea that appears to her, grey, green-grey and endless. She sleeps, dreamlessly, the fronds high above her sometimes making a noise like rain though no rain falls.

*　　*　　*

In the early morning, uncoiling from the base of the tree, she looks about herself, the grove, the visible world, its colours bleeding through the muted air – the red of the earth, the tattered green of the palm fronds, some bird threading the grove, a blur of living yellow.

The ground is cracked, almost grassless, and not, as she might have hoped, strewn with fallen coconuts, though the trees have some sort of fruit, high up and well out of reach. She eats a handful of raisins, drinks more of her water, then walks about the grove hoping to find a building of some sort, or failing that, a wall, a fence, a fresh track, something – anything – with writing on it. She finds nothing except the blackened remains of a fire with an empty fire-blackened tin at the edge of it in which a large insect is living. She returns to the track. For the first hour she is listening for the engine note of a truck, a car. After that she just walks, her trainers red with dust, her shadow shortening, the light starting to dazzle so that for long periods she keeps her eyes lowered to the surface of the track. There is no shade. She thinks of the hats on the boat, Gosse's hat, her own. She takes sips of water, falls prey to the idea she is walking in circles, then lies down in the shade through the worst of the heat and sets off again in the mid-afternoon. Her watch says nine o'clock; her watch is useless to her. As the day cools, the whiteness of the sky settles to blue. A half-dozen clouds appear though none obscure the sun, even for a moment.

On the right-hand side of the track there are cacti, some as tall as two men. On the other side, and for some time now, she has been walking next to bushes of small yellow flowers, and beyond these the vegetation is denser and greener, the bare trees replaced by trees with broad leaves that reflect the light like green mirrors.

She longs for the sheltering dark, the cool of the night. She keeps going because the track keeps going and because stopping feels like the harder choice, certainly the more dangerous one. The gathered heat of the day radiates from the track and comes up to her in warm gulps.

With the dusk, bats appear – frantic dartings at the edge of sight. A beetle whirrs across the air in front of her. A moth, large as a saucer, settles for a second on her shoulder, from each wing a false eye staring. And there – at last! – the moon, moving through the upper branches of the trees then rolling clear into a sky that's briefly green, then ten different blues with black at the back of them.

Again, she has that stubborn fantasy of arriving at the edge of a town, a city, with its subways waiting patiently for the first train of the morning, but it's a fantasy thin as celluloid. The rest of her is head down and head deep in the actual, in red dust and moonlight, in the tide of her own breathing.

And then – like an entirely unexpected move in a game you thought you were starting to understand – the track divides. It's the first thing that has frightened her. One way curves into the bare country on her right, the other enters the woodland, the green place to her left. Each path is of a similar width. There is of course no post or sign. Or perhaps there is a sign, for *something* is there, at the tip of the island where the ways divide, but sunk in such deep shadow she has to go close – close enough to smell it – before she understands what it is. A cow's dry hide, propped up on a maquette of sticks, the long skull (she's turned her torch on it now) growing through the skin, a thing transitioning, a thing leaving itself behind.

She chooses left again – isn't that how you find your way out of a maze, always turning in the same direction? After twenty yards she's under the canopy of the trees. This way, she decides, will lead her back to the coast. She should not have allowed herself to lose sight of it, to become lost in palm groves, to walk on a track that leads nowhere. She thinks of the boat, of how much she wants to see it again, the thing that almost killed her, the thing that saved her. Was it still there? Or had it dragged its chain and drifted into deeper water, an unlit boat wallowing off the coast, a menace to navigation?

She tries to work out how many hours she's been walking since the palm grove. Ten? Twelve? She trips over roots, walks several paces at a time with her eyes shut. Twice, she wanders off the track entirely and has to find her way back (there are cells in the hippocampus that help her to do this).

In the treetops and at ground level she hears the movement of small creatures, or creatures she prefers to picture as small. She hears – a bare yard away! – something climb on quick claws the trunk of the tree she is passing. Then the track enters a clearing and she looks up to see stars, the freewheeling night, a patch of it at least, its edges like cut paper where it meets the leaves and branches of the trees. She sinks down into the rough grass, gets the pack off her back, lies down and draws up her knees. Certain tedious songs are playing in her head, the kind children are supposed to like and perhaps do. Part of her is still working on a plan; most of her suspects the time for plans is over. She cannot move a finger. She is pressed to the ground, crushed to it. The life of the forest, its ten thousand separate sounds, pass through her unencumbered . . .

At the edge of the clearing a sleek head slides past the wall of tangled black. Eyes that do not flinch, that do not waver, take in the shape of the sleeping woman. Nostrils quiver. The forest holds its breath. Then the head withdraws and the surface of the forest closes over it like water.

*   *   *

When she wakes there are butterflies overhead, and on her leg a centipede long and thick as a pencil. She flicks it off, examines the rash it has left behind, then forgets her leg and looks at the car. The forest has tried to tidy it away so it looks like a car that might have appeared on a 1970s album cover, the unmistakeable shape of a car but bound with vines and tendrils and studded with large red flowers. She crosses the clearing towards it. She is not so confused, so far gone, that she does not know some things are unreal. Close to, however, it's real enough. She feels the sun-reflecting heat of its metal, sees the light ripple on the windscreen – there's even an aerial, neatly wound with some delicate climbing plant. She walks around it. It's a long car, an estate of some sort, a shooting-brake, long and low. Beneath the greenery the sides of the car are a sort of mock wood or, examined more carefully, real wood. There's no hope of getting any of the doors open, not without a half-hour of sawing at stems, some of them as thick as her thumb.

She parts the curtain of leaves by the driver's door. The glass has its own ecology, a fur of green – a type of lichen? – and she rubs some of it away with the heel of her hand, puts her face close and peers inside. Whatever has happened to the outside of the car, the interior seems untouched, or just to be changing more slowly. There's a steering wheel bound in what looks like padded maroon leather, red trim on the doors, broad seats of a paler colour. A radio, an open ashtray. A key in the ignition, a second key dangling from it. Bench seats, and on the passenger side a pack of cigarettes and Zippo lighter, a flag on the side of the lighter which, pressing herself to the glass, she identifies as the flag of the Confederacy. A fine dust over everything, everything sleeping in the red shade of the trim, the green shade of the creepers. When she circles the car again (studying it like a prospective buyer) she finds the part-devoured remnants of a bumper sticker that reads *DO YOU FOLLOW JESUS THIS CLOSE?*

She wants the car to tell her something. Someone must have driven it to this place. Did they come down the track she walked yesterday? Or up the track, the way she will have to go today if she is not to retrace her steps? But the car is facing neither one way nor the other. The car is parked. It has no clear message, offers her no clue. As for who drove it there, where did they go? Where *is* there to go?

She returns for the bag. There are only two or three mouthfuls of water left, perhaps a fifth of a pint. She drinks, screws on the top, eats the last of the raisins, put the bag on her back, the straps immediately finding yesterday's rawness. The rash on her leg is swelling. She can also feel she has been bitten on the face – mosquito bites, or one of the other insects that thickened the air above her as she slept.

She stops in front of the car again. It is, she now realizes, a tomb of some sort, albeit an apparently empty one. The scent of the red flowers is not sweet, nor are the flowers themselves pretty. They sit with their large petals open in a mime of exhaustion and make her think of those carnivorous plants that close at a touch, though above them a score of yellow butterflies (not the yellow of English brimstones but as if cut from yellow card or scraped from an old yellow-painted wall) drift on the car's thermals and do not look threatened. She takes her leave of it, walks backwards for several steps, then turns and enters the shade of the track, its curving descent between the trees. It must be possible to find food in such a place – berries, roots, leaves, types of fungus – and throughout the morning, the first hours of walking, she breaks things off, scrapes things between her teeth, begins, in a small way, to eat the forest.

At noon – call it noon – the light plunging through gaps in the canopy, she hears the whooping of monkeys and going closer looks up to see a crowd of them on a tree whose bark is mottled like a eucalyptus, but on this tree there are clusters of black fruit the size of ping-pong balls growing directly on the trunk in a way she has never seen before. There's a term for it, this sort of growth, but she cannot remember now what it is. The monkeys are eating the fruit, feasting on it, and though they scream at her and bare their gums, she shrugs off her pack and climbs into the lower boughs, picks the fruit and breaks the skin with her teeth. Inside is a veined, milky pulp, sweet as a grape. She spits out the seeds, then takes off her T-shirt and makes a bag of it, fills it with the fruit and clambers down to sit at the base of the tree, ignoring the monkeys' rage and pressing the fruit, one after the other, against her teeth and tongue. She puts the remaining fruit into her pack, puts on her T-shirt and starts to walk again. A large green bird flies down the track. It carries the light on its back. It's like learning green for the first time.

She has gone no more than five hundred yards when she is seized with stomach cramps and squats at the side of the track gasping and emptying herself, then goes on for a while in a waking nightmare in which the car, riding its heavy suspension, is coming down the track behind her, coming very slowly yet closing on her all the time. But the mood, the fear, ebbs away, and something else begins, some fresh effect of exhaustion, of the black fruit perhaps, and she walks as if gliding, without effort, without pain. 'I can't stop!' she cries, her voice, her English words, more exotic in this place than any green bird. At times she is almost running, her feet pressing lightly on the deep litter of the track, a woman right at the edge of flight. Everything that she is travels with her. There is no long scarf of memory, no extraneous thought. She walks, she runs, her hair in damp whorls plastered to the skin of her face and neck. Her heart is a wingbeat, her mouth dry as a stone. And like this she dances out of the forest to find the world has stumbled into night, that there are stars at the level of her feet, a horizon of some pale violet colour, and the sea, slack, tipped with starlight, the smell of it like something poured out of her own veins, like sucked brass.

Ten steps to the left would take her into the air. She stands there a minute, her breath frayed almost to nothing, to rags and threads, bare threads. Then she lies down exactly where she is, curls up on the path listening to the deep reflection of the sea while above her the Milky Way glitters in a blue smoke and lines of light streak for a second and burn to nothing.

2

Though she is a girl as curious as the next she has learnt in her short life to have a proper caution. She is, after all, in charge of the goats, and the animals, twelve of them, spill around her as she squats on a convenient rock and looks at the figure sprawled across the path at the point where the path enters the forest. At this distance she cannot be sure if it's a man or a woman but she's certain it's not a child and not anyone she knows.

She's a blonde, gap-toothed girl with a band of freckles across her cheeks, a straw hat on her head, an oversized black T-shirt with a picture of Luke Skywalker on it. And though barely past her tenth birthday, she has already seen a good many dead things – dead goats, dead cattle, dead chickens, a dead turtle once. Not yet, not properly (because it doesn't count when they're under a sheet and you can't see the face) a dead person.

The old billy, who has been cropping the dry brown heads of plants at the edge of the path, stops, wary for a moment, then picks his way past the open, outstretched hand, and the others follow him, one by one, into the shadow of the forest. The girl slides off her rock. She doesn't want the animals to get too far ahead of her. There are things in the forest that will eat a goat and only a month ago she did lose one and did not dare (she who dares a great deal) go far from the track to search for it.

So who is this, who does not wake at the sound of goat bells? She can see it's a woman now. Shorts and T-shirt, a green bag beside her. Her face burnt and bitten, sores on her lips. Her shoes red with dust.

'*Você fica cansada?*' she says. She prods one of the woman's legs with her stick and the woman makes a noise in her throat. It's a little funny to watch someone coming so sleepily up the long stairs of themselves, to see them squirm in the dust of the track as if they had, two minutes ago, been made out of that same dust.

The eyes open, brown like the brown hair.

'*Você tem sede?*' The girl has a camouflage-green, military-style drinking bottle across her shoulders and she unslings it, unscrews the cap, squats and holds it to the woman's lips. Most of the water slides down her cheek but then she's suckling like a baby. When the girl decides she's had enough she takes the bottle back, screws on the top. For a moment she's distracted by the woman's arm, the black writing there, then she remembers her manners and asks, '*Qual é o seu nome?*' She waits. For long seconds the woman says nothing, just looks at her with eyes that could swallow you whole. Eventually she pushes herself into a sitting position, looks about herself, looks at the sea, looks back at the forest. When she speaks the girl does not understand her then, suddenly, she does, and in her head the honeycomb of words is changed.

'My name is Leah,' she says, listening to herself, the charm of her own voice. 'Please wait here. I must find my goats.'

*　　*　　*

With frequent stops, the girl and the woman make their way along the coast. The path leads them down to the edge of the sea and after that the only path is the girl's own footprints and those of the goats. They cross a spur of headland, descend to a second beach, then up a shallow rise to where the sand gives way to ochre earth and a white church stands looking out to sea like an old white boat drawn up out of the surf. At the side of it is a second building, also white, with a row of small shuttered windows above three dark archways.

As they come closer, other children appear. Some are about the girl's age, some much younger. They do not speak to Maud. They look at her with grave expressions, expressions of wonder. In whispers they ask Leah questions and several times Maud hears the girl speak her name, or a version of it – 'Moor . . . Moor'.

The walk from the edge of the forest has taken two hours, perhaps two and a half, and has cost Maud the last of her strength. She leans on Leah's stick and waits for one of the children to bring an adult and for that adult to tell her where she can lie down. One of the children – a boy running furiously – has been sent as a messenger to the church but instead of an adult, two older children step from the door, an adolescent girl and boy, and for a while they simply look on as if they were expecting someone else. Then the girl strides forward, parts the circle of children and stands in front of Maud. She is, perhaps, thirteen, though at least as tall as Maud. Copper-coloured skin, her hair a slightly darker version of the same colour. The dress she is wearing, with its orange polka dots, has at one time belonged to somebody larger, heavier, and has, at the waist, been gathered into pleats and tightly belted.

'*Ola*,' says the girl.

'I need to sit,' says Maud, and does so, almost tumbling to the ground in the middle of the children, the goats.

The older girl speaks to Leah then kneels at Maud's side. 'You are American?'

Maud nods. American will do.

'You are lost?'

She nods again. She has shut her eyes. When she opens them and looks up at the girl, the girl smiles. She is missing one of her front teeth but it doesn't make her less beautiful. 'I am Jessica,' she says. 'I will help you.'

Before Maud can answer, the girl has stood and begun issuing orders, scattering the younger children, one of whom returns a moment later with a plastic beaker of water and a slice of mango. Maud drinks some of the water but she cannot manage the fruit. They watch her, then one of them takes the cup from her and they raise her up – the older girl, Leah, and two other girls, twin's surely, black girls with bright astonished faces. They prop her onto her feet. Maud reaches an arm around the older girl's shoulders, and they set off, step by halting step, towards the nearest archway.

Inside the building they climb a flight of wooden stairs to a corridor or gallery where three unglazed windows, their shutters partly open, look from the back of the building, a view consumed by light. Opposite the windows are four or five doors and the older girl opens the first of them, the one nearest the top of the stairs. 'This is my room,' she says. 'You can stay in here.'

It's small and simple, a narrow bed along one wall, a table and chair under the window. The window, like those in the corridor, has green shutters but no glass.

Maud sits on the bed. Life is happening to her; she has no part to play, or her part is like that of the blind men, madmen and cripples in the Bible stories, people lowered from a roof or touched miraculously in passing.

A small boy comes in carrying, with great care, a bowl half full with water.

'Thank you, Caleb,' says the older girl, in English, perhaps for Maud's benefit. The boy sets down the bowl, spilling some of the water onto the boards. He has a yellow, short-sleeved shirt on, red shorts down to his knees, bare feet. He looks as if he has some Indian blood in him.

'It's not polite to stare,' says the girl, and though it's hard to tell if the boy understands the words, he understands enough – the tone of voice, the young schoolmistress – and he looks down, leaves the room.

'You can go ahead and wash now,' says the girl. 'The children won't come bothering. I'll have Leah sit outside. When you need me you just send her to get me.'

Maud nods.

'You got all you need?' asks the girl.

When she has gone Maud sits there looking at the trembling in her legs, the thinness of her legs. She does not wash, she does not undress, does not take off her shoes. Eventually she lies down. She can smell the girl in the rough linen, can smell herself too, the bitterness of her skin, or a bitterness that rises from somewhere deeper. Outside, the children are calling to each other and the sounds are like the cries and whoops and chattering of the forest. She listens. Surely now some man or woman, some clear, rational voice, will speak over them and she will hear the heavy footfall on the stairs and she will ready herself to tell her story.

She listens. She waits.

*   *   *

Once she has fallen asleep she is like a child into whose room the parents can come and go without fear of waking her. Leah, the doorkeeper, in exchange for small gifts, admits, one at a time, her particular friends. All the friends are girls; certainly no boys will be allowed. So Jenna, a black girl, seven years old, stands at the end of the narrow bed imagining herself as a baby again. So Bethany, pale as Leah, daring to lean over Maud to examine her dirty face, her broken fingernails, the writing on her arm that seems almost readable but not quite. So Summer, eight, snub-nosed and frizzy-haired, not knowing if the woman is twenty-five or fifty-five, and wondering why she wears around her neck a piece of string with a child's hair clip on it.

Jessica is also a visitor, and like the younger children she stands over the sleeping woman, but on her face the expression shifts between something like anxiety and something like relief, profound relief. In the evening she covers Maud with a blanket then holds out her hands, palms down above Maud's sleeping head and speaks a dozen words, hushed and fervent.

Below, when the girl comes down, the children are waiting for her. They pester her with questions, hang from her hands, tug at the polka-dot dress. She shakes them off, gently, and crosses to the church, walks down the unlit length of it to the door beyond the altar.

She opens the door; the boy is in there. By the light of one of the wind-up lanterns he's doing something with the boxes on the bench and she stands very still until he has finished. He has on a baggy checked shirt and a pair of jeans as tightly, as awkwardly belted as her dress. The room is whitewashed, a small window just above head height. There's a desk with metal legs, a metal filing cabinet, a pair of tubular steel office chairs, a calendar for the year 2007 open at the month of December, a photograph of snow on the mountains.

272

'She's still sleeping,' says Jessica. 'Maybe she has a bad fever. Should we give her something?'

'Give what?'

The girl shrugs. 'An Advil?'

The boy laughs at her. 'Did you look in her bag?' he says.

3

Through the middle watches of the night, delirium flourishes. Old Rawlins is a regular visitor, slumped at the end of the bed like the night itself, a man lit only by stars but unmistakeable. He seems pleased to see her, though also distracted by what he calls tactics. His chest bubbles. He addresses her as Minnehaha, as he used to in the Nissen hut in the car park of the boys' school where they trained. He laughs to himself. Did I ever tell you about my dog? he asks. My dog, Lady? One, he says – sitting up in his tracksuit and coughing his way towards song – one is the loneliest number.

At another time she can hear her parents outside the door, a sharp to and fro of anxious whispers, and even, seeping from somewhere, the warm plasticky whiff of the laminating machine.

Other voices, speaking to her or about her. Bella saying, Anything at all. You need only ask. The woman from Human Resources saying, That would involve childcare for a very young baby.

The last voice is the man from the cutter in Falmouth, or that man transfigured to a grey-bearded Captain Slocum leaning over the stern rail of *Spray* and demanding, with terrible urgency, where she is headed. She does not have the breath to call back an answer . . .

She sleeps for a while but it's still dark when she wakes again. There's a blanket over her and she pushes it down to her waist. Her T-shirt is stuck to the skin between her breasts, her hair is damp on her forehead. She feels nauseous but does not think she will actually be sick. For long minutes the only thing that ties her to any sort of reality is the whine of a mosquito somewhere by the window. Then something joins it (as if out of the hollow wire of the insect's throat), a noise that makes her remember lying in bed as a girl in Swindon, those nights they were firing on the ranges, the rumble of artillery, bombs too, a drumroll that stood outside all other sounds – the night bus, a neighbour's television – not because it was loud when it reached her but because of what it was where it started out, a force that opened up the sides of hills. And here? Here perhaps it was thunder or some trick of the sea. She holds her breath, tilts her head, listening until it's impossible to know if she is still hearing it or if the sound now plays only inside her own head.

The next time she wakes, a bar of sunlight is simmering on the wall opposite the window. She sits up, spends half a minute wondering why she is not on the boat, and with a grunt of effort swings her legs out of the bed.

The wash bowl the boy brought in – yesterday? Two days ago? – is still beside the bed. She cups her hands to drink from it, then strips and crouches by the side of it to wash herself. As she can see no towel she dries herself with her T-shirt. The rash on her leg from the centipede has blistered – four, five little sacks of fluid.

The backs of both ankles are blistered raw. There are numerous fine cuts on her arms and legs and hands, though none look to be infected. She is, she considers, in better shape than she might have feared, though her ribs – as they remind her when she stands – can still stop her dead, make her gasp.

Draped at the end of the bed is a pile of clothes. She does not think they were there when she lay down. She picks through them. A nylon dress that she is neither tall enough nor wide enough to wear. A nylon slip, a white nylon blouse, a pair of tan slacks with a waistband that would circle two of her. The only wearable item is a shirt of heavy, faded blue cotton – a man's shirt, surely, and perhaps brought in by mistake, part of an armful carried from a wardrobe, some deep drawer. When she puts it on it hangs to just above her knees, but with the sleeves rolled up it's comfortable and cool.

She leaves the room (her feet are bare) and in the passageway pushes back the shutters of the window opposite the bedroom door. The view is over the building's landward side, and to the right, some hundred yards away, is a piece of walled-in ground, half an acre perhaps. Over the top of the wall she can make out tilled beds, low trees, trellises strung with climbing plants. Also the heads of three or four children, one of them with a pitchfork taller than he is, much taller, another with the blade of a machete resting on her shoulder like a broadsword. Beyond the garden is the shallow dome of a water cistern, and at the side of that, a line of palms, their trunks shaped by the onshore wind.

Leaning a little and looking the other way, she can see a single-storey building of mud and sticks, a clutch of hens investigating the dust around an open door, a young girl squatting in the building's shade, apparently in conversation with the cockerel. There's a flagpole where no flag is flying, some pieces of a dismantled tractor, and a track of red earth like the one she walked on that first night, heading in an almost perfectly straight line towards low, round-topped hills. There are no houses in the distance, no telegraph poles. Nothing like that.

She comes down the stairs and arrives in a large open room cross-lit by the light coming in through the arches, brighter on one side than the other. At the far end there's a long table and against the wall, rows of shelves where plates and cups give off the dull gleam of themselves. An animal she mistakes at first for a cat is scavenging on the floor – the packed earth – between the chairs. Noticing Maud, it trots to her on quick small feet, tail erect, and she can see it's some other kind of animal, the size of a cat, but looking more like a monkey or even a small, fur-covered pig.

She walks out through one of the archways and shades her eyes to look at the sea. There's a little boat coming in – blunt prow, dirty-white lateen sail. She's seen pictures of this kind of boat before, knows it as a craft peculiar to these coasts – a jangada. As it reaches the surf the lone sailor slips into the water and leads the boat like a horse, pulling it up onto the sand. She can see who it is now – the older boy who watched her from outside the church when she arrived. From a box on the deck (it's as much a raft as a boat) he lifts two large fish the colour of red coral. He whistles and she wonders for a moment if he's whistling to her but then a child comes sprinting past her, a boy who can be no more than five, his feet kicking up the sand in little spurts as he runs. He takes the fish, holds them with his hands through the gills. They look too heavy for him but he manages them, just, a grimace of concentration on his face. As he passes Maud he squints up at her then disappears with the fish along a path of sunlight between the church and the building with the arches.

Maud waits for the older boy to come closer. He must have

seen her, but he sets off along the edge of the beach and only once he has walked beyond the tree that grows where the sand gives way to the red earth does he turn away from the sea and towards the church. Maud takes the shorter line across the front of the church and meets him as he arrives at the steps of a trailer home. She was not expecting this – an oversized caravan parked on salt-whitened breeze-blocks along the far wall of the church. She stares at it, the plastic and metal flank of it much punished by the sun, then looks back at the boy and says, 'Do you speak English?'

'Of course,' he says.

He has on a T-shirt at least two sizes too small for him, his belly taut and brown between the shirt's hem and the waistband of his shorts. His forearms glitter with fish scales.

'I came on a boat,' she says. 'I lost the mast in a storm. I left the boat along the coast here.' She points in what she hopes is the right direction. 'Have you seen it?'

'No,' he says. His eyes keep flickering over the shirt she is wearing. Something about it obviously disturbs him.

'It's red,' she says. 'A red boat.'

He nods and turns to go up the steps to the door.

'Will you look for it?'

He nods again.

'What is this place?' she asks.

'The Ark,' he says.

'The Ark?'

'Yes.'

'Who looks after the children?'

'They are not here now,' he says.

'When will they be back?'

He shrugs. 'Soon.'

'Today?'

'Soon,' he says, and turns away, opens the trailer door and goes inside.

She stands there a moment examining the trailer, the yellowed sticker above the door that reads, *The Ten Commandments are not multiple choice*. She cannot tell if the boy is shy or for some reason angry with her. She turns and looks down the beach to where his boat is drawn up. If she took it now and sailed it along the coast would she find *Lodestar*? And if she did, what then? Despite the damage (not all of which might be obvious and visible) she still believes the yacht could be salvaged, that a well-equipped yard and several weeks of work could make it sound again. There is, of course, the question of cost, of how this hypothetical yard would be paid. She does not think she has more than a thousand or two in her account, even if she could find a way of accessing her account (this place where she has not yet found a farm, let alone a bank).

She walks to the door of the church and slips inside. It's cool as evening in there and as dark. What little light there is – the light from the door and from the shuttered windows above – lies in shallow pools on the tiles of the floor and in frail, trembling grids on the grey walls. There are no pews, just a dozen chairs that look to have come from an old schoolroom, gathered in a semi-circle below the pulpit. The pulpit itself is some tight-grained wood riddled with wormholes and something about its appearance suggests to Maud the timbers of a ship, and that it was, conceivably, once part of a ship and cut away by people who dismantled their vessel on arriving, who did not intend to return anywhere.

She moves around the walls squinting at memorial tablets. The earliest she can find is from 1658, the latest 1780. Ribbons of faded Latin; some imagery, including what seems to be a whale.

The Portuguese names are like tables laid with too much silver. Other names look as if they might have belonged to servants or slaves. Nearly all of them – slaves and masters – appear to have died young.

Outside again, she walks to the tree. It's a mango tree, a pair of macaws in the head of it helping themselves to the fruit. She watches them, and they tilt their yellow faces to watch her as they eat. Then she curls up in the shade of the tree and sleeps. When she wakes, the older girl is sitting beside her.

'You just sleep and sleep and sleep,' says the girl. 'You're the most tired person I ever met.'

First, they clear up the question of her name, so that the girl learns to say Maud rather than Moor. Then the girl tells Maud where they are, though it seems to Maud the girl's geography is a kind of hearsay, and that she carries no clear map of things in her head. She wants to know about Maud and Maud tells her about the boat, the voyage, the storm, her landfall on the coast. All of it, it turns out, can live in a score of simple sentences.

'I talked to the boy,' says Maud. She points towards the trailer.

'Theo,' says Jessica.

'He said the people who look after you are away. That they are not here.'

'Pa,' she says. 'He means Pa.'

'Pa? Your father?'

'He was Pa for all of us.'

'Where has he gone?'

The girl shrugs. 'Maybe Huntsville?'

'Where?'

'Huntsville, Alabama.'

'Pa's American?'

'There was Ma too,' says the girl. 'But she passed.'

'She died?'

'Yes.'

'And Pa went away?'

'You're wearing his shirt,' says the girl.

'Is that Ma's dress?'

'Yes,' says the girl, looking down at herself and lightly touching the material.

'The boy,' says Maud, 'Theo. He said Pa would be back soon.'

'Oh yes,' says the girl. She smiles. 'He will.'

'Do you have a phone here?'

'Pa has the phone.'

'He took it with him?'

The girl nods, grins. 'Pa can make anything,' she says. 'Pa will fix up your boat.'

'Was it Pa who taught you to speak English?'

'Pa and Ma.'

'How long have you been here?'

'Oh, a long time,' says the girl.

'And Theo?'

'Yes,' says the girl. 'And Theo. Since babies. Since little babies.'

At the Ark, the day's main meal is in the late afternoon, the last full hour of light, and for the first time Maud sees all the children together. They gather at the ringing of a goat bell and take their places at the table between the arches. There are fourteen of them, the youngest a boy of four. Each child seems to know his or her place.

Maud is sitting next to the older girl at one end of the table. The boy, Theo, sits at the other end. When he arrives, walking quietly through the end archway, appearing to them as if sinking – calmly, a philosopher – from the world of light (the beach) to their world of shade and shadow, the children become hushed and respectful. The food has been cooking for the last hour on a brick-built griddle at the back of the building. The fish, their pink skins charred, are brought to the table and divided up, quickly and neatly, by Jessica. There's sweetcorn and sweet potato, bowls of rice, a chewy, unsalted flatbread, a salad of leaves (a type of spinach?).

Before anyone starts their food they bow their heads while Theo says grace. 'Heavenly Father we thank you for this food we are about to receive for the nourishment of our bodies. Please cleanse it from impurity in Jesus' name.'

The little animal is present, the one Maud mistook for a cat and which Jessica now tells her is called a coati. Theo shoos it from the table then throws it a piece of sweet potato, which the animal eats, turning the food in the dirt with its sensitive-looking snout. Throughout the meal the children stare at Maud for as long as they dare. Beyond the arches the building's shadow stretches towards the beach. No one comes, no one goes.

After the cooked food there is fruit – mangoes, and something that looks like red bananas and may be, in fact, bananas. Then Jessica leaves the table, and after a theatrical pause, a shy grin at Maud, she pulls up by a rope ring a trap door in the floor, descends with a wind-up LED lantern and returns two minutes later with a biscuit barrel. Each child is given a biscuit – a charcoal-black Oreo – then the barrel is closed and returned to whatever place it has below the floor. A second grace ends the meal. The children carry their plates to a metal tub into which Jessica pours water from a pan that has been heating on the embers of the griddle. Each child washes his own plate, cup, fork and spoon. Three chil- dren – Leah is one – have cloths and are in charge of drying. Two others carry the clean things to the shelves where Jessica oversees the stacking. No instructions are given; all of them clearly know what is expected of them. By the time they have finished, all that is left of the light is a narrow band of paler blue at the horizon.

With the work done, Jessica places a chair over the trap door, winds up the lantern, sits and places the lantern on the floor in front of her. This is a signal. The children, like a flock of sparrows, settle at her feet, the faces of those at the front etched with light, while those further back are almost hidden.

She begins a story – Jonah and the whale. She tells the story in English, though now and then some word of Portuguese or some brief aside in that language is added. Maud, whose knowledge of the Bible is like her knowledge of certain cities – accurate and even detailed for small areas, entirely vague for the rest – is unsure if the girl is telling the story as it is written or some more private version of it. She leans against the end of the table, and at the point where the whale vomits Jonah onto the shore she looks through one of the arches to the beach and sees the glow of a cigarette. For several seconds she assumes it must be Pa, that he has made his expected return. Then the ember arcs into the sea and she sees the boy's silhouette slouching towards the church or the trailer.

The story ends. The children are readied for bed or ready themselves, trooping off in small groups to the lean-to latrines beside the garden wall or wiping their faces with makeshift squares of cloth, cleaning their teeth with small brushes. To Maud, Jessica says, 'Every night I tell them a story but they've heard all of them many times. Do you know stories, Maud? Maybe one night you could tell the story?'

She invites Maud to see the children in bed, and together – Jessica holding the lantern – they go in and out of the rooms off the corridor where the children are lying in metal-frame beds, four or five to a room, the younger children mixed in with the older. They look up at the light, at the girl, at Maud. Some of them have tattered soft toys in their arms. Some call out their goodnight in English. One boy, as Maud passes his bed, shouts, 'Goodbye Mama!' and immediately pulls the sheet over his face.

When they come downstairs again, Maud asks Jessica where she will sleep and the girl says she's in the trailer now and that Maud can use her room as long as she wants. It can be her room now.

'Does Theo sleep in the trailer?' asks Maud.

'The trailer's big. We got plenty of room.'

'That was Ma and Pa's trailer?'

'Pa drove it down one year. All the way from Huntsville.'

The lamp is drawing in a haze of insects. Some with their white wings look like the ghosts of themselves, others seem whimsical, balletic. The girl shows Maud where the lamps are kept, hanging from nails between two of the arches. She turns off the lamp, and for a moment they are invisible to each other, then the white walls of the building begin to glow and with a quick goodnight and the merest touch of her fingers on Maud's forearm, the girl takes her leave.

Maud goes out the other way, towards the latrines. All around her on the path, the slow zig-zagging, the green light of fireflies. The latrine has four cubicles with doors like the swing doors to an old Western bar. There are drifting green lights inside the cubicles too. The toilets themselves – it has already been proudly explained to her – are compostable, the dried humus used in the garden.

When she comes out she can hear a dull ringing from the jostling of the goats, though she does not know where they are penned and cannot see them. She looks along the path, wonders what would happen and where she would reach if she followed it towards those hills that are nothing now but a starless dark beneath a dark pitted with stars. She has seen no maps at the Ark. Perhaps there are none, or the maps travel with the man, with Pa.

She walks back through the fireflies, past the hen house, through an archway. She feels her way to the water container, drinks the water that tastes of iron, rubs at her teeth with a finger, then goes up the worn wooden edges of the stairs to her room. She does not take off the man's shirt but slides under the blanket still wearing it and drifts into a dreamless sleep, only to be woken, minutes later, by a child crying in the room next to hers. A voice speaks over the crying, a fierce whispering until the crying stops. After that, nothing but the small sounds of the ocean.

In the morning she is again the last to rise. It seems strange that so many children have passed her door without waking her. Are they under instructions to pass voiceless on bare feet so that the stranger, the sleeping woman (this woman who has, they might imagine, walked out of the sea in fulfilment of a prophesy none of them even knew about) can wake in her own time?

Downstairs, she finds the trap door open and looks down to see a flight of metal steps such as you might find leading to the engine room on a ship. The older girl appears in a pool of light at the bottom, and though the steps are steep she comes up them nimbly, the wind-up lantern in one hand, a large saucepan of rice grains in the other.

'You want to see?' she asks. She puts the saucepan on the end of the table and climbs back down with Maud following her. The space below is larger than Maud had pictured it, some fifteen feet by ten, and high enough for someone taller than either of them to stand upright. She thinks immediately of the treasure room at the Rathbones' – an odd, dislocating thought that seems to spread her hair-thin across the whole Atlantic – though on the shelves here, in place of watercolours and African masks there are rows of tins, of packets, labelled boxes. She follows the lantern – Hershey's cocoa, California olives, red bean gumbo, instant grits, pancake mix, Oreo biscuits, SpaghettiOs. There are even cigarettes, four cartons of Lucky Strike, three of them still in their paper wrapping, the fourth half empty. At the end of the room are bins of rice, dried beans, flour, demijohns of maize oil, red palm oil. None of these are full – none of the shelves are full – but even without the walled garden and the fish the boy catches, there is enough food here to last the children many months.

Between the bins, a door opens to a second room. Drums of whitewash, loops of cable, hand saws, drill-bits. Also, exercise books, boxes of coloured chalk, of pencils. Against the far wall there's a generator with wires hanging like pale roots from the ceiling above it. Maud lifts one of the steel jerrycans.

'No gas,' says Jessica. 'No gas for a long time.'

On a shelf beside the generator there's a small machine of some type half hidden under a drape of black velvet. When Maud raises the cloth she sees that it's a film projector, a Bell & Howell super 8 that looks to have been well cared for, its glass and steel parts gleaming with a medical brightness.

'Oh, we have movies,' says the girl, and she points with the light to a pile of slim boxes on the shelf above the projector. 'We miss them.'

They climb back into the upper air. The coati is waiting for them. It sniffs them, observes them with sad, gum-coloured eyes. Jessica closes the trap door, locks it with a combination padlock, the shank threaded through a stout U bolt.

'You want me to tell you the number?' she asks.

'I don't need to know it,' says Maud.

For a moment the girl looks crestfallen, unexpectedly checked. Then she brightens. 'The children will eat something now. Us too. Then we have school time. You want to teach the children a lesson?'

'A lesson?'

'Yes. School time.'

'What should I teach them?'

The girl laughs. 'You're an adult. You know lots of things.'

'Do they all understand English?'

'Some more, some less.'

'Ma and Pa taught them.'

'Then me and Theo.'

'What happened to Ma?'

The girl shrugs. 'Snake bit her.'

'A snake?'

'Pa's bit three, four times and never even gone to the doctor.'

'Did Ma go to the doctor?'

'There are no doctors here, Maud.'

'Is she buried here? Her grave?'

The girl points through the middle arch and out along the path. 'Pa chose the place. Worked all night making a box for her. He said her dying like that didn't mean he was wrong about things.'

'What things?' asks Maud.

'Oh,' says Jessica, picking up the goat bell with hands, ringless like Maud's, that seem to belong to a fully grown woman, 'about everything, I guess.'

After they have eaten they gather in the shade of the mango tree. Maud has her back to the trunk, the children sit in a fan around her, all except for two boys whose absence is not explained, and Theo who is out in the boat. She teaches them how a body breathes, how the lungs are like bags filled with little structures like the roots of a plant, how oxygen travels in the blood pumped by the heart, how the air we breathe out is different from the air we breathe in. She teaches them that a tree like the mango also does a kind of breathing and that the energy of the sun makes this possible. At one moment – sliding into some state parallel to sleep – she hears herself talking about plasma membranes, and looks at the children only to find them listening to her as if she were telling them about Goldilocks and the bears. She talks for twenty minutes. At the end, Jessica claps and the children join in.

'You're a good teacher,' says Jessica when the younger children have scattered.

'I've never taught children before,' says Maud.

'A real good teacher,' says the girl.

'Thank you,' says Maud.

'You want to do it again tomorrow?' asks the girl.

In the afternoon Maud finds the children who missed her class on breathing. She has been walking – first along the beach in the direction she had not taken before, then inland, through sharp-edged grasses and the remnant of some long-disappeared settlement, the keels of ruined houses, the outline of what might have been a street. After walking the best part of an hour she comes to the church again, the back of the church, where she sees, propped against the wall, a hutch or pen with a sloping metal roof and two wood-frame doors covered in chicken wire. She goes up to see what kind of animal is kept here, and finds the children, boys of about eight who she remembers from the previous evening's meal. She does not know their names. One is a black boy with a bounce of ginger hair. One is paler, naked apart from a pair of pants or swimming trunks. When she crouches in front of the chicken wire she can see how the whites of his eyes are pink, the eyelids raw.

'Why are you here?' she asks but gets no answer. On their cheeks, through the dirt on their cheeks, there are tear stains, though long since dry. They look at her with expressions beyond resentment or fear. They are like machines turned to their lowest setting.

The doors are held in place by small steel bolts. Maud draws the bolts and opens the doors. 'You can go,' she says, but neither boy moves. 'It's OK,' she tells them, and thinking it's her being there that stops them coming out she straightens up and walks around the far side of the church, passes the trailer home and goes down to the mango tree in time to see the jangada riding up to the beach on the smallest of breezes, and the boy, who may or may not have noticed her under the tree, stepping down into the surf.

At the evening meal, he does not join them. Jessica says grace. The children are unsettled, uneasy. Throughout the meal they look at Jessica, look at Maud, look later at the embers on the beach.

'He's mad,' says Jessica to Maud when the children are in bed. 'Someone opened the forno.'

'The forno?'

'Behind the church. When the children are bad.'

'I opened it,' says Maud.

Jessica nods. 'I know.'

'One of the boys has an eye infection,' says Maud. 'Do you have eye-drops?'

The girl shrugs. 'Pa says the best medicine is prayer from a pure heart.'

'He needs to keep it clean,' says Maud.

'Jesus heals,' says the girl, though she seems to be listening.

They walk outside together. A warm muggy night, starless and very dark.

'I'd like to smoke,' says Maud. 'Can I have some of the cigarettes from the store room?'

'The store room?'

'Where you keep the food.'

'Oh, sure,' says Jessica. She sounds pleased. 'I'll go get them.'

Maud walks towards the sea, the sound of the sea. When she sees the grey edge of it sliding towards her she takes off the shirt, takes off her pants, makes a bundle of them and puts them down where the sand is dry. Her body is a poor light she follows into the water. She has to walk a long way before the sea covers the tops of her hips and she can lean in and start to swim. Though her ribs ache as she pulls – the muscles on that side feel shortened, tight – she keeps it up for fifteen minutes, then stops, floats onto her back looking up into the black mirror of the sky, her hands pooling the water.

She has slept many hours since she came here, to this house of children, but she is tired still with a tiredness she has begun to suspect she will never quite be free of now; a weakness, like a withered arm or palsied foot she will have to find some way of going on with. And she supposes that she will find a way – for isn't that what she does? The thing that marks her out as her? Strange then, this sudden longing for stillness, for surrender, for letting this swell that gently lifts her up and drops her down, keep her.

Who or what has ever held her as the sea does?

Her parents must have held her when she was small. Held her, sang to her even. And she has a memory of Grandfather Ray, something retained not as a picture but a loose knot of sensations – the rise and fall of his big smoker's chest, the heat flooding up from the gas fire, drugging them both . . .

Tim, of course, and she had liked that and not questioned it, though it was only really restful a dozen times or so somewhere near the beginning, those occasions when they had not wanted anything from each other beyond bare presence.

The last person to hold her was the crane driver (whose name she cannot remember). The thump of his heart, the thump of hers. Those minutes that could not be kept entirely free of tenderness.

Is that a lot? Is that what others can remember, more or less? She doesn't know, has no idea. It is, she thinks, the sort of question she would have to ask Professor Kimber, who would laugh at her and sit her down and say, 'Maud, dear Maud, let's go through this step by step . . .'

And she is thinking of Professor Kimber, the pretty shoes on the big feet, the silk camellia she sometimes wore in her hair even to work, when she hears, not far away from her – though it's difficult to judge – the water moving, some sound not made by the sea itself, and her head empties out and her whole being becomes a kind of arrow. She lets her feet drop and tries to see what's there. She knows that sharks hunt at night, that there must be sharks off this piece of coast, but on *Lodestar* she developed a feeling for them, their presence, and would often look up a second or two before they showed themselves. She does not think it's a shark nearby. A turtle? Wrong season. A dolphin then, or some big fish, a marlin or tuna, come to investigate what manner of creature is out here in the dark with it.

She can feel herself standing in a current of cooler water she imagines running parallel to the shore but the shore itself is invisible – utter darkness both ways – and she is no longer confident of the direction she is facing. If she struck out now she might be swimming further and further away from the land, a mistake not understood until it was too late.

And there, again, the movement – a swirling she both hears and feels – a tremor like the flick of a big tail, and she prepares herself for some manner of contact, turning and turning, not wanting to have her back to whatever is with her. Her heart rate is up but there's no panic, not yet. If it wanted to attack her she thinks it would have done so without announcing itself, and she has a series of compressed, possibly confused thoughts, one of which is that this life circling her own is lonely.

Then, from far off, she hears her name called, the sound of it coming to her like one of those birds that fly so low over the water the tips of their wings seem to touch the waves with each beat. A fragile spark of light appears, growing stronger as the lantern is wound. She starts to swim, wondering if she has left it too late, if she has the strength to get back. Then she finds the strength and burrows through the water, its dense black grain, until at last she sees the lines of surf, untethered in the dark, and her feet brush against the ridged sand. The first time she tries to stand she falls and the surf breaks over her head. She tries again, steadies herself, looks over her shoulder at the sea and walks up onto dry sand.

'Maud?'

'Yes.'

'Oh, Maud, I was scared.'

'I wanted to swim.'

They look for her clothes with the lantern, find them. Jessica casts shy glances at Maud's nakedness, then runs to one of the archways and comes back with a towel. Maud dries herself and dresses. They walk up the beach together, sit down where the sand is soft and still warm. They sit side by side. The lantern is off now, now that Maud has been found. Jessica gives her the pack of cigarettes and Maud strips off the cellophane, takes one out. Jessica lights it for her with a match – a quick blue flaring, their blue faces anonymous as masks.

'Are these Pa's cigarettes?'

'Yes.'

'The cigarettes Theo smokes?'

'Yes.'

'Will he be angry?'

'Pa?'

'Theo.'

'Theo's always angry. He's angry since Pa went away.'

The chill from the swim is slowly wearing off. Blue smoke from the cigarette floats just above their heads. There's no breeze to blow it away.

'Maud?'

'What?'

'Can I ask something?'

'If you want.'

'Why do you wear the thing around your neck? It belongs to a child.'

'Yes.'

'To your child?'

'Yes.'

'A girl.'

'Yes.'

'Maud?'

'What?'

'Has she passed?' Something in the girl's voice here. Kindness, yes – but something else, something alert and sinuous.

'Yes. She's passed.'

'I can tell things like that.'

'Yes.'

'Are you angry with me?'

'No.'

'What was her name?'

'Zoe.'

'Zoe?'

'Yes, Zoe.'

'And is that why you were on the boat on your own?'

'That was part of it.'

'Because you were sad?'

'Yes.'

'Maud?'

'What?'

'What happened to her? To Zoe?'

'She was in an accident.'

'You were with her?'

'No.'

'She was alone?'

'Her father was with her.'

'Has he passed too?'

'No.'

'Didn't he want to come on the boat with you?'

'No.'

'How old was she, Maud? When she passed?'

'Six.'

'You must think about her all the time.'

'Not all the time.'

'You dream about her?'

'Sometimes.'

'Maud?'

'What?'

'You ever feel she's reaching out for you?'

'Reaching out? How can she reach out?'

'Well, you ever see her, Maud?'

'No.'

'You ever think you *hear* her?' The girl waits. She's not a fool, did not spend nine years of her life with Ma (Ma's ways, Ma's games) and end up a fool. She listens for a catch in Maud's breathing, for the cigarette to tumble to the sand, for something. When none of this happens she says, 'If Pa was here he would help you.'

'Help me?'

'He would know how to help you.'

'How would he help me?'

'Maud?'

'What?'

'Maybe I can help you?'

'I don't need you to help me.'

'I'd really like to help you, Maud.'

'It's too late for help.'

'No,' says the girl, emphatically. 'No, you just have to want it. Don't you want it?'

For a minute, as if they have forgotten whose turn it is to speak, they are silent. Then, out of the dark, comes a sudden breeze. 'Rain wind,' says Maud, lifting her face to it, and almost before the words are out, it begins, fat drops, just a scattering, striking the sand around them. One breaks on Maud's cheek, one on her knee. As they get to their feet the rain begins in earnest – black sheets chasing them up the beach as they run, drumming on their skulls, blinding them.

The girl and the boy are not lovers, though Ma and Pa used to joke about it. They have not kissed, would never think of letting the other see them naked. So the boy is troubled and does not know what to think when Jessica sits on his bed in the dark and leans over him, rain dripping from her hair onto his face, her hair smelling of rain, and her face so close he feels her breath on his skin.

'What?' he says. '*O que você quer?*'

'The woman,' she says.

'She's gone?'

'Where could she go?'

'Then what?'

'I think she's here for a reason. A purpose.'

'What purpose?'

'I don't know,' says the girl, 'but maybe it's a test for us.'

4

The only sign of the rain on the following day is a speckling of flowers, some of them appearing out of cracks in the ground or from the mouth of a stone-coloured pod – something, the previous day, you took for dead. The sea has shifted its blue a little, and from the window of her room (water pooled on the floor beside the table) Maud guesses that offshore, beyond the bay, a big swell is running. The air is fresh, cool, but by the early afternoon the heat is back, the flowers wilt, and those woody fists that broke open to show intemperate colour have sealed themselves again.

Today, under the mango tree, Maud teaches Evolution. 'Think of two birds,' she says. 'They both want to eat the same food but one bird has a beak' – she makes the shape with her hand – 'that is good for eating the food, while the other has a beak with a different shape that's not so good. The bird with the good beak grows stronger. The children of that bird are bigger. It has more children, and most of those children have the good beak too.

'Everything changes,' she says. 'Everything is moving very slowly from one state to another, one condition to another. Birds, mountains, rivers. People like us. Like you. Like me. Very slowly . . .'

She mentions Darwin's name and when she has finished the lesson Jessica smiles at her and says, 'Devil Darwin. Pa told us about *him*.'

Neither of them speaks of their night on the beach. In the afternoon Maud helps Jessica prepare the evening meal. They walk up to the walled garden together. The rain has washed the dust from the leaves of the plants. They pick sweetcorn, tomatoes, cassava, gourds. They light the griddle, boil water, start to cook. Later, they lay up the table with forks and spoons and cups and plates. They put out the precious bowl of salt. They make loaves of flatbread with flour from the store cellar. They talk a little as they work, mostly about the characters of the younger children, about Pa's prodigious skill of fixing up, the way a screwdriver looked small as a pin in his hand. It's sisterly, easy enough, entirely sane. Now and then Maud leans against one of the arches to smoke, whole minutes in which nothing urgent needs to be achieved. When they are ready, Jessica offers Maud the goat bell. She rings it and the children appear as if out of the day's slowly cooling crevices. They gather, they circle around Jessica. The bolder ones come up to Maud. They say, 'Hello, how are you?' then scatter before she can answer.

They sit at the table. The food smells wonderful – smells like the kind of food she sometimes dreamt of on the boat. The coati is under the table; some of the hens wander in and two of the girls get down to harry the birds back to the coop where someone has forgotten to close the door. They are waiting for Theo. They look out through the arches, the empty beach, and Jessica is about to send one of the children running to the trailer to fetch him when he comes into view, Theo, or some version of him, sauntering along the beach parallel to the building, the arches, the table, then turning and walking towards them. It's a game, a piece of theatre. He is wearing a suit, a dark suit – a black one, in fact. A black suit with a white shirt underneath (bare brown feet below). Unlike everything else Maud has seen him wear the suit seems to fit him perfectly. A black suit. A tuxedo with satin lapels. He stops at the end of the table. He does not sit down. He looks at them all. The children are silent, Jessica is silent. He looks very briefly at Maud as if (what is he? Fourteen?) she has not yet earned it, the weight of his regard. Then he reaches into the right pocket of the jacket, brings out a spilling fist and flings red petals into the air above the table, red petals that shimmer down, one of them landing, like some fat splash of blood from an upstairs murder, on the back of Maud's wrist.

Next morning she waits on the beach while he drags the jangada down into the surf, then she wades into the water and climbs onto the boards with him. It takes her a few minutes to become used to the boat's skittishness, then they sit together, hunkered down side by side (the boy back in his usual clothes), as the church, the house with the arches, the figures on the beach, lose all particularity and are folded into a landscape. The boy does not talk, or no more than a few words. He has his fishing gear with him and perhaps later he'll fish. They have also brought the two steel jerrycans from the store cellar, and these give off a tired though undispersible whiff of fuel.

It takes less than two hours to reach *Lodestar*. Her route away from it – that march along the red track and through the forest – must, viewed from above, look like a tangled thread and not at all the line, the almost straight line, she thought she was walking. The yacht has shifted a little, dragged its anchor some eighty yards across the face of the bay but looks, at a distance at least, much the same as when she abandoned it – a vessel carrying its history, a vessel that seems to have been shot at, but still recognizable as the boat that made her stop that day in the yard with Camille.

A pair of large white birds are sitting on the coach-house roof and only take to the air once the jangada comes alongside. Maud pulls herself onto the deck, takes the jangada's line and ties it to a cleat. The boy, in a single neat movement, climbs onto the deck behind her.

When she goes below there is water up to the level of the benches. Has the boat, technically, sunk?

She goes down, splashes about. She flicks on the VHF – more life in a stone. She picks Captain Slocum's journal out of the water, puts it on the chart table. She can hear the boy in the cockpit rummaging in the lockers there.

Her sleeping bag is still in the quarter berth. She hauls it out and hangs it over the companionway steps; it might be useful. She finds some of her clothes and puts these up with the sleeping bag; finds – floating like the last remark of some urbane and drowned man – the straw sun hat. In a drawstring PVC bag in the heads are two bottles of wide-spectrum antibiotics and an antibiotic cream, together with a hundred US dollars rolled tightly in cling film that she had completely forgotten about. She searches for her mobile phone adaptor but cannot find it. There is no trace of the suitcase that was in the cockpit, nor of any of its contents. She does not ask about it. It's the boy's prize for finding the boat.

They bring the jerrycans up from the jangada. Maud finds the fuel-cap key hanging in its not very secure or secret place in the starboard cockpit locker. In the same locker are oddments of hose. One length of hose will carry the fuel; a second, slipped into the tank alongside it, is to blow down to start the fuel running without swallowing a mouthful of diesel. They fill both cans and lower them onto the jangada along with the other things Maud has pushed inside the sleeping bag, then cast off and sail back. With the fuel on board it takes both of them to draw the boat up onto the beach. They unload; the children touch the sleeping bag, the soaked book, the clothes, even the old sun hat that has dried on Maud's head on the sail back.

They have been out for half the day. Maud – as usual now after any exertion – finds herself reaching for reserves of energy she has not yet recovered, and after eating she goes upstairs to sleep for an hour. When she comes down again the trap door is open and she descends the metal steps and goes through to the second room where the boy, lit by two of the wind-up lanterns and stripped to the waist, is looking furiously at the generator, both fists balled in frustration.

'It won't work,' he says. 'It has the gas and it won't work.'

There's a blue metal tool box beside the generator (one of those that you open like a mechanical mouth, and in the act of opening, on either side of the box, a series of hinged drawers appear). Maud gets on her knees in front of the generator. Some manner of albino lizard scurries away between the film projector and the wall. If the generator was run until it was empty there is almost certainly air in the fuel pipes. She works her way along the black rubber tubing, loosens off clips and bleeds out air until the diesel seeps over her fingers. The boy is watching her, her or what she's doing. She has noticed already how much heat the boy gives off, how when you're close to him you feel it. She loosens the nut by the fuel injector, pushes the run/stop lever to run, turns the key and cranks the engine. Nothing wrong with the pump. She tightens the nut, finds in the tool box a folded rag, wipes up the fuel she has spilt. She takes one of the lanterns and runs its light over the engine then puts the light down, unscrews the electric fuel valve on top of the pump, sniffs it, decides it has probably burnt out and removes the plunger. She tells the boy what she is doing, explains the function of the valve, explains that from now on he will have to use the throttle lever to stop the generator. She turns the key again. The engine starts. The boy knows the rest of it. He hooks up the dangling wires. One of these powers the extractor fan (where does *that* come out?). When they speak they have to raise their voices though they do not need to shout. Jessica comes down. She's laughing with pleasure. They let it run for several minutes then Maud shuts it off and cleans her hands on the rag.

The children have heard the generator and most of them are there to witness Maud rising out of the ground, her dirty knees, her gas perfume, a speckling of fuel oil on her right arm, black as the lettering on her left.

Now that the Ark is electric again they long for darkness. Thirty litres in the fuel tank will give them forty hours of power, probably more. Maud takes her pack of Lucky Strikes onto the beach, sits cross-legged, lights up and looks at the horizon. The sound of the generator has started something in her. She thinks of the batteries on *Lodestar*. If they can be charged – or just one – then, in theory, the engine can be started, the boat pumped out, and she can limp along the coast until she reaches a port. And she's picturing this, picturing it while knowing full well the boat is going nowhere, that it needs a crane rather than a battery, when Jessica sits in the sand beside her and says, 'Tonight we're going to do something special. OK? We're going to do something for you.'

'If you want,' says Maud.

The girl puts her hand on Maud's shoulder and though Maud may be mistaken it feels like the girl is trembling. They look at each other; it's a little like the moment before a kiss, then the girl jumps up and runs back to where Theo is standing in one of the archways, half in, half out of the light.

They eat at the usual time. There are pancakes, biscuits, even some little rubbery sweets in the shape of simple objects like clocks and guns. Then Maud goes down to the store room with Theo and starts the generator. The projector has already been carried up, the screen also, unopened on its stand but in position by the bottom of the stairs. The projector bulb with its snapped filament has been replaced. The film has been chosen, wound on. The older children have seen it many times; the younger ones once or twice. They gather on the floor under the screen. Some find it impossible to sit still, and one boy, seized with the spirit, hops from foot to foot, his little shadow on the screen, a thing in itself, so that soon the others jump up to join him, dancing and watching their shadows dance, the wildness of it. Only when the screen bursts into colour do they sit down, holding hands, their mouths gaping. Below them the generator thrums; they can feel its vibrations through their sitting bones. On the screen now a night sky, a drawn sky – *Through the snow and sleet and hail, through the blizzard, through the gale, through the wind and through the rain, over mountain, over plain, through the blinding lightning flash and the mighty thunder crash, ever faithful, ever true, nothing stops him, he'll get through . . .*

Storks. Then a whole arkful of baby animals dropping by parachute. Dumbo's mother unwraps her package. Dumbo looks at his mother's feet then up, up, up, to her face . . . It is not just the young children who are watching this as if it were life itself unfolding in front of them. Theo and Jessica too are taut with attention, and even Maud, half sitting, half leaning against the end of the dining table, stares at the screen, the richness of the old film's colours unlocked by the light. Everything around the frame of the screen is flat, silent, nothing but a canvas backdrop. The children laugh. They shriek at the scenes of chaos, at the precariousness of everything, the speed, the hooting, the flames, the flights that always threaten to end in disaster. It is not a long film. When it ends the children want to watch it again, immediately. They are all crying out for it and Jessica is trying to explain that they must not use up the fuel in the generator watching *Dumbo* all night, and then, with no warning, there is something else on the screen, and the children fall silent. A man in a checked shirt is smiling at them. He has a cigarette in one hand and is talking, bantering, with the person filming who, talking back to him, turns out to be a woman. The man is in his forties perhaps, a heavy handsomeness, his hair thick, black as an old telephone, and swept back in a wave from his forehead. A rockabilly. A man you can imagine dancing and dancing well. He's in high good humour. The sound quality is poor and his accent heavy with the south but some of it carries clearly enough. 'Hey, Ginny, what shall we do in the dry?' And the woman answers, 'Blow away, I guess.' And the man says, 'Asses to asses, bust to bust,' and the woman, laughing, says, 'A-men to that,' and the man looks away at something out of view and his smile fades and you see how big his face is and how shadowed. Then it's over. The film flicks out of the gate. Theo turns off the motor, puts out the light. Maud takes one of the lanterns and goes down to the generator.

When the children are in bed, Maud swims again. There's a crescent moon, thin as the paring of a nail. She has a towel with her. She doesn't know where Theo and Jessica are, but she doesn't mind much who sees her. She makes a pile of her clothes and goes into the water. She doesn't swim far tonight. She's killing time, something like that. She swims towards the moon then swims away from it. There's no one on the beach when she comes out. She finds her clothes, her towel, dries herself, dresses in her shorts and a sweatshirt she brought from the boat and dried in the afternoon sun. She smokes a cigarette then starts up the beach towards the building with the arches. There are no lights in there, none she can see, and she has stepped into the building's greater dark when a hand grips her arm. She breaks free immediately. She knows it's the boy, can smell him, feel the heat of him.

'Jessica's in the church,' he says. 'She's waiting on you.'

For some seconds there's a silence between them, then she says, 'OK,' and walks out of the building, walks across to the church door, pulls it open and goes in. At the far end of the church a single candle is burning.

'Maud?'

'Yes.'

'Can you see?'

'Yes.'

She walks towards the candle. When she reaches Jessica, the girl takes her hand and leads her into the small room with the desk and chair, the little window, the calendar on the wall from December 2007.

'Sit here,' says the girl, pulling the chair away from the desk into the middle of the room. Maud sits. The girl puts the candle on the floor. She is wearing make-up. Maud has never seen her with make-up before. She looks excited. A girl on a date, a first date.

'Don't be afraid, Maud,' she says.

'I'm not,' says Maud.

'Didn't I say we would help you?'

'What are you going to do?' asks Maud.

'You only have to open your heart,' says the girl. 'Can you do that, Maud? Can you open your heart?'

Maud looks away from the girl to the boxes on the bench at the side of the room opposite the window. There are three of them, the size of foolscap box-files, each with a pattern of small holes in the top and each with a hasp and lock.

'Where's Theo?' asks Maud.

'He's coming,' says the girl.

'What's in those boxes?'

'Oh, Maud,' says the girl, 'I'm going to put this little light out now.' She squats and pinches the wick between her fingers. 'Think of your little girl, Maud. Think of her and open up your heart.'

'I'm going now,' says Maud. 'I'm going to go to bed.'

The girl fumbles for Maud's hands, clasps them. 'Wait,' she says. '*Please . . .*'

Very faintly at first, but so unexpectedly Maud makes a small, involuntary noise in her throat, the clear bulb hanging directly above their heads begins to glow. The boy has started the generator. The light grows brighter. A minute later the boy himself comes in, swiftly and softly, shuts the door behind him. He's wearing a clean checked shirt. It's not the one Pa was wearing in the piece of film they saw but one very like it. It hangs off him, his narrow, hard frame. 'You ready?' he says, perhaps to Jessica, perhaps to both of them.

He goes to one of the boxes (the young technician, the young master of ceremonies), quickly frees the lock then, more slowly, opens the lid, peeps inside, closes it again without locking it. He comes and stands at the side of Maud's chair, takes one of Jessica's hands, takes one of Maud's. He starts to pray. He's speaking in a rapid, low voice. The words spill over each other. The girl is staring at Maud, her face bright as morning. It's hard to look away from her.

The boy is working up to something. He's getting louder. Maud stands. It feels awkward to be sitting, foolish. She looks at them both, looks from one to the other, these children who have opened some secret cupboard and found things they ought not to have found. She should tell the girl to wash the make-up off her face. She should send them both to their beds. She does not understand why she has not already done it.

The bulb with its faultless skin fades and brightens; the room's shadows soften then grow hard again, hard-edged. The boy lets go of her hand. He goes to the box, he nods to himself, opens the box and reaches in. When his hand comes out it's wearing a living branch of snakes. Now, truly, they have her attention. The snakes, with their slender, triangular heads, look like vipers of some type. The boy pours them gently from hand to hand. He gazes at them, enraptured. All this is real enough. And she's heard of something like it, those little churches in the hand-written, misspelt far south of the United States, the stubborn descendants of slow readers, people Christ himself might have been uneasy about but understood and even admired. These are Pa's snakes or Pa's example or both. But who would have guessed the power of it, or these children's ability to channel it? The snakes move slowly, drowsily. The boy holds them up like a slow green fire. The girl is cooing. Whoever she was before, she's someone else now. Her face with its make-up (Ma's make-up?), its sheen of sweat, seems caught in a panic of happiness, some-thing urgent, bodily, ancestral. Maud has dreamt none of this, has had no convenient previsions. It turns out, however, that none of it is out of her range.

The boy holds out the snakes to her. She does not flinch but her breath does something odd – goes from shuttling in her throat to sinking like a glass rod to somewhere, some point in the knot of nerves between her legs. She takes the snakes from him, threads the fingers of both hands through their looping bodies. Cat's cradle, carding wool. The boy is moving like a figure in an old film. He is moving like a man with Parkinson's disease, a boy with Parkinson's disease. She holds the snakes. They are not heavy. How many are there? Five, six. Not easy to see where one ends and another begins. The girl touches her own breasts as if they're beginning to hurt her then puts her hands above Maud's head. Maud passes the snakes to the boy who brushes them against his forehead then carries them back to the box. The rest of it feels very private, though in some way the gibbering of the children makes it possible. She sits on the floor under the bulb and begins to cry. It breaks out of her, comes out of her in waves. Her eyes, her nose, her mouth. She speaks her child's name, mutters it thickly. Zoe, Zoe . . . The boy and girl are kneeling either side of her now. They are chattering and crowing, touching her shoulders, her head. All three of them are rocking, swaying. All three in a small boat adrift. And then it stops. For a moment Maud imagines the bulb has gone – blown – but it hasn't. The boy is standing. He's staring at her, clownish in his big shirt. The girl is also staring, though she is still on her knees and her expression is different. Maud looks down at herself. On the inside of one of her thighs there's a heavy web of blood; blood too through the cotton of her shorts, blood on the floor beneath her. She's shaky but she manages to stand up. She's never bled like this before. She goes to the door. She crosses the unlit body of the church, trips over a chair, bangs her knee, gets up, reaches the door to the outside and walks down to the sea, walks straight in until the sea is around her waist in a black skirt on which the moonlight shines like threads of silk.

5

In the night she hears again the sound like distant artillery. Hears it at the edge of the audible but is sure this time it is not thunder. When she wakes in the early morning she lies a long time looking at the light on the wall. She cries again, though without any violence, the tears following the creases at the corners of her eyes and finding their way down to her throat.

Before getting into bed she made a rag for herself by tearing the back out of one of her T-shirts. She looks at it now, looks to see if she has bled onto the sheet below her, then gets up, dresses in jeans (the denim stiff with salt but wearable) and goes down the stairs. She's very hungry and goes straight to the cupboard where, in tupperware boxes and old biscuit tins, any uneaten food from the main meal is kept. She eats cold roast vegetables, a piece of flatbread, three of the little plantains, two tomatoes. She goes out to the girl looking after the chickens to ask if she has any eggs and the girl gives her two, which Maud breaks and swallows raw. She sees Jessica coming down from the walled garden. The girl greets her with just a moment of unease. She looks somehow younger today and perhaps feels it.

'Where's Theo?' asks Maud.

'He's in the trailer.'

Maud goes to the trailer and knocks at the door until he opens it. He's just wearing shorts.

'Can you take me to the boat?'

He will not look at her, not directly.

'I'm tired,' he says.

'OK,' she says. She smiles at him but he is already turning away from her, closing the door.

She goes back to find Jessica and has her take the lock from the trap door. In the room below she tops up the fuel in the generator and takes an empty jerrycan down to the beach. She does not believe she will find the jangada hard to sail. She drags it into the surf, climbs in over the stern. The boat is steered with a rudder oar and there's no more to the rigging than a mainsheet but for the first twenty minutes she thinks she's made a mistake and has to reach back to skills learnt in her teens, the club days when she raced shallow-hulled Lasers and Fireballs on the Thames. Even so, the church is out of view before she starts to feel comfortable, to know where to put her weight, how to aim the sledge prow at the swell, how close to the wind she can go.

By the time she reaches *Lodestar* there's almost no wind at all. She brushes alongside the yacht, ties on and climbs aboard. She fills the jerrycan with diesel – there's still plenty in there – then goes below into the water. In the sliding-door cupboard in the heads she finds the tampons she took from the bathroom of the cottage, and pushing down her jeans (she's up to her knees in water) she unwraps one and makes use of it then and there, a side-glimpse of herself in the mirror, her face darker than her hair, the white line of the shock cord around her neck.

Back in the saloon she looks for what else she can take. As before, she makes a pile on the top step of the companionway, then packs the smaller items into a pair of canvas buckets and puts the rest into a sail bag. She collects the boat's title document, registration and insurance (all in a plastic file still above the waterline). The last thing she does is tear out an endpaper from the *Book of Landfalls* and with a pencil she finds floating between the benches and rubs dry until it functions, she writes a note that will serve as the final entry of the log she did not keep. *My name is Maud Stamp, joint owner of the yacht* Lodestar. *I set sail from Falmouth on the English coast at the end of May 2009, was dismasted in the mid-Atlantic and driven south by a storm . . .* It's a short account, at the end of which she writes Tim's phone number and the address of the Rathbone house. As an afterthought she also puts down Chris Totten's name and the address of the yard. She hangs the page from one of the brass hooks holding the curtain wire at the window above the chart table and is about to step through the companionway when she sees, below the framed photograph of the boat, a piece of buoyant light in the water and she wades over to it and lifts it. It's the bulb she picked out of the sea south of the Azores. General Electric, sixty watts, the glass skin undamaged, the filament unbroken. She turns it in her hands. She is almost afraid of it. She is also smiling at it, and for a moment she considers taking it with her – this object carrying its own improbable news – but she settles it onto the water again and climbs the companionway steps for the last time, drops in the washboards, and after tugging, hard, three, four times, drags shut the hatch on its runners.

The boy is waiting for her on the beach when she gets back. He runs into the surf to take hold of the boat, take possession of it. 'You must never take it!' he shouts. '*Isso não te pertence!*' Something strangled in his voice. He's close to tears.

'You were tired,' says Maud.

'It's not yours!' he shouts. He grabs one of the canvas buckets and flings it onto the beach, scattering the contents. Maud walks around the front of the boat to where he is standing. 'I'm sorry,' she says.

He stares at her, then looks down at his feet. 'It's not yours,' he mumbles.

She lifts the other bucket from the boards, lifts the sail bag, puts them on the sand and crouches to collect the contents of the spilt bucket. Some of the children have been drawn to the sound of shouting, and outside the door of the church Jessica is looking on. No one comes any closer – then one of the children breaks ranks and runs down the beach towards Maud. It's the boy with the bounce of ginger hair she found in the punishment box, the *forno*, at the back of the church. He flicks a nervous glance at Theo, then picks up one of the buckets and carries it behind Maud to the arches. Three other children carry the sail bag. It's like the head of a giant they have just watched slain.

There is no film that night. At the evening meal Jessica tells them they must save the gas. Next week perhaps they will watch another; it will depend on how good they are, how obedient. Theo says nothing other than the grace at the start of the meal. As soon as the meal has finished he leaves the table. The atmosphere is exactly that of a household where the parents have reached some impasse.

Maud, carrying one of the wind-up lanterns, goes to her room half an hour after the children are in bed. She did not accompany

Jessica on her rounds. She's tired, drained, restless. Has she become unused to bleeding? So much blood last night she half imagined a miscarriage. She undresses, puts on Pa's shirt that she now uses as a nightshirt and lies on top of the bed with Captain Slocum's journal. Most of the pages are stuck together and when she unsticks them they feel, between finger and thumb, like old fake money. She props the lantern at the head of the bed and reads paragraphs at random, moths touching the edges of her face with the edges of their wings. *After righting the dory for the fourth time, I finally succeeded by the utmost care in keeping her upright while I hauled myself into her and with one of the oars, which I had recovered, paddled to the shore, somewhat the worse for wear and pretty full of salt water . . .*

She settles the book on her chest, looks up at the ceiling where a house lizard is looking down at her. All there is, she thinks, is this, just this. This and nothing more.

The lantern, unwound, is growing dim, and she puts it on the floor, switches it off and has rolled beneath the thin blanket when she hears her door being quietly opened. She waits – it's too dark to see who's there – but when they do not speak she sits up and asks – with no great kindness in her voice – who it is.

'It's me,' says a small voice. A child's voice, a girl's.

'You want to see me?'

'Yes.'

Maud feels for the lantern, winds it, holds it up (as Captain Slocum might on a wilder night to see what rattled the dog-house door). It's Leah.

'Come in,' says Maud.

The girl comes in and behind her come two black girls, the twins, who helped Maud to stand that first day. They gather at the end of the bed while Maud looks at them and they look at her.

'Are you OK?' asks Maud. Leah nods.

'Did you have a bad dream?'

The girl shakes her head.

'Are you hungry?'

'No,' says Leah. 'No,' chime the girls behind her. (Everybody knows the word 'hungry'.)

Then Leah – perhaps prodded – comes around the end of the bed and stands directly in front of Maud, in front of her knees. Only now does Maud understand what they have come for. She opens her arms, the girl steps in and Maud holds her for some ten or fifteen seconds. After her comes one of the twins and in her turn, her sister. When it's over, and without another word, the three of them file out and the last carefully shuts the door.

This, then, becomes the pattern of Maud's nights. The tap on the door, the face of the boldest child leaning in. Three or four of them at a time, each one patiently waiting his or her turn to be held, then quietly leaving. She doesn't tell Jessica about it but somehow she finds out. 'So you're a mother now,' says Jessica, coming to sit next to Maud under the mango tree.

'I was a mother before,' says Maud.

'But now you're their mother.'

'No,' says Maud. 'They have their own mothers somewhere.'

There's a long silence between them. The girl rubs a piece of red earth between her fingers.

'You,' says Maud, 'you're like a mother to them.'

'When Pa comes back,' says the girl, kneeling up and grinning, 'maybe you can marry him.'

'Do you think he's coming back?' asks Maud, in whose head

has appeared, in all its weird detail, a picture of the car in the forest clearing.

'Sure,' says the girl. 'Why wouldn't he come back?'

That night she hears it again, those guns firing at the edge of sound. It wakes her and she lies listening to it for a while, then gets up and goes to where her watch is on the table. When she opens the shutters there's enough moonlight to see the dial, and though the time it shows is local to itself – she has seen no clocks at the Ark – she makes a mental note of it and goes back to bed.

In the morning she walks out with Leah and the goats. She asks her about the noise, thinks it unlikely the girl will know what she's talking about, but she nods immediately, looks at Maud and says, '*O trem.*'

'*Trem* . . . train?'

'Yes. Train.'

'Have you seen it?'

'One time. With Pa. He likes to walk at night when it is cool.'

'Is it a train that carries people?'

The girl points to the sky. 'On top,' she says.

'People on top of the train?'

She nods.

'And inside?'

She shakes her head.

'It passed last night,' says Maud. 'When will it come again?'

'Not tomorrow,' says the girl, nudging one of the goats with her stick. 'Not tomorrow tomorrow. Not the next tomorrow. The tomorrow after that.'

Maud holds up her hand, her fingers. 'Four days?'

'Four days,' agrees the girl.

*　　*　　*

For two of those days she's undecided. She's keeping an open mind, or that's what she tells herself. There are practical questions, of course, but she's Maud Stamp, and the practical holds no terrors for her. So what else? The children? The children were on their own for months before she arrived. And she cannot be certain Pa will *not* return, though she no longer wants to see him, the magician, the old dancer, the man whose shirt she has been sleeping in. There's food, water, shelter. Looked at from a certain point of view, their situation is enviable.

On the third day she puts on her trainers and walks up the path towards the hills. As she passes children – children working, children playing, children making work into a game and getting the work done – they stop to watch her and some run over to her and she spends a few moments talking to them before moving off. After fifteen minutes of walking the ground starts to rise. On either side of the path the land looks barren, though here and there some leathery succulent grows, or patches of silvery grass, or a cactus (one with a small white bird on its highest limb she mistook for a flower until the sound of her walking put it into flight).

Halfway up the hill she enters a belt of trees, their trunks no higher than her head but with large, intricate crowns of branches and tangling twigs where cicadas sing their tireless, mechanical song. Beyond the trees, she comes to the bare summit of the hill and climbs onto a cinnamon-coloured rock to look out over the country. No buildings, no herded animals, certainly no sun glinting off rails, just the low hills repeating themselves and rolling on towards the watery outline of bigger hills, mountains perhaps. She should have brought the Zeiss with her though she does not think she would see more than emptiness magnified.

She turns back, gets among the trees again by a different route, and there, at the base of a larger tree, one that rises above the others like a yellow fountain, she finds a wooden cross and a grave covered in patterns of fallen leaves. Carved into the wood of the cross, the lettering still sharp: *Ginny Plautz August 2 1967 – December 13 2007. A True follower of Signs.* She had known it was up here somewhere, the grave, but she was not looking for it, and to come across it like this, by chance, feels important in a way she could not easily explain. She sits beside it. She's tired and hot and the shade of the tree is welcome. And there is the sense of a meeting, overdue, with this woman whose presence has not quite ebbed away from the old buildings on the beach. Ginny Plautz, dead of a snake bite. Ginny Plautz not healed by Jesus or Pa or anyone. No way of knowing what kind of woman she was, what kind of guardian to the children. Maud has not even seen a picture of her, has nothing to go on other than her clothes, her voice on a clip of film, and cannot quite remember what she said. '*What shall we do in the dry?*' Or was it Pa who asked the question and Ginny who said something about blowing away? It would be good now to have her company, to sit here in the shade of the tree with her, talking in low voices, the sort of conversation Maud has had so rarely but now feels a sudden appetite for. Ginny Plautz might offer confidences about Pa (there would be many, surely). And Maud, when her turn came, would tell her things you cannot tell to children; tell her, for example, about that winter morning she drove through the rain to the Rathbones' house, Mrs Slad in the kitchen, Bella reading to Tim that book with the man and woman on the cover, dancing. And she would tell her about Tim's father waiting for her in the kitchen and leading her through to the little drawing room. The fire, the drinks table, the way the whisky burned her lips. And she would tell her what he said and before Ginny Plautz (the dead woman is her friend now) could cry,

'Why, the devil!' she would say that she did not think he was wrong, not entirely. Had she ever been interested in being a mother? In motherhood? Interested in the way the other mothers were or seemed to be? Was she not, in truth, perfectly content to let Tim be the one who fed Zoe, who bathed her, comforted her, knew which of her soft toys was her current favourite, knew which drawer her winter vests were in, knew when she was tired, when she had had enough? A bad mother, then. Or not a good one. And this perhaps should trouble her more than it does. A bad mother who worked long hours, who sailed, who liked to sail on her own, who liked to be on her own. The simple reason Tim was with Zoe that morning on the way to school was that he was with her most of the time, whereas she, her mother, was not. But about the rest of it, her being cold-blooded, unmoved, about that he knew nothing at all, and she would not let him knock her down a second time.

She lays a hand on the grave's wooden crosspiece, lets it rest there a moment, as you might on another's shoulder. Then she gets to her feet, looks down through the twisting avenues of trees. If you have a talent for surviving – as poor Ginny Plautz did not, as Pa, too, may not have done – it does not seem wrong to use it. Is it wrong?

Anyway, she'll use it.

In the room that night, after the children have visited, she goes through the things she brought from the boat, puts some of them – clothes, her phone, her passport, the boat's documents – into the green backpack, then lies awake a long time wondering if Leah's counting can be relied upon. In the morning she cuts up the sail bag and uses the cloth to make two parcels. Into one she puts the antibiotics, fifty American dollars (the other fifty is for herself), the last of the Fennidine with clear, careful instructions written on the side – how much and in what circumstances. Also, half a dozen tampons – nothing in the store rooms below to suggest Pa or Ma had thought that far ahead. In the other parcel she puts Captain Slocum's book, the tattered charts, the binoculars, her Green River sheath knife and two of the hand flares – then changes her mind and puts one of the flares into Jessica's parcel.

They watch another film that evening – *The Empire Strikes Back* – and though several yards of the film seem to be missing (at one point the soundtrack gives way to that of another film entirely – *Mutiny on the Bounty*?), the children cheer as if watching a football match and afterwards run on the beach, flinging themselves at each other, tumbling over each other in the sand.

It takes almost half an hour to round them all up but when the last of them has washed and the last boy, weary on his feet, has wandered back from the latrines, Maud goes up with Jessica to say goodnight, then says goodnight to the girl herself at the top of the stairs, a quick touching of hands in the dark, a dozen soft words. Ten minutes later, four children come in to be held – Jenna, Conner, Caleb and Faith. She holds them and they go. She checks the time, straps on her watch, lies on the bed, sleeps for an hour dreaming of a night sky thick with the migration of fabulous birds, the moon rippling on their wings as they pass. Then she gets up, changes into jeans, T-shirt and sweatshirt, though does not yet put on her trainers (what's left of them). She has been tempted to cut her hair again, cut it short, but instead she uses a strip from the sail bag, pulls her hair into her fist and binds it.

The parcels are under the bed. There's a T on one, a J on the other. She takes them downstairs, listens, then goes to the door of the church. The door does not open silently but she does not need to open it far. Once inside she turns on her torch and follows the beam the length of the nave to the room behind the altar. She imagines suddenly confronting the boy there but the room is empty.

On the bench the boxes are where she last saw them. She lifts them in turn. Two she can immediately feel are empty; the other is heavier, a weight that wakes in her hands. This one she sets on the floor and in its place puts the sail bag parcels, then grips her torch between her teeth, picks up the box and goes back to the church door where she stops, turns off the torch and slides it into one of the back pockets of her jeans. She has thought carefully about what she is going to do next. Her first instinct was to release the snakes but the thought of leaving behind a half-dozen pit vipers combined itself in her head with pictures of the children's bare feet. Nor could she carry them with her. Nor could she leave them in the little room – it's barely even a matter of conscience. Without Jessica the children might not survive. Without Jessica, Theo might simply follow the shade of Pa to wherever it is he thinks Pa has gone.

She carries the box down to the surf, walks out and sinks it in the water, holding it there until the weight of water running through the air holes is enough to anchor it to the sand. It only takes a minute, perhaps two.

In her room again, she sits a while, getting her breath. What's done is done. She looks at her watch, puts on her trainers. She is starting to tie the laces of the second shoe when the door opens and a figure slips inside. It's Leah. She's dressed. They had no arrangement, or perhaps the girl thought they did. Either way, Maud is pleased to see her. She puts on the backpack. Everything now is touch and whisper. They go down the stairs and out through the back of the building, past the chicken house, past the walled garden and the latrine. Leah has her stick in one hand; her other hand has hold of Maud. She guides her away from the track towards the shallow grey dome of the water cistern and the palm trees. The half-moon throws thin shadows from solitary trees, or from cacti or black rocks. They do not use the torch, nor do they speak much. Maud has water with her, some mangoes and biscuits, a piece of flatbread. Leah has brought her camouflage canteen, the one she held to Maud's lips the first time they met. The walking is not difficult. The ground is solid and true, though walking at night is never like walking in the day. The eyes change; the brain too, presumably. Some afternoon in her third year at Bristol, sitting in the library, Maud skimmed through a paper on it in a journal – *Cell*, perhaps, or *BioEssays* – and can remember things about cones and rods and photoreceptor proteins; can remember herself, too, sitting by the window with a view of afternoon clouds over office blocks and ancient churches, a young woman who sometimes disconcerted people though never tried to . . .

Leah stops. They don't seem to be anywhere.

'Here?' asks Maud.

The girl points. It looks at first – the metal smudged with moonlight – like rivulets of water, little streams, but it's the rails, a hundred yards away, running on a shallow bank between the open country and the rising ground beyond.

They sit in the dust and take a mouthful of water each, eat a biscuit. They wait; the moon glides; the train, of course, is not coming. It is impossible to even imagine a train. The girl rests her head against Maud's shoulder, then slides down to her lap and sleeps. Maud looks at her watch again. She did not really have a plan for the train failing to come and she cannot stay out here all night with the child. Another hour, an hour at most, and they will have to go back. She will have to face the boy's rage.

Then a new sound enters the world. The child opens her eyes and sits up. She leads Maud by the hand to the cover of a low, scrubby tree, a thing within a thin, twisted trunk as if its growing had been an agony. It's not clear to Maud which direction the train is coming from but Leah knows and is staring down the track – south? – for several seconds before the light appears. Everything now depends on the speed of the train, on whether Leah's memory of it (out here in the cool of the night with Pa) is a true memory, but from the way the light – a neat cone of yellow light – is creeping towards them it's clear that it is, as the child promised her, a train you can outrun.

But the noise of it! Rumbling, jangling, screeching. It's like an old world army on the march, a column of conquistadors with their siege towers and loot and tarnished armour. The light sweeps the dark before it, shows the land unreal, martian. They stay hidden by the trunk of the tree, watching, fascinated. Then Maud leans down to the girl and into her ear says, 'You want to come with me?' The girl shakes her head, says something in which Maud can only catch the word goats (in fact it sounds like 'ghosts'). Maud nods. It's too late for speaking now. She lifts the cord from around her neck, the hair clip, and puts it around the girl's neck.

The engine is almost level with them, a soft wash of light behind the double windscreen, a ten-second view of the driver sitting as if stunned in a dream. After the lead engine a second, pouring fumes through high vents. Then the first of the wagons, some painted white, some a darker colour, some with words on the side – ALBRAS, HANJIN, FMC Chemicals – some swirled with graffiti. And on top of the wagons, huddled as if at the top of a high wall, the shadows of people, scores of them, dark blue against the paling blue of the sky . . .

How many wagons have passed? Forty? Fifty? The base of the

wagons is at least four feet above the rails but all of them appear to have mounting steps and little ladders, a whole superstructure of handholds and footholds. A red glow, soft and somehow lovely, indicates the end of the train. Maud reaches round to touch Leah's hair, the warmth of her. Then she squats with the pack on her back, and when the red light draws its colour across her face she rises up and starts to run.

In truth, the girl does not see her climb aboard, not the actual moment when she must have leapt and seized hold of something, but the train, which took so long to arrive, takes only a few minutes to disappear, and when the lights have gone so has the woman. She calls her name, two or three times, but nothing comes back. The track is empty and the world has settled into silence again.

6

In the car park at the boatyard, Chris Totten and Robert Currey are standing either side of a cherry-red Honda. They lean, peer into the car, can see the other's blurred face through the opposite window. Robert Currey tries the door but it's locked of course. They walk around the car, change sides, peer in again as though, from a new perspective, they might see something helpful. Thirty yards away, a man in a yellow hard hat and hi-vis jacket is waving directions to the rear-view mirrors of a reversing concrete-mixing lorry. When the beeping stops you can hear the gulls again.

Recession has meant a scaling-back of the plans for the marina. The hotel will only have one restaurant and there is a new emphasis on conference facilities, but the money doesn't come from British banks or banks in Zurich or in America. It's money moving to a different music altogether, and stage one – the clearing of the ground – is underway and on schedule. A film of dust from the work has settled over the Honda. Notices have been left on the windscreen ordering the owner to move the car. The date mentioned on these notices has already passed. It's the only vehicle remaining in this part of the car park.

There's not much inside the car. A water bottle on the front seat, a road atlas on the back seat, and what looks like a little box of business cards on the rubber mat below. Next to the tax disc (only a month to run) is a pink and green parking permit for Croydon University Hospital.

'It can't stay here,' says Robert Currey, as both men slowly circle the car again.

'Nothing can stay here,' says Chris Totten. He's in a suit and has good shoes on, though the toes of the shoes are scuffed.

'I've got room at mine,' says Robert Currey. 'We'll just have to get it lifted.'

'To yours?'

'Yeah.'

'You've got room, then?'

'Yeah.'

'OK,' says Chris Totten, bending down for one more look – that bare, that unremarkable interior. 'Sounds like a plan.' They step back from the car. The lorry is reversing again. This is the future.

'See you at close of day,' says Chris Totten, his voice smothered by the beeping. Then both men turn their backs on the car and walk towards the water. On the side of the car, the driver's door, one of them has drawn a small heart in the dust.

ACKNOWLEDGEMENTS

With thanks to James McKenzie, to Liz Baker and Jon Pritchard. Thanks also (once again) to Beatrice Monti della Corte and the Santa Maddalena Foundation in Tuscany where this book was started. And thanks, as ever, to my agent Simon Trewin at WME, and my editor Carole Welch at Sceptre.

Writing is a solitary task; it is also a communal one.